MICHAEL BLAINE's fiction has app[illegible] *New England Review, The North American Review, New Letters, Shenandoah* and *American Fiction '97*, among many others. Both Raymond Carver and Joyce Carol Oates have selected his short fiction for anthologies. His stories have been nominated several times for Pushcart Prizes. *The Linoleum Sea* was noted in *Best American Stories 1993*, edited by Louise Erdrich, as 'among the year's most distinguished.' He has written on books, media and politics for *The Village Voice, American Report* and other magazines.

Michael Blaine is a two-time winner of the New York State Foundation for the Arts Fellowship in Fiction Writing. A prizewinner in Katherine Anne Porter and *New Letters* short story competitions, he has also received the City University of New York Fiction Writing Fellowship three times. He is the founder and Editor in Chief of the literary magazine *New York Stories*.

Michael Blaine lives with his wife, the artist Rose Mackiewicz, and Willy the Wonderdog, in the wilds of upstate New York.

# WHITEOUTS

Michael Blaine

HEADLINE
*FEATURE*

Published in the United States under the title
The Desperate Season

First published in 1999
by HEADLINE BOOK PUBLISHING

First published in paperback in 1999
by HEADLINE BOOK PUBLISHING

10 9 8 7 6 5 4 3 2 1



ISBN 0 7472 6159 8

Typeset by Palimpsest Book Production Limited,
Polmont, Stirlingshire

Printed and bound in Great Britain by
Mackays of Chatham PLC, Chatham, Kent

HEADLINE BOOK PUBLISHING
A division of the Hodder Headline Group
338 Euston Road
London NW1 3BH
www.headline.co.uk
www.hodderheadline.com

To Rose

*Love for Life*

ACKNOWLEDGMENTS

Many caring and uncompromising readers had a hand in bringing *Whiteouts* to completion. First and foremost, I must thank Rose Mackiewicz, who brought an artist's eye to the language, landscape and characters here. Her critical sensibility is reflected on every page. Through it all she could still make me laugh so hard it hurt.

Anna Tasha Blaine's intense support and belief in *Whiteouts* helped keep me going. An old hand in publishing, she agitated fiercely for this book's publication, provided psychotherapy when necessary and has the phone bill to prove it.

No writer has ever had a more passionate and tenacious advocate than my friend and agent, Mary Evans. Without her tireless support and energy, *Whiteouts* might never have gained so wide an audience. The day after a long and bitter snow storm she called and said she would do her all. Did she ever.

My American editor Rob Weisbach gave me the chance to refine the voices and find the real conclusion to this story. He discovered the flaws, the mis-steps and encouraged me to go back to the work three more times. In an age when editors are supposed to have lost the will and the art, Rob defies the clichés.

Bill Massey, my English editor, sends off some of the finest e-mail on either side of the Atlantic. When he wrote and said he was walking along the Thames with this book raging in his imagination, I was astonished and touched. He gave me hope that the vision of *Whiteouts* could be understood by even the most foreign cultures.

I also wish to thank Joyce Carol Oates, who edited *American Fiction '98* and chose the short story, 'Whiteouts,' for that 'best American fiction' anthology. Other readers who helped and provided encouragement include Edward Blaine, inspiration's progenitor; Marge Blaine, a kind and critical reader; Tanya MacKinnon, Mary Evans' cool top gun; Stephanie Staal, the vital and tasteful link; Peter Rondinone, astute chapter switcher; Phyllis Van Slyke, a supporter without peer; Daniel C. Lynch, generous with praise and time; and Joseph Blaine, who can read for hours without moving a muscle.

# CHAPTER ONE: MAURICE

## Friday: February 26, 1990: 10 a.m.

Dr Greenberg's beard is patchy and you can see islands of eczema on his cheeks and neck. He looks like a human goat. 'So what are we going to do if we have a bumpy period, Maurice?'

'Make sure I'm taking my meds, doc,' I say. *Blithely*. I watch people who are supposed to be sane and this seems like one of their characteristics. Anything they do they do it *blithely*. They say it *blithely*. They act so *fucking blithe*, as if everything were so easy.

'You'll call me right away if you're feeling bad?'

'Yeah, sure. Definitely.'

'This is a cyclical illness, Maurice, we can control it if we want to. Your mom and dad are good people, they're going to help no matter what.'

I wait for him to say something about mom visiting me exactly twice since I've been in the bug house but he pretends like everything is okay. With my dad, it's true, with him it's Unconditional Love. My dad is always saying, 'Don't worry, I understand Maurice, he listens to me.'

He wishes but I don't listen to anybody, even myself. I feel like my body is just smoke puffing up my clothes and I can leak away any second.

My dad is supposed to pick me up in the Cherokee at around noon so after Dr Greenberg does the paperwork on me I stuff the forms into my jacket and take a stroll. There's a hard crust of snow on the ground and my duck boots crunch when they break the surface. When I get to this mossy stone wall that runs around the Breitman grounds, I just toss my knapsack over, lift myself up and melt like a radio wave into the trees. I like thinking about waves. Electromagnetic waves. Heat waves. Cosmic rays. X-rays. They can see right through you.

It only takes three rides, with a redneck and his police dog, then on a town truck hauling a bunch of rock salt and then with some kind of Sloughter in a '73 Pontiac Bonneville that's so rusted you can see its skeleton. *Sloughters*. That's what they call these people who've been living in the hills and hollows for hundreds of years, cut off from everybody. They're part Indian, part white and maybe a little runaway slave, and this dude Ronnie giving me the ride, when he wiggles on his ripped front seat, he gives off a stink that practically chokes me so I get off at Stick Willow, near Natale's Pizza, right before Accordia because I can't stand riding with him all the way home.

Anyway, his eyes are slits, you can't see them and I hate that more than anything.

The first thing I do is dump my meds into the stream that runs next to Natale's Pizza Place. I haven't taken them for days. Ice flows dam up the water. Dead yellow reeds. There's a lot of run-off from the farms around there and the water looks blue and sudsy so I figure my meds aren't going to hurt the environment much more, maybe they'll make a few cows see double and go down to their knees and see through this veil, this filthy veil they call a cure.

What I want to do is get in contact with my old mind, the mind that saw the edges of things sharp and clear. I used to be able to multiply eleven digit numbers by eleven digit numbers. In my old mind. Now a calculator goes soft in my hand and I forget what I'm doing.

Stick Willow's worse than Accordia, creepy old houses collapsing and burning down and no stores anymore except Natale's Pizza, a Quikway, Myrtle's Unisex Hair Shack and Al's One Stop, so I walk over to the Quikway and buy a Snapple and two packages of chocolate Hostesses with chocolate icing and I sit down and I watch the old cars and pick-ups and milk container trucks pull in and out and I wonder what I'm going to do because I feel like doing something. I want something to happen but I don't. It's like the lure of Black Thinking but very faint cause it takes a while to get the meds out of your system.

In my old mind I can feel my dad picking me up higher and higher to the roof beams of the converted barn and I love him so much all I can do is laugh. I am his Flying Boy. Laughing, lighter than air.

Al's One Stop Shooting Shop is right across from the Quikway. It's really just a hundred-year-old house with an electric sign hanging off the living room window. Snow starts falling light and easy, I fade in and out and it feels so good, it's me, not being on the meds and I can't wait to be myself. I was in Al's a couple of times with my dad to get ammo and Frankie Cole, this kid I went to high school with, a sophomore, bought a Chinese AST off of Al and around midnight on a Sunday he blew out every window in the school library with one hot spray. With the silencer on he said it sounded like a cat hissing.

In fifth grade Frankie Cole blacked out every single word in his reader with a magic marker. Really neatly until the book was solid with black lines.

'My dad owns the bank,' I tell the Quikway girl with the paper hat.

'Oh yeah?'

'Really. Accordia National.'

I can tell she doesn't believe me. 'Uh-huh.'

The girl with the paper hat isn't the world's leading conversationalist. Her eyes are dead olives.

So the entertainment is either Myrtle's Unisex or Al's One Stop, so there's a choice of one. I don't need a haircut anyway, I've got the new buzzcut. When I open the door a little bell tinkles but it doesn't disturb Al. He's got the Nature Channel on, polar bears, but he's snoring, hung up high on his Lazy Boy, half a Genny Pale Ale in his fist. The room stinks of beer and cigarettes. A pair of mangy old twelve-pointers hang on the opposite wall where he's got the gun cases. Their horns look moldy. I'm not really thinking about buying anything, I'm just looking for some distraction. I mean, what's there for the youth in Stick Willow to do?

Lying there, Al's like the boa that swallowed the boar, his stomach a big hump of a thing. I cough, shuffle my feet. Nothing. If I had a truck, I could back it right to Al's front porch and rip off his whole stock, that's how dead to the world he is. The rumor is he's got grenade launchers and anti-tank guns. Little bubbles of spit puff out on his lips.

'Mr? You open?'

The Lazy Boy heaves and rocks as he tries to get up, then settles as he falls back, blinking. 'Whatcha want ? You twenty-one?'

'Yes sir. I've got my driver's license with me. Twenty-two almost,' I lie. Usually, I can't even pass for seventeen, but he doesn't ask me to show him anything. I wonder if he knows me but he doesn't seem to recognize my face. Maybe it's the buzz cut or I got older.

'Well . . . Get some coffee,' he adds to himself.

While he rattles around in the kitchen I look in the cases. There's a lot of junk, Davies pistols that could blow up in your hand but he's got a hundred round Caleco semi and the usual Smith and Wesson .38s. With those you pay for the name and the feel of the handle. That's what my dad says.

'Got any Glocks?'

Al waddles back in. 'Nope, no Glocks. Got a nice Caleco .38 though.'

The store bell tinkles and in through the door comes a shambling Sloughter farmer in shit kickers and overalls and his little boy with a haircut that's mostly scalp.

'Mind if I look around, Al?' The farmer has that people-shy, Sloughter air, with a face like somebody squeezed his features together. Stick Willow must be the Sloughter capital of the world.

Barely above a whisper, his son asks, 'Daddy, the video . . .'

Al breaks out in a grin. Everybody's favorite uncle. 'How many times you seen this thing, Davey?'

But Davey looks away, as shy as his towering dad.

'You got the Ingram M10, sir?' I ask.

'What do you want with a gun like that?' he asks, straightening up, his stomach bobbing. 'You ever seen an animal shot with one of those things?'

The room gets very quiet for a second while Al fusses with his stack of videos, finds the right cassette and pops it in. It's as if he's ignoring my question. A century passes. I can hear how loud Al breathes, and the phlegm in his lungs. I can feel the shiny black eyes of the farmer on my face, wet marbles rolling on my skin.

His suspicions are crawling all over me, my skin itches with them.

'No sir.'

'Just like pulp. A real mess. I mean, give the buck a fighting chance, am I right, Sam?'

'They're shooting 'em from their cars nowadays.'

Dimly I'm aware of music in the background and quick flashes of color on the screen. Some sort of elaborate cartoon. Then I see the flashy Disney title, *The Little Mermaid*. 'This isn't just for kids, is it, dad?' Davey asks.

'Naa. It's got a real message, don't it, Al.'

'Anything Ingram puts out is just for show, appeals to a certain type of mentality.'

'I just saw it in a magazine.' I stare down at the floor, trying to sound respectful. This is the same asshole who sold a Chinese AST to Frankie Cole, which he might as well be selling AK-47s while he's at it.

'All you gotta do with the M10 is file down the trip, the bolt springs forward and you got yourself a machine gun. You a big time drug smuggler?'

Before I can say anything, Al flings his head back, and I can see a mouthful of silver and greenish fillings. The room is too small and close, I can't breathe. Without saying anything I'm swimming to the door through a soupy haze. Then I'm out on the porch, the snow falling shhhhhhhhhhhhhh on the empty street and I can breathe, ahhhhhhhhh. Across the way, weighed down with ice, the black power lines sag.

The Stick Willow Hotel, which used to be an old stage coach inn, has been boarded up for years and next door The Ron De Voo is shut up also, piles of rubble on its porch. The last time I was in Stick Willow at least The Ron De Voo was open. All these little towns up in the mountains are like this now, old people rattling around in big falling down houses, gaps on Main Street where the burnt down buildings used to stand. If I squint I can see the ghosts of wooden hotels with towers and huge covered porches and I can remember one of them on fire, too. Black, oily smoke and hardly a flame. Me and dad stood across the street and heard the rafters come crashing down.

Then there was a gas explosion but my dad said the insurance company wouldn't pay off.

The Sloughter slides up beside me on the porch without a sound.

'Hey kid,' he whispers. Shhhhh. The snow falls, it's a white screen between me and the Quikway. White is the sum of all the light waves in the world.

'Huh?'

'You interested in some firearms?' He sounds very formal, like a science teacher I used to have named Mr Glanz.

'Yeah, sure.'

Down the block in front of the Stick Willow Hotel, he's got a 70s Chevie parked up on the curb. The back window's all plastic and brown tape. We don't say anything, just walk. It's funny how I hear my own feet slap in the snow but the big man seems to glide beside me as if he's not touching the ground. I'm starting to wonder if he knows some kind of Sloughter magic. They're supposed to do voodoo like Haitians.

He pops the trunk and nods for me to stick my head inside it. 'Don't want to get the ordnance wet. Night operations,' he adds, picking up a thin black ski mask. 'Goes over your head.'

'You got bullets, too?'

'Clips, bullets, whatever you want. You say you like the M10? How bout this one?'

He's got it tied up in a black garbage bag but when he gets it unwrapped he shines a flashlight on it, like a spotlight kind of, and I can see a squared-off black steel body with a stubby barrel, the grip slightly back from center. It's ugly, like a black plumbing fixture. One look and I know what it is, it's the Cobray. The ads in the gun magazines used to call it 'The gun that made the eighties roar.' But I just play dumb and listen.

'Thirty-two shot magazine. We can do a private sale, no forms, no government shit. And lookit this, see these holes? Somebody went and drilled out the serial numbers before I bought it. What can I do? Here, see how it feels.'

I take the machine pistol in my hands, try to extend it with my right, but it's heavy, unbalanced.

'Lemme show you,' the Sloughter says. 'This is a hands gun. Gotta hold it with two hands. Then all you gotta do is spray it in a range. All that firepower, you'll hit something.'

I lift the gun again, this time with two hands. It feels better. The sight sucks, but like the guy said, all you gotta do is spray. 'How much?'

'Five hundred,' he says, trying to keep a straight face.

These people think just because your boots aren't covered with cow pies, you don't know shit about guns. 'Cobray costs three hundred new. I'll give you two hundred if it works.'

'Two fifty.'

'Two twenty-five. That's more than it's worth.' The gun's a piece of crap but it'll scare the shit out of anybody when they see it at first. 'You got some place to try it out?'

'Sure, you got the money?'

'Don't worry. We can go to the cash machine at Accordia National.'

My dad always leaves a thousand dollars in my account in case of an emergency. Dr Greenberg is right about him.

Nobody visits Breitman as much as dad. He's always keeping up with new drugs and therapies for me, too, he always brings me presents and letters from Crissie and he's a good listener. That's why I'm trying to get back in contact with my old mind, for dad. He didn't even mind when I stabbed him in the kitchen. After that I think he loved me even more.

# CHAPTER TWO: VINCE

## Saturday: February 27, 1990: 3:45 p.m.

I squint, trying to make out a shred of the double line, but it's fucking useless. Halfway between Merwinville and Accordia the snow starts hitting harder, in sudden bursts. Up near Gaiter's Dairy, past Pindar's boarded up building and supply, the two-lane highway disappears under blow-off from the blanketed fields. Shit. An ancient Chevie pick-up with a cap tilts ass-up, nose-first in a ditch. These local boys never have any liability, and when they get juiced they love to ride the roads. If they lose control on their bald tires and ram you, you're screwed. I know because the court's appointed me to defend half the booze hounds in Iroquois County.

Wind-driven snow blinds me. In the powerful gusts even the heavy Lexus jerks sideways in small, heart-stopping skids. My wind-shield wipers slow down under the weight of the white stuff. It's the dangerous time, almost too warm to snow. You think you're looking at scraped pavement, but it's fucking sheer black ice. Holding my breath, trying to fight the instinct to hit the brake, I downshift, forcing the car to crawl down the steep drop.

But the hill is almost a straight incline, the gears whine, and we pick up speed anyway.

All I can think about is keeping Lonnie safe, and showing no fear. Next to me, staring silently out the Lexus's window, he taps his finger against the glass. WGY, the only station I can pull in this high up in the mountains, has been promising the ski report for fifteen minutes. I switch it on, but Mark Moranus, the rabid talk show host, is raving as usual. 'I don't think the Councilman ought to be performing that type of sex act in his closet on our tax dollars. That's our closet. What do you think?'

I switch it off fast.

'What a jerk. You reading anything?'

'Yeah, *Dr Jekyll and Mr Hyde*. It's kind of simplistic, but it's cool.' I can hear my ex-wife Janet's tone in this remark. Lonnie is her protégé, her prodigy, even if he does have my Mediterranean complexion and a nose straight from Napoli. 'You think the trails'll be mobbed like last time?'

'Could be the way this winter's been.' For months the weather has done an imitation of early fall, then a hairy storm dumped a foot and a half of snow on the northern Catskills. On its heels, a lousy, gray thaw took hold. The skiers are pissed off, wondering what to do.

As we fall, a shiny red Blazer materializes in the middle of the road. It hulks, huge, at a dead stop. Now there's no choice. Sonofabitch. My heart in my mouth, I feather the brake, but we speed up anyway. Below, the Blazer looks like it's rushing backwards to collide with us. Now there's no alternative. I stomp on the brake, steeling my legs, preparing for the spin-out, my right arm flung across Lonnie's bony chest. In the long second before the crash, I think: *What a joke, I keep trying to give him everything, and I end up fucking killing him.*

Somehow, though, the studded snow tires bite something and we glide to a stop, just kissing the Blazer's high bumper. In a blur I'm out in the thick storm, ready to strangle somebody. Snow blows into my face, I have to shut my eyes the shit is blowing so hard. My chest is about to explode. Then I see the roadblock.

A pair of stone-faced troopers are talking to a man in pink and black ski pants. Maybe there's been an accident. Reflexively, I stick my hand in my coat pocket, fishing for my card. You never know when the big payoff's going to come along. I know a lawyer from Jersey City, he collected a judgment for two mil and five on a pothole. Car swerves out of control, whacks a pedestrian, the family sues the shit out of the city.

White mist swirls around the ankles of the geek in ski pants. The trooper is trying to calm him. 'We advise you to turn back then, sir. We expect this to take quite a while. Try Hunter Mountain.'

'God damn it!' he shouts. 'I called in sick! I been driving for hours! From Bayside!'

'Sir, we have a very serious situation on our hands. We've got Ten and Twenty-Three blocked off. If you want to get a bite to eat, if you want to stay in town, that's up to you. The motel may be full up already, though. And there's no way out of Accordia except the way you came.'

Edging in, I try to find out what's going on. 'Officer, we

live here, can't we just get to our house . . .' This isn't strictly true as Lonnie lives with Janet in Hurley, but he visits me on weekends when I can convince him.

Skiing is the big lure. If he doesn't want to see me, he does want to take to those hair-raising trails. The kid's fearless, which I like about him, but it takes a lot of discipline for me to keep my mouth shut and let him fly.

In that stupid, nasal upstate accent, the trooper calmly repeats himself.

'Fuck! I spent all that money at Herman's!' the bald man mutters, pointing to the skis on the roof of his 4X4.

The trooper turns to me, showing his back to Mr Bayside. 'Not at liberty to say, sir. For your safety, though, we can't let you beyond the town.' That means I'm out of luck. My mangy farmhouse is two miles up Redbone Road.

Every table at the Hungry Heart is taken, the small cafe stinking of smoke and grease and mildew. We stand near the door, stamping snow off our boots on a runner made of flattened cardboard boxes. Late on a Saturday afternoon the restaurant is usually deserted, getting ready to close up shop. But this crowd's made up mostly of stranded downstaters. You can tell by their new Land's End clothes, by their fidgety impatience, and their unfinished meals. They're not hardened to Hungry Heart cuisine.

I grab Kiki, the teenage waitress with the nose ring, before she can scoop up another platter of hot dogs, sauerkraut and potato chip specials. 'What's going on, Kiki?'

'Nobody knows. Some kind of shooting over at the Colemans. All we got left is chicken grillas and Jell-O.' Her upstate twang makes no distinction between gunplay and the depleted menu. Stabbed right through her nose's cartilage, the ring dangles like a tiny, silver trapeze.

Lagging behind me, Lonnie hasn't heard a word.

For his sake, I cover my fear with a flip tone. 'Jell-O sandwiches sound fine.'

Lonnie never knew about Moira Coleman and me. Anyway, our endless, on again, off again thing had finally ended a couple of years ago. I can still smell that extra bedroom in her house. She worked with piles of dried flowers. Musty and sweet, they hung upside down from the rafters. Globe thistles and hydrangeas and stuff I kept forgetting the names of. I never told her, but the smells got me hotter than any hundred-bucks-a-pop perfume.

'Vincie, over here,' O'Bannon calls to us from a rear booth. 'C'mon, we've got room.' The town pharmacist, O'Bannon made my A-list years ago by opening his store on Sunday morning and filling my usual scrip even though it had expired.

His pretty wife Julia slides over on the red leatherette seat.

'Julia, you know my son, Lonnie?'

'Hi,' Lonnie says, pulling his dog-eared Robert Louis Stevenson from his back pocket and burying his nose in it.

'The world's last thirteen year-old reader,' Julia says, glossing over the kid's lack of social grace.

'Just the usual teenage, antisocial behavior,' I joke.

Lonnie shoots me a sour look from behind his novel, the kind of look that makes me cringe. Nothing I say seems to live up to his standards nowadays, a fact I can't help attributing to his mother's iron-clad brief against me. And Janet can write one wicked brief. If you marry another lawyer, avoid experts in matrimonial. Of course, she did have some ammunition against me, the usual *flagrante delicto*, and a false claim of desertion which she tried to use to restrict my custody. I deserved everything else she dished out, but that one I fought tooth and nail.

In fact, I got so crazy over the divorce I lost a pair of nice soft tissue injury cases back to back. To say I was a stupid, self-involved, arrogant asshole would be to merely state the obvious, but it's been years now, and I wish she'd let up. All I can do is focus on the main message to Lonnie: *I'll never desert you, no matter what*.

Glancing up and back at me and the kid, O'Bannon lowers his voice to a whisper and leans towards me. 'There's some wild shit going on, Vincie. The troopers are all over the Colemans' place, their hunting camp.'

'Moira there?' Suddenly I'm shivering and sweating at the same time, but I retain my all-too-practised professional mask.

At the same time I remember lifting up from her boat of a bed and realizing that her floor sloped away at a good fifteen degree angle. Across the room the dormer window angled in the opposite direction.

From under the down quilt, she stuck one hand out and waved away my paranoia. 'Oh, don't worry, the house is sinking, but I asked a friend of mine, and he said it won't collapse for another thirty or forty years. So let it sink!'

O'Bannon nods his head towards the back, and we both get up. 'Two bladders, no waiting,' I say. Lonnie just ignores us.

'Your old man, what a guy.' He winks at Lonnie, too damn jovial for comfort.

In the rear of the restaurant we slip into the storeroom. On an extra gas stove red potatoes bob in a huge pot of boiling water, the back window all fogged up with steam. It's hard to breathe.

'We don't know who was there, all we know is that Harlan, you know, the guy who does body work across the road from their camp, he called the troopers cause he heard some shooting or he saw something.'

Shifting his weight, O'Bannon knocks a restaurant-sized can of tomatoes off a shelf with his shoulder. Dented, the can wobbles across the wide-plank floor.

'Nobody calls the troopers if they just hear gunfire. Shit, it's hunting season all year round at my place. Bow and arrow. Snowshoes. D.E.P. catches 'em without a license they say they were only shooting woodchucks.'

'Well, I heard Harlan was back there near the camp in his snowmobile. Maybe he got a look at something.'

'Troopers aren't running around for nothing.'

'Just sit tight, I guess. Maybe it's all overblown.' He gives me a searching look. Does he know? Since I moved upstate, Moira and I have barely seen each other.

'Probably. Everybody's going nuts right away. They see this shit on the boob tube, they start hoping for the worst.'

O'Bannon snorts. 'She's a funny woman. She's got this silver thing shaped like a finger she stole from her mother. One of those holy doodads? She says it's got the crotch hair of St John the Baptist inside.' I think it's got her crotch hair, actually. 'She makes those, she clips those hedges, whattayoucallems?'

'Topiaries,' I say without thinking. Not something I should know, but O'Bannon's so lost he doesn't even blink.

Moira's tall, I always like that in a woman, and she has those off-beat looks that are almost beautiful, only better. A very wide face with a slightly flat nose. Wide-set green eyes. A slightly thin mouth that's out of fashion nowadays since they started shooting up the models' mouths with collagen, but very even, very good teeth. You'd almost say with her long neck that she looks aristocratic, which is pretty funny since she comes from real shanty Irish in Milwaukee.

When I first met her in California she had reddish brown hair straight down to her ass. Very shiny. When she'd get on top of me and let it down, I'd be in a tent of hair. That I loved. For years men would stop dead in their tracks when they saw her, five eleven in her bare feet, her arms rattling with bracelets, walking with her shoulders flung back alongside me like some Egyptian queen. Face it, you never get over the kick of that as a man. She's your prize. Every poor sucker wants her, and they know you're fucking her every night.

'Vincie, let's go out front. I'm choking in here.' Creeping out the back door, we negotiate the icy stairs like men who've taken a few falls.

We huddle under the World War I gazebo. A peculiar sign

under there lists the town's casualties from the Great War in white plastic letters like the times for the next movie. On the other side of the park, Main Street is deserted. Across the way stands Massey's renovated Victorian. He bought high in the boom, like me, and now we're stuck. Next door he's got the Autumn Leaves Rest Home. Jabbering geezers in wheel chairs. What a mess.

The mountains are barely visible in the snow. In his shirt-sleeves, O'Bannon hunches his big shoulders, and stamps his feet like a horse. 'It's bad, it's really bad . . .'

'What the fuck's going on, Jimmy?'

'We're not sure, we don't know who was in the camp, but Maurice got out of the hospital, those stupid psychiatrists . . . I called Moira, no answer. Christ, nobody can find her. Any of them.' To my shock O'Bannon with his inflamed Irish mug is crying, snorting up snot, rubbing his eyes with his shirtsleeve, but he manages to go on. 'Gotta stop . . . Julia . . . You see this crap on some cable movie . . . It's not a joke. You know I had a thing with Moira five years ago, not too long but serious . . . Almost left Julia, but Moira didn't want me to . . .'

O'Bannon, too? And then I think, why am I surprised? She's been alone, without me anyway, long enough. Still, I feel jealous. How could she let this rube put his hands on her?

Moira sat up in bed and extended her arms to me. Without makeup she looked pale, all the energy drained out of her. One of her breasts flopped out over the quilt. 'Now I know where I saw you,' she said. 'On one of those Pompeii frescoes.'

I spit the words out. 'She dead?'

'I don't know, maybe, could be . . . Sweet Jesus . . . The cops are talking out of both sides of their mouths. How does a certified lunatic get his hands on a semiautomatic? Know what? Yesterday Julia was telling me she had an idea to give Moira some business . . . Today, phhhttttt . . .'

The dead quiet gets under my skin. In all the years I lived in Manhattan I never witnessed a single act of violence. Pretty grotesque when you consider that I've spent half my life in that scummy Criminal Courts building on Centre Street trying to figure out how I could convince juries that my little monsters were poor, abused, misunderstood tikes once upon a time. Then I move up here after that insane Martini case, to this retreat . . .

'Shit. What am I supposed to tell Lonnie? You think we're going to be trapped here all night?' How can I entertain him? The baseball museum in Cooperstown? Ty Cobb's dried-up mitt? Who gives a shit? Then I think, Moira's dead, and my knees turn to water. I'm surprised I'm still standing.

'Who knows? As far as I can tell they haven't caught the little murdering sonofabitch. Schizophrenia, bullshit! At the store I'm giving out psychotropics like candy, nobody goes and . . . Yeah, he's still on the loose. You'd think those dumbassed troopers could catch one kid with a rifle, there must be thirty or forty of them up on County Eight.'

'Yeah, but little Maurice knows the terrain . . . he's been hunting with his dad for years.' Narrow-faced little Maurice with his sucked-in cheeks, his hedge of black eyebrows, his brilliant black eyes. You couldn't take your eyes off him.

He was a deceptive little bastard in his khakis and pin-striped shirt and V-neck pullover, rattling on about hacker friends of his or new theories about how the universe started. He talked in such a rational way even I started to believe him.

'I'm sorry, Jimmy. Don't jump to conclusions, we don't know anything yet . . .' This sounds so empty I try to think of something else to say, but I'm struck dumb. Vince Vitale, of all people. Give me five minutes and I can get a whole bar pissing in their pants.

'You know whose fault this is, don't you? It's that jerk Nathan's fault. Jesus H. Christ. They get divorced he moves right across the road. Ten years and he still won't let up on her.'

'Maybe I should take Lonnie back to Hurley.' Oh, man, this is what it feels like to disintegrate. Am I?

'Damn Nathan. The guy's an obsessive maniac. He probably put the kid up to it.'

'Oh, c'mon, Jimmy, don't go off the deep end.' Disintegrating, but my performance is professional to the end. 'Jimmy, the kid's a fucking schiz, it's chemical. You of all people should know that . . . C'mon, I gotta go inside. I'm freezing.'

I search his face, and I can tell he doesn't know a thing about Moira and me. And a good thing, too because I don't want to hear myself put a spin on our affair in that convincing, completely phony way that only I can. Sickening.

'Yeah, wait a sec, lemme wipe my face. My God! Poor Moira . . .'

He shakes his head hard, like he's trying to get rid of all his worst fears.

I grab him by the shoulders. 'Jimmy, we don't know shit yet. She's probably okay.' I'm convincing myself and seeing through myself at the same time.

'You want to laugh? I keep thinking I'll get back with her. Pretty stupid, huh?' He makes a strangled noise deep in his throat. 'People go and then they're gone. She could.' Without warning the heavy man lunges and starts puking. When he's finished I kick some snow over the yellow bile.

'It's okay, big guy.' I pat his back.

'Yeah, well.' He looks around, trying to figure something out. 'Jesus, it's cold. What're we doing out here?'

Back in the Hungry Heart booth Lonnie, his novel at arm's length, suddenly lets go with a burst of laughter.

'Lemme guess. Mr Hyde is pillaging and murdering?' When I say this the words come out just right.

'He's a baaaad boy that Mr Hyde.' Lonnie smirks. Under the wavering fluorescent light he looks very thin. His skin is stretched tight, almost transparent along his jawline.

'I offered to feed him, but with little success,' Julia says brightly.

'Know what, Lon? I think this thing's gonna drag on. Maybe we should head back to your mother's.'

'That's okay, I can wait. I really want to do some downhill, dad.'

'Yeah, well, nobody's skiing this weekend. I think we ought to hit the road.'

'Why can't we just wait? What's the big deal?'

'For one thing there's a storm coming. I can't afford to be stranded. Lake effect they said,' I improvise, but the moment I say it the fear comes over me. Up in the Adirondacks I drove through a whiteout that sucked every sensation out of the world. In a blast of snow the windshield went dark, the wiper blades just choked. What the fuck do you do? You're blind but if you stop you can get rammed from behind. If you go forward, you could go off the side of a cliff. All I could do was slow down to ten miles an hour, open the door and look for the edge of the mountain.

'My favorite, I like to ski downhill in that stuff.'

Irritated, I toss down a few bucks. 'Thanks folks. Maybe I'll see you in a few days.'

Sullenly, Lonnie follows me. We're the only ones out on the street. 'Hurry up, let's get in the car. Can't you see there's something wrong?'

'You always make such a big deal. You look like you're having a heart attack.'

The back of my neck is soaked. My armpits are dripping. Alone with Lonnie my studied composure starts to crack, but I insert the key and the car whispers on. In five minutes we can make Accordia disappear, we'll be back in the countryside, driving past the dairy farms, collapsed outbuildings, scuzzy trailers, picture-perfect auto graveyards.

I'm driving a shade too fast, but under control, whipping

past the abandoned Victorian department store, Accordia Liquors, Christian Notions, the Image Zone Tattoo Parlor, The Last Tangle Hair Salon, Constantini's Truck Parts.

'I don't know why I bother,' Lonnie mutters.

Without warning, I lose my cool. 'There's a fucking lunatic loose with a gun, you want to hang around for the show?'

'Really? Why didn't you tell me?' For the first time all day he sounds animated. 'Who is it? Why didn't you tell me?'

We're arguing. Great. At least we're having a real conversation. That dead cool routine of his reminds me too much of some clients I've known and loved.

I'm almost going too fast to stop at the roadblock. In a neat bit of footwork, the trooper dances out of the way, but he's none too pleased. I roll down the window.

'Turn around! Nobody goes through!' he snaps. His hat is knocked sideways, he has a panicky look in his eye, and suddenly, despite his Marine-like demeanor, he looks like a kid.

'You just told me I could go back this way an hour ago.'

'No more. We've got police activity here. Get back into town. Now!' he barks.

As I struggle to turn around we hear the pop of real gunshots, flat and matter-of-fact. I keep backing up, turning the wheel, looking around wildly. Then I see the small black figures running along the ridge near Gaiter's dairy barn, racing towards the silo's long shadow. A chain of figures rushing towards the edge of the world. More shots. It's all a blur. Who are they? Did they fall or just disappear over the white hill? Don't want Lonnie to see. Any of it.

'Don't look! Don't look!' I'm shouting, but of course Lonnie ignores me.

'EEEOOWWWW! EEEOOWWW!' he bellows, pounding the dashboard with his bony fist. 'You see that? You see them?'

Skidding around me, a van full of troopers disgorges five cops with rifles. In a panic I try to maneuver the car into a U-turn, but my front tires start digging a trench in the icy shoulder. On the other side of the windshield the kid trooper is shouting, waving his arms angrily as I spin my wheels. Finally, the Lexus lurches forward, but gets stuck again. My blood pounds in my ears.

At a crazy angle the white fields turn into a white sky, and for a second I lose my bearings. Surging forward by itself, the car reaches the shoulder of the road then slams to a halt, wheels digging a fresh ditch.

Twisted around, Lonnie gapes at the distant figures as they rush into the shadows. Far away the gunfire seems to recede. Poppoppoppop, toy guns in a game of war. Slamming the car into reverse, I'm flung forward, the tires spitting slush and road salt. Forward, back, then forward again, till finally the tires seize the pavement.

Once we're safely out on the highway, I can't help looking over my shoulder too, but all I can see is Gaiter's silo and its weathered yellow and blue dome. A heartbeat later the farm's three acre pond swings into view. This warm, you could go right through that milky ice.

Without thinking, I head straight back to Accordia Memorial Park, with mechanical concentration aiming the car into a spot against an ancient, laid-up dry wall. Silently, we sit there, the fan droning on and on.

The pressure to say something builds, as if it's supposed to be my duty to explain the unexplainable. 'We better try the motel before they sell out. We're stranded.'

'What's going on, dad?' Lonnie's face looks dead. No color at all.

'I wish I knew. Maybe we can catch something on HBO.'

He brushes aside this transparent attempt to act normal.

'You know what mom calls you? The Big Meat Puppet. I used to watch the *Dating Game* with her, that's what she called them, guys like you. You know the first memory I have of you? Really, honestly and truly? The day you packed up and left us. That's what I remember.'

It's like getting kicked in the balls by the past; you can't kick back.

'Okay, I'm a meat puppet. I confess. Let's talk about something else. We've gotta find a place to sleep.'

'That's another name mom has for you. Mr Change-the-Subject.' He shifts uncomfortably in his seat, looking away.

A cold anger seizes me. I'm beyond strategizing, maneuvering, or protecting his tender feelings.

'Well, listen to this. I'd cut my right arm off for you, whether you want me to or not. You want my time, my help, money, you can call me any time of the day or night. You know that. So stop breaking my chops. Your mother is a very, a very fine person, but she's not perfect either. Anyway, what're you gonna do, shoot me?'

In the brief, awkward silence that follows I wonder how I could say something so idiotic.

'I thought of that, dad, but I decided to let you live.'

He's fast and wicked this kid of mine. We both start laughing, just for a second, but even then I'm afraid somebody'll see us.

# CHAPTER THREE: MOIRA

## Saturday: February 27, 1990: 8 a.m.

All curled up on the couch in her flannel nightgown, she looks like a sleepy cat. I've made the coffee just the way she likes it. Half expresso, half hazelnut, cream, one sugar. 'Thanks, mom,' she says, reaching for the new mug. 'It's as big as a bowl.'

'Special at Violet's. How about an omelet?'

She stretches, the foggy look on her face clearing. Crissie has such beautiful skin. 'Can you put in cilantro like you do?'

'Got some. If you drive forty miles you can get anything around here. That new Shop 'n Save in Tuscarora had some beautiful arugala.'

'It's great when you wait on me, mom.'

I throw an old pillow at her head, but I miss. When the phone rings, it sounds like a fire alarm.

'It's him,' she says. Her mouth tightens as she hands me the receiver.

At the base of her neck there's a love bite she's tried to cover with foundation, but I can still see its raw outlines. If I told her

I thought the bite was cute, she'd start in again. Just like her father. A dental drill of reason.

'What're you laughing at?' Irritated, she thrusts the cell phone right at my face. If I could have her taut skin, her smooth forehead, her pristine throat again, I'd lie down with the devil anytime. Anyway, who knows? Maybe he could do things with that forked tongue.

'Who?'

'Maurice. It's Maurice.'

Two syllables and I'm stunned. I haven't gone to visit him in weeks because I can't live through another tirade, another hail of accusations. And why should I? Is it fair to let his illness tell me what I've done to him? And the worst part is he looks so handsome with his black hair and those magnetic black eyes, and he sounds so much like Nathan. Both of them, human scoreboards. On June 14 of 1982 you did this to me. I said that to you. You ignored me, you broke promise number 1437.

On the other hand, he's probably sitting in that awfully clean day room suffocating in the stink of deodorizers and the drone of that incessant daytime TV, watching those awful TV hostesses. Supposedly, the Breitman Institute is above mindless institutionalization, at least in its four-color brochures. But I trust Maurice's descriptions more than the shrinks'. They're the ones making money off of sickness.

'Oh, give it to me.'

Crissie has the strangest look on her face. She covers the receiver. 'He's out,' she says.

All I can think of doing is running. Hopping in the car, heading for the airport in Albany, disappearing into Italy or Greece. I'll become one of those threadbare biddies who lives in a one star hotel on a vanishing income. Who can say we don't have the right to make up a new life?

At the same time, I want to race to him, say just the right words to quiet his torment. My monkey boy, skinny spider monkey boy, sucking, soft-boned in my arms.

'Hello, Maurice? Where are you, honey?'

'I'm at Stewart's. They've got Hazel Nut now. I wanna go hang out at the camp, okay?' I can hear the manic edge in his voice.

'Is your father there?' I'm so transparent, and he's so smart, even disturbed as he is he can see through me.

'No, he's not around. He was supposed to pick me up, but there was some kind of foul-up. Can you meet me over at the camp in a couple of hours? I'm hitching over there. It's really fantastic to be out.'

'Can you get the heat on? Is there any propane?' I know I'm trapped, but maybe there's a way to get Nathan over there. I can't be with Maurice alone. It isn't fear, fear would be easier to deal with. One or two episodes don't make him dangerous. And under the influence of his medicine he's so calm he seems like a Buddhist. No, it's finding a way to speak to him. Groping for something to say is agony.

If I could only hop into the car and start driving south, slip into another life. I've got to write away for another credit card.

His voice is wispy in a shower of interference. 'Yeah, sure, no problema, momsie. But there won't be a shred of food. Could you bring me a sub or something?'

'I thought you weren't eating meat.'

'That was then, this is now. I've constructed a new simulacrum.'

When he starts talking like that he makes my skin crawl. But Nathan is right. You love no matter what. The best I can do is love the Monkey Boy, the Cub Scout, the fifth grader who wrote a poem about photosynthesis and shouted it out without a microphone to a whole assembly:

When sunlight passes
Through Chlorophyll
God makes
Carbohydrates

Nathan used to read him science books like they were fairy tales. The Nathan whose tight muscular torso and long, tennis player's legs used to turn me on. He had just the right amount of hair, dense on his chest but tapering down to his belly-button. His ass was tucked under, strangely flat, but I'd ignore that and concentrate on his whole body, the smooth hard length of it. We fit in our way for a time.

'How long have you been out, Maurice?'

'Did you see Arsenio last night? Andrew Dice Clay was crying. Can you believe it? I don't have any money. Maybe you could pick up a pizza from Natale's. Could you bring Crissie?

It feels like years.' The phone goes dead. Maybe he's hung up, maybe it's electronic gremlins. All I know is I'm thankful. It's easier to drive over to the hunting camp than to call him back, easier to see him in the flesh than to listen to that spacey voice of his.

'Would you run over with me, Crissie? It'll only take a few minutes.'

'I swear, you don't hear a thing I say. You're in your own little world. I'm not his damn mother. You are.'

'What were you saying?'

'Never mind.'

God, I could use a joint. Joe, the bartender at the Seasons Cafe, was explaining to me the other day why the local, mountain-grown is so good, something about extremes of temperatures and excretions of resin. Oh, to feel that swooning sensation. A bottle of decent Cabernet and pasta *al dente*. Mushrooms lightly sautéed in olive oil and garlic and sprinkled with basil. The apricot aroma that clings to chantarelles.

I can't tell Crissie how nervous I am. And why should I? She'd just use it against me. 'Well, I just have to finish packing up these arrangements for Exurbia. Thank God for orders from that store. At least they have decent taste.'

I don't say another word, knowing she'll come around. She's really too sweet to say no.

* * *

Back in the workroom on the plank table I assemble the five extra orders that came through, putting together the strawflowers, sumac and teasel with a sprinkling of sea lavender, tugging at a stem, varying the palette of dry grass and flowers, searching for the shape hidden in each half-random bunch. The stems crack and abrade my hands as I snap them into forms I didn't know were there. It isn't even the final composition I crave so much – though I love to see what finally appears out of nowhere – but the mental state I fall into when I'm making things.

When I work my eyes go out of focus, I drift into a light trance and something opens up deep in my chest. I forget Maurice for a while.

I love working on this dark, battered table, I love the view of the snaky road and the leafless maples that line it. While I work, I play my tapes, mixtures of Motown and Latin and Rock and before I know it I'm letting loose, new steps flowing out of me that I never planned. I always dance better when I'm alone. Dancing seizes me and I don't think about anything at all except slipping my body into the beat. I do karate kicks, Bob Fosse, I moonwalk. I'll try anything, my tap routine, my meringue, my silly imitation of Twyla Tharpe, dancing til I drop. I'm myself again, not the strange woman with the lined face and lank dyed-auburn hair in the bathroom mirror. Better to be nothing but fast, mindless feet.

Almost an hour passes, maybe more. I forget to look at my watch. But it will take Maurice a while to even get to the camp. Then Crissie wants to take a quick bath. After that I have to wait for the water to recycle so I can do my hair. Otherwise, I'll look like a wild witch on a heath.

'Can we go in two cars?' In her baggy sweatshirt and droopy jeans, Crissie hides her body. Just as well. The poor farm boys would faint if she wore a Danskin top. She has my figure, but more athletic, her breasts higher, her legs even longer. In Catholic school I was always at the end of the line. Somehow, the nuns made me feel that being tall was a sin.

'Sure. Oh shit! No. We'll have to use your Toyota. I can't get the Honda into reverse.'

'Ohhh, mom! I'm supposed to meet Harry! Why do you do this to me?'

'You can meet Harry. We'll just stop by to see Maurice, his father will come over, and then we'll go to town to the post office. You can drop me off on the way back.'

'God! I feel so bad for him I can't stand it!' Now she's stripped bare, angry, haunted, just like me. I know I'm the adult, I'm supposed to say something wise, make it better, but I feel exactly the same way.

'He was such a brilliant boy, I never suspected—'

'Oh, don't start that, I knew he was strange when he was ten. Everybody did except you and dad.'

'That's really not fair. And he didn't start having symptoms till he was twelve, almost thirteen.' This isn't quite true either, but it's a point of honor. I knew, I knew as soon as he started to eat alone on the basement steps every night, I knew as soon as he started playing with the Lesh boy, who was so many years younger. All of a sudden my Maurice, who could name all the constellations in the sky, starts playing marbles in the dirt and war games in the woods for hours and hours.

Later he started repeating my words in this maddening way. Echoing. At first I thought he was being nasty, and once I lost my temper and slapped him as hard as I could. The anger just boiled out of me, my palm leaving an angry red smear on his face. 'Now will you stop it!' I shouted, my whole body shaking.

'Now will you stop it,' he repeated calmly. No, in an inhuman, machine-like way.

Oh, I understood then, and I wanted to take him in my arms, heal him, strangle him, but we just stood staring at each other behind the tilting house, under the red maple.

He looked so normal in his plaid shirt and jeans and brown Nikes. But I knew, I knew long before he ran away and ended up sleeping under a bridge in Syracuse, long before he dotted his forehead with the pattern of pin-pricks. Even now faint scars in the shape of a pentagon are visible in his skin. Could you love someone like that? Fine. You're a better person than I am. I do everything I can bear.

'Actually, we should go to town first, I've got to send these arrangements overnight. You could call Harry and have him meet us in town.'

'Harry doesn't have a license, remember mom?'

'Of course.' Skinny Harry with his big black glasses, the least fashionable boyfriend Crissie could find, a farm boy interested in physics. She could have all the conventional prizes, the quarterback or the Boy Most Likely to Succeed, but instead she sticks to Harry, marches him defiantly around the mall, bony

Harry whose toothpick legs swim in his muck boots. I'm proud of her. I shouldn't, but I wonder what his hairless body looks like, his skinny, innocent erection.

And just like clock-work, she says, 'Maybe I can stop by Junk Heaven. Harry needs a few things for school.'

'If they'd change their stock once in a while, I'd tag along with you.'

'Don't you have to go to the post office?' Her not-so-subtle hint to buzz off. It's still hard to remember I'm the mother, not the girlfriend, especially because Crissie is exactly the kind of friend I always liked. Even though I know every one of her terrors, she has a confidence and grace about her. Well, maybe you won't believe me because I'm her mother, but all my friends tell me it's true. Anyway, she *does* like to hang out with me, otherwise why would we have those three hour heart-to-hearts in my bedroom, drinking tea, wallowing under my pile of quilts, and why does she ask me, so shyly, whether she can teach Harry to do it a little slower, a little longer.

Before we go out Crissie grabs her boxy Carhart coat and ties her plain black scarf at her throat. She won't cover her head, so why even bother trying to convince her.

'Oh, shit, I forgot to feed the horses.'

'Oh, I'll do it, mom. You'll take forever.'

'See how Baltasar is doing. He was off his feed.'

She rolls her eyes, but I know she loves the Icelandic with the wild, heavy mane that falls over his eyes. My five-gaited beauty. Ten thousand was too much for him – I don't want to think about the cash advance on my Visa – but with stud fees I could make some back. Half, anyway.

Flakes stick to Crissie's thick, wavy hair. I never had a single curl in mine. Black Irish to the core. But for some reason my mother kept an Infant of Prague statue on top of the Kelvinator refrigerator. Maybe she liked the Infant's prissy little man's face with the gold curls or the satin brocade garment she dressed him in. Like a christening dress.

Down below I can see Stone Creek Road, skinned asphalt streaked with ice. I wonder if there's any fuel in the cabin. If it's bitter cold, Maurice could get uncomfortable, change his mind and head over to Nathan's. 'We should have warmed the car up before we started.'

'You always say that, but you never do it,' she snaps. 'That's the way you are.'

'Hey, don't go global on me. How is he?'

'He's a horse, mom. He's fine. You could brush him once in a while, though.'

We drive without speaking, the snow swirling down then stopping entirely, as if we're entering a hollow in the storm. By the time I get to Steadman's Corners though, it's blowing harder again, blinding me, enveloping the light, skidding Toyota. Nothing frightens me more than hydroplaning. Once, in a wild thunderstorm, I sailed right out of my lane on the Palisades Parkway. First I was in the left lane, and then suddenly I was in the right. If there had been a car next to me, I would have been killed. There's not much protection in these tin can Toyota Tercels, no rear wiper in this model, either. And the side windows are smoked with mist. I can't see a thing except the twisting highway directly in front of me.

'When we get to town, do me a favor. Call your father to see if he's heard from Maurice.'

'Mo-om, why don't you call him yourself?'

I don't say anything for a while, the car skidding and sliding a foot in this or that direction. We could plunge right over the bridge on Semanski Road and nobody would find us for days. In the winter hardly anybody drives that way. 'You know why.'

She refuses to respond, but I can sense, by the tone of her voice, that she'll give way. Anyway, I can't talk to Nathan. Years ago he started confusing himself with Moses or the Pope or somebody. He'd write me these precise notes explaining step by step why I was the most selfish, immoral bitch to cross the face of the earth. If there's one thing Nathan knows, it's what's right and what's wrong.

'You're only doing twenty miles an hour, mom.'

'I can't see a thing in this car. I don't know how you drive it.' On either side of the narrow road white fields swell up to the low sky. In the distance a few, scattered maple trees break the monotony.

'You know, when I was little I really used to admire you,' she says after a while. 'You were the most beautiful of any of the mothers, and you were always in such a good mood. My friends just died to come over because you let us make a mess, and you really didn't care—'

'I'm glad you felt that way.' I try to head her off, knowing what's coming next. To distract her I pop in a Smokey Robinson tape.

'Do you have to play that? It's so . . . it's so clean!'

'Well, I've been accused of many things, but that's a first!'

She laughs, almost a low growl in the back of her throat. 'Remember when I was nine and you gave me the Spanish dress and the maracas?'

I flip her a Latin shoulder dip. 'Celia Cruz! Tito Puente! Mon-go San-ta Ma-ri-a!'

'Azucar! Azucar!' Even her voice, a timbered alto, makes me love her. This isn't like loving a man, seeing his inevitable imperfections but rationalizing. This love is embarrassing, it's too much love to explain or control.

Worse even than Vincent. He used to say I was like an electric charge, but it was him, his all-night talking jags about his cases, his compact, athletic body. With his husky thighs and behind, he reminded me of a Centaur. When we made love he'd pound himself in the chest and say, 'my whole body's coming.'

Well, I don't like to get sentimental, but I can't help surrendering to the sweet memories sometimes. It's better than wondering if Maurice changed his mind and is looking for me in town. He's appeared out of the blue dozens of times, right in my face in the specialty foods aisle at the Grand Union, from behind stacks of bird seed bags at Agway or at the counter at the Hungry Heart, spinning on a stool.

Junk Heaven – a pill box cement building next to the Fire Department. The whole parking lot is like a bumpy ice skating rink. Only one other car sits there, some ancient, enormous American thing. 'Oh, they'll be closed till one now.'

'Who?'

'The Post Office. Well, you get out, I'll go see Julia anyway. If you get bored just come over. See if there are any new mysteries.' Junk Heaven contains everything from Bag Balm for irritated cow teats to remaindered hard backs for $2.99. Smear a little Bag Balm on your face and those crow's feet fade away. It's been a beauty secret of mine for years.

'We can't take forever,' she says, just to hold the moral high-ground, but she doesn't want to face Maurice either. By the time we get there, Nathan will have shown up. Being reliable is a religion with him. Why don't I want to give him credit for it? Because he tells me how reliable he is, that's why.

'If I don't get these orders out overnight, we don't eat next week.'

'I need some money.'

I crush a ten dollar bill in her hand, and she slides out. Even after she disappears into the store I sit there, wondering what to do after mailing my orders, worrying that I'm taking too long. When did Maurice call? Not more than an hour ago? No, an hour and a half now. But there is really no choice. I either sit in the car or visit Julia, who will make herbal tea and have a plate of ginger snaps on hand. She'll play her sensitive, tedious folk song tapes – God, whoever called that *music*? – and go on and on about the way the town used to be in 1909 when the hotels were full of financiers, and Broadway dandies like Theodore Dreiser's brother Paul, who wrote *On the Banks of the Wabash*.

Nathan's great-grandfather sang a sentimental love song and danced in one of Dreiser's shows, and lent him money, too, a fact Nathan loves to point out.

But I've known Julia so many years there's a comfort to our friendship. Julia is a good listener; she's the only one who can understand what a topiary is, and how I can spend two months creating an original one. She went into transports over the turtle I clipped out of hedges at Jack and Amy Zelakowski's farm. (Now that Amy left Jack, I worry about the turtle. She was the gardener in the family.)

And who else but Julia, prim, erect Julia, would never imagine I had slept with her husband? Of course, now that it's over it's a relief. I'd much rather have Julia than O'Bannon anyway. There's nothing worse than a needy man.

But Vincent hadn't worked out, not even that last time around, and that hurt so much I could never admit it to anyone. Vincent, who always made me think of that Pompeii boy in the Roman mural. Vincent, who had that casual, confident way of arching his back above me. Oh, I could get a hold of his full behind, and arch up to him, and hang on, taking him in, taking him in, and we would be suspended in the heat of it, both of us faint, laughing in shock when it was over. Vincent, who I always fled to, who I always escaped from. I'm a mystery to myself. Now, all of a sudden Crissie is on her way to college, and I'll be alone, completely alone.

I like to tell myself that I'll enjoy the solitude, and it's true I can spend hours and hours by myself in perfect bliss, but to be without anybody, to live the rest of my life curled up in the corner of my sagging four-poster? The best thing to do is change the subject with myself.

O'Bannon was just something that happened. Well, not exactly. I put my hand on the inside of his thigh at dinner one night while Julia was in the kitchen. I didn't plan it, I didn't think about it. But it wasn't his thigh I found my hand on. Just sitting next to me he had a hard-on like a horse, and my fingers without thinking just wrapped around the shape of it, and he went so red I thought he'd have a heart attack. After that, I had to be polite and go to bed with him. I mean, you can't do something like that to a man and then pretend you're some kind of virgin, can you?

You can read the years of little boys in Julia's floors. Wide-planked, uneven, they are gouged, scraped, and pitted by cleats, roller skates, ice skates, bats, clubs and sticks. Clean-cut, healthy, moderately bright boys. Franky and Mike. Julia says she wishes they were more intellectual, more off-beat, more creative. Is she gloating or patronizing me when she says these things? What I wouldn't give to be simply disappointed by a son.

In a minute she has me wrapped in an afghan by the fire, apple spice cinnamon tea in a mug beside me.

'Can't we call him out at the camp? We can invite him over here. I was going to stir fry some veggies. Maurice always liked me,' she adds with such delicacy. Why didn't I think of that? I won't have to go out there at all.

'For some reason I thought the phone was dead. But Nathan could have put it on. I don't know if he's hunting much anymore.'

'You want me to give him a ring?'

'Would you . . . I don't know if I'm up to it.' Julia is such a good friend. Numbly, I rattle off the number. What a perfect solution. Julia calls Maurice and Nathan is already there. But no, that's too good to be true. Suddenly, I smell the dank, mildewed air of the hunting cabin. The stink of mouse shit. Maurice wouldn't even notice it, but it makes me ill.

I pray someone will pick up.

Without make-up Julia's face reveals its bony structure. Her thin eyebrows rise as she presses the receiver to her ear. 'It's ringing. Let's wait. Maybe he's nearby.'

She lets the phone ring over and over, for a whole minute. I hold my breath. 'Maybe Nathan already met up with him. They crossed wires at the hospital or something.' But I can see Maurice sitting all alone at that wobbly table, staring off into space, playing obsessively with his fingers, biting his cuticles. I smell that dreary, dead air.

'We could try again in a while,' she says, carefully placing the phone back in the cradle. It's as if she's afraid that the slightest sound will set me off.

'Oh, no big deal. I'll just have to go out there. I'll take him shopping for clothes at Penny's.'

'There's a clearance sale, but they're so overpriced to begin with. But where else can you go? K-Mart?'

'Yeah, our malls aren't even malls.' Without warning I'm crying, tears boiling up out of nowhere. 'It's okay,' I laugh in the middle of the sudden outpouring, but I'm shaking as if there's a powerful storm inside me. 'The longer I avoid him . . . the harder it is for me to face him . . .'

Julia is kneeling in front of me, holding my hands. 'Here's a tissue,' she offers.

'But I have to.'

'What?'

'See him. I feel like a big old snot-bag.' For a while I can't stop shuddering. Chills run through me. Why do chills make me hot? This isn't like me, and I simply have to stop. I take out my compact. A web of fine red veins spider out through the whites of my eyes. My make-up is running all over the place.

'You've got a right.'

'Waterproof mascara, ha.' Rummaging in my make-up bag, I find some old Visine. A Kohl pencil, too. Just going through the rituals calms me down. 'Maybe I should get going.' I can't even get up from my chair.

'Oh, take your time. I want to show you something.'

'This is ridiculous.' I sip some tea and slowly the shaking shrinks to a small point inside of me. A small pulse of panic that won't stop.

On the end table next to me, Julia spreads out a series of vintage photographs of Accordia's Main Street. Turn of the century probably. Their surfaces are brown and yellow, something to do with the fixing or the chemistry, but the images are intact. 'Oh, I want you to look at these,' she says eagerly, as if nothing has happened. 'You see the hanging baskets. They run all the way down the street.'

What a relief. Something else to concentrate on. She hands

me a magnifying glass. Elaborate mixed arrangements pour from the suspended cedar boxes. Petunias, geraniums, ivy. 'Let me guess. You want me to recreate these for the spring.'

'I thought they might spruce things up. I consulted with the mayor and the budget committee, and there could be a small contract.' She's beaming now, knowing I could use every cent she can squeeze out of the town.

'The old girl network, huh?'

'Why not? They've been doing it long enough. Do you know how much that creature Ray billed for gravel last year? Eighty-five thousand dollars!'

'How much are they willing to pop for flowers?'

'Five thousand for you, plus the expenses. The whole budget is only ten, but maybe I can get a few thousand more when we work out a real estimate.'

When I hug her it's like holding a bag of dry sticks. Woman of Sticks, my protector. She's wearing some sort of musky powder that reminds me of old sour ball candy in cut glass dishes. Then I'm rushing to the door, the way I do things, taken over by some surging impulse before I can think. 'I'll work on some numbers for you,' I shout over my shoulder, picking my way out from under her portico, down the wooden stairs.

In my first moment outside I take in a breath of hard, icy air. The door to the Toyota is frozen shut, and I'm afraid the puny plastic handle will snap off in my grip, but all I can think about is getting to the camp. I can't explain it. It's not as if I've thought it through, it's not as if I've decided to do the proper thing, or that I'm being driven by some buried maternal instinct. I'm simply ready to face him now. Him.

Finally, the door gives way with a crisp peeling sound, and I'm behind the wheel, turning the key. Giving it gas. But all I get back is a single click. I floor the clutch pedal and try again, just to make sure, but the battery's dead as a doornail. For the fiftieth time this winter, I've left on the lights. I'm frozen in place.

# CHAPTER FOUR: JULIA

## Thursday: May 8, 1987: 1:10 p.m.

Willistone, home of my childhood, is underwater now, its streets deep in silt. Settling to the lake bottom, the feed store, the Willistone Inn, Sinclair's bakery, the Italianate town hall, Vic's hardware, the barn-like Rollerama still stand. The church steeple lists, a rotted mast in the murky water. The house where I was born is a shipwreck. The roof is a mat of green weeds. Fish swim through my old bedroom. I left a white dress with a scalloped hem in my closet on a hanger, and I wonder if it still floats, fluttering in the currents, empty of me. I left soft, fat crayons in an old highboy, I left a broken-spined Uncle Wiggly book with color illustrations, I left my armless doll Nellie with the human body and the rabbit's head. I cannot touch the things that made me.

People hundreds of miles away drink the water that drowned my town, unaware that they are swallowing bits and pieces of Willistone.

Accordia lives above the waterline, but it isn't terribly different from Willistone. Or I am not any different than I might be if I drifted through the rooms of my old school on Schenectady Avenue, running a finger across a wet, mossy blackboard. Deep in the watery past I see the wall of Artie's Auto Parts where seventeen year-old Jimmy O'Bannon pressed against me, half in terror, half in lust. He was going to buy a manifold gasket for his Chevie Impala, and I had tagged along. Inside the caved-in aisle of Artie's drowned storeroom manifold gaskets rust and stick together like old lovers.

I put on a light sweater and go out on the porch with my alumni magazine. May. Sixty-two degrees. People in the Hudson Valley don't believe us, but as far as we're concerned, they live in the tropics.

With an eagerness I'd never admit to anyone, I turn the glossy pages. Cecilia St John is running a small bio-tech firm with her husband, Philip, outside of Seattle. Myra Gombrovicz has been named director of a social service agency in Atlanta. Joan Birdbaum is an editor at a small publisher specializing in wildlife books for children. She lives in Santa Fe. I live underwater, in Accordia, sleeping more than I'd ever admit. I have nothing to submit to the alumni magazine. Or at least nothing they would print.

Julia Pindar, who formerly won honors in literature, attracts secrets. Her research has shown that winter hides what is already dead. That long affairs are flies in amber. That good-looking women are blinded by their own light. One of the subjects of her study, Moira Coleman, is a case in point. Julia Pindar, who starts to write novels, stories and histories of small places reports that she finishes none of these. She has perfected, however, the ability to stare off into space for hours at a time, and to live underwater without breathing at all.

Julia Pindar O'Bannon, class of '71, writes that she is thankful for Moira Coleman's visits, and her husband, who Julia always calls by his last name. She wants O'Bannon to be happy, and when Moira left him adrift he went into a dark mood that lasted a whole winter. Julia Pindar reports that her husband's affair with her best friend began well, but like all of her designs it petered out, leaving only a fragment to turn over in her mind.

O'Bannon shatters my reverie, slamming the door and pounding his boots on the floor of the mud room. He's late for lunch as usual. I race to the microwave to heat up last night's meat loaf and potatoes. By the time he gets into the kitchen I've opened a bottle of Merlot.

Absent-mindedly, Jimmy takes the glass and hurls himself onto the couch. 'Viruses. Nits. Herpes. Worms. Cancer of the month. I swear, every man over fifty's got the prostate. Violet Longo pulled that shit again, too.'

'Benny?'

'What am I supposed to do? Her husband's going in for angioplasty, I'm going to withhold his nitro? I don't think that woman has told the truth once her whole life. It's always some excuse.'

'She'll never pay. And you know you're not going to hold back Benny's medicine. Maybe you should just accept it.'

This is O'Bannon at his most attractive. He won't admit it, but he worries about his customers; he's always afraid somebody is going to die on him, as if he's the doctor, not just the pill pusher.

But he's getting that bloated face of his father's, permanently red from all that Genny Pale Ale. I hate to judge him, but I think he's starting happy hour right after breakfast.

I pick at my green salad.

'Nathan called me at the store. A week after they commit the kid, he's trying to get me to agree they should let him out of Breitman. He starts asking me questions about side effects, he knows more than I do.'

Now I'm shocked from my reverie. But I'm not surprised. Just the other day Nathan swore he'd barely been scratched, even though I know better. 'Was he serious?'

'Oh, yeah, he's driving over there now to argue with the shrinks. If you ask me, the kid's like that because Nathan's around the bend. He's got all the answers. He won't even let the kid get treatment.'

'What does Moira say?' I ask with sickening innocence.

'How do I know. She's your friend.' Face down, he concentrates on the meat and potatoes.

'Well, I think you ought to talk him out of whatever it is he's doing, Jimmy. It's irresponsible.' And, I neglect to add, it frightens me. I like to keep up the polite fiction that I have a certain rapport with Maurice, but that's just for Moira's sake.

'Naaaa. I don't want to have anything to do with it. This store's closed.'

Secrets are a bittersweet pleasure. I find myself daydreaming, though their affair is long over, of Moira servicing O'Bannon. I've even wondered if he is acting in my imagination as a surrogate lover, but that would be all too simple. I feel no desire for Moira, just envy and admiration. But on those summer days when I drive up Rose Lane, a far field from the renovated barn, and I make my way through the sticker bushes and cat-tails to the back door hidden from the road, I prove that even a skin and bone woman can catch fire.

# CHAPTER FIVE: NATHAN

## Friday: February 26, 1990: 11:45 a.m.

Dr Schwartz plays with his red paisley tie. The corner of his mouth is blue. He's been chewing cheap pens again. But he knows better than to try to manipulate me.

'Well, frankly, I'm pissed off, Nat. And embarrassed. There are procedures for weekend passes, and obviously they weren't followed. Dr Greenberg should know better. But the first thing we've got to do is track Maurice down. Usually they don't get far from the grounds.'

Schwartz is subtle. He'd make a good PR man if he'd cut that rag of a beard off his face and buy a decent suit. Admit error up-front, go for the damage control. But what he's pitching is junk bonds. 'Maurice isn't just another patient, Mark. He knows the country like the back of his hand. I taught him survival skills. If he gets back in the hills he'll think he's outsmarted everybody, and he might freeze to death.'

'I know that,' he says, too impatient for my taste.

'So what do you propose to do about it?' Bore in and keep an eye on your objective. It's the only way.

'There's only one main road and two directions. North and South. I called the local police and notified the troopers. I gave them a full description.'

Now my heart skips a beat. Maurice, alone on the highway, listening to the contradictory voices he hears. Voices that just rip into him. My heart sinks. 'What kind of condition was he in when he left?'

'Not bad, according to Dr Greenberg,' Schwartz says guardedly. 'He certainly wasn't delusional. Just a trace suspicious.'

'Well, anybody with a brain in his head would be suspicious. You're the jailer, Mark. Or don't you get it? I'd try to escape, too. What was he taking?'

'Stelazene. And his bipolar medication.'

'Lithium?'

'Yes. Lithium.'

'So what do you propose to do, sit on your hands while he freezes to death in a snow bank?'

'I can't leave the grounds. I've got thirty-five other patients to attend to.'

I actually like Mark, but there's something holier than thou just under the surface. Maybe it's because he used to be a cancer researcher before he was a shrink. But for mental problems these drug treatments can go only so far. How can a shrink give himself to a kid the way a parent can? The boy's your mirror image, he's you. Only a parent who's willing to give everything, go over the top, can really heal a boy like Maurice.

'You don't have the vaguest idea where he is, do you?'

'Not yet anyway. Where do you think he'd go?' At least he doesn't try to bullshit me.

'I haven't the faintest. Remember when he hitched a ride all the way to Syracuse and we had to pick him up under the bridge?' That just popped out of my mouth. The less I say about Syracuse the better. The cops can claim anything they want about a patient. The kid was talking pure word salad by then. And who knows what happened to that derelict? He was frozen solid before Maurice got there. 'He could be at the video arcade at the mall, he gets fixated once he starts. He could be at the bus station in Tuscarora.'

'Maybe you should try the mall. Get Moira to check out the station.'

'Fat chance.'

'Right. I forgot for a second.' He gives me a soulful look that says, I know what a good father you are, you've been through hell. That's the last thing in the world I need. Life is hard. Big deal. He picks up the phone. 'I'll call the cops again and have them keep an eye out in Tuscarora.'

As he places the call the fear I've been keeping at arm's length takes over. Without his medication, and he'll definitely stop taking it, Maurice will start getting delusions all over again. One winter morning he was running up and back in the yard in nothing but Bermuda shorts. Barefoot. Naked to the waist. When I finally grabbed him I had to hold him down like a wild animal, but he rolled away into a patch of sticker bushes. They tore red scratches all over his arms and chest.

I reached down to help him, but he reared up and bit my face.

He bit my face, my right cheek. That was the strangest feeling, my own son biting me like a dog. I could feel his teeth rip into my skin, going deep down. There was something about that bite, where it was, that made me understand everything. Later, in the house, when he sat rocking and watching his tape of *A Brief History of Time*, I noticed the bloody patches on his scalp. He'd pulled out whole fistfuls of hair.

Then he looked up at me suddenly, totally oblivious to what we'd just been through. Blinking. 'I'm the only one in the world who can see leptons, dad. Isn't that amazing?'

Schwartz's whole response seems so feeble. Does he always send the parents out after his escapees? Probably saving money on staff. There's no one to go out in hot pursuit these days. Blue Cross won't come across for search parties.

I'm trying my best to keep my temper. 'You have the troopers' number?' As he reads it off to me, I start wondering what the line on the Knicks game is. 'So this is the best you can do, Mark? How about calling back some attendants. I'll run the search party myself.'

'This is it. If I could do more, Nat, I would. I wish I could, believe me.'

'Yeah, sure. You and Pinnochio.'

'No need to get nasty. I understand you're under a lot of pressure.'

In a rage, I snatch the troopers' number from Mark's desk. You pay through the nose for facilities like Breitman, believe you me, and then they poor-mouth you. Maurice could have been run over by some redneck on Lavergne Hollow Road, try to find that one even with a map, and what the hell does Mark care? But I can't think negative. Not to be superstitious or anything, but when you start thinking negative, you spook the odds.

Until last week, I'd never been nervous about playing with the overnight deposits because I'd always been able to shift funds and cover any serious losses, but who could possibly expect the Lakers, the Suns, and the Pistons to lose on the same night? Every one of them favored, too. But if you love the action, you've got to take the heat.

And the difference between a shark like Milken and me is that I always cover the deposits. Ten, twenty, thirty thousand people lose their jobs because of his dicey paper, and what does he do? He raises his fee. A mil five just for a letter of credit.

If I had to there's some foreclosed property I could grab, a nice eighteen-eighty Greek Revival with over a hundred acres and a creekside meadow. I know the area so well around here, I look at the landscape and I automatically see the property lines. I know a farm that's not worth diddley because Niagra-Mohawk is going to run some power lines right through it, and I know a cute-as-a-button Cape with radon in the basement. What I also know is who's sick and desperate to sell, and who's a complete fool and asking for the moon.

Maurice costs a ton of money, that's another thing Moira conveniently neglects to notice. Well, don't go down that road. What's she got to contribute anyway, the Queen of Dried

Flowers? She clips the shape of a dog out of a hedge and we're all supposed to fall down and worship her. She says she's worried about pesticides, and we're supposed to notice how sensitive she is. Only she conveniently forgets to visit Maurice, who's in pain every second of his life. It's the old story with her, public liberal, private fascist.

Down at the end of the hall a woman with dyed blonde hair stops me, her face full of those complicated tics caused by the psychotropics. They're hard to look at, especially when I think that in a few years Maurice's face will be creasing and twitching in the same way. 'Aren't you the man from the bank?'

For the life of me I can't figure out who she is. 'No, must be somebody else.'

She wags her finger as if I'm a child. 'Ohhh, no. You're the man from the bank.' Her speech has that thick-tongued sound of over-medication. 'Your son's in my . . . group therapy . . .'

The idea that Maurice has to spend his life with critters like this turns me inside out. In a way I don't blame Moira for wishing the whole nightmare away. I'm not looking for any medals. If I could keep myself from visiting I would, but he's my son, and abandoning him would only make me feel more disgusted with myself. You have to face it. Your genes did this, nobody else's. Call it enlightened self-interest. Moira pays a higher price for running away.

On the other hand, I wonder if she has any feelings at all. Maurice was about a year and a half and could pull himself up and stand a bit, but one morning he was crying, falling down, in a terrible fever. I remember his soaked hair sticking to his scalp. I wanted to hit the road ASAP, but Moira just said, 'Oh, it's a little fever, it'll go away.'

Then she jumped in the car and took off to Tuscarora for some damn art appreciation course at the college. I suppose I was in shock because for a couple of minutes I wondered if she was right, that I was making too much of a small cold, but then I looked at his dripping, red face, and I knew it was bad.

After examining him for half an hour, the doctor came out to the waiting room and told me, 'You have to be prepared for the worst. It could be meningitis.'

And there I am, all alone in a waiting room sitting on a plastic bucket seat. For two hours I sat there chewing my fingers off, sure Maurice would become an idiot because of the fever, while Moira was off appreciating Monet or Manet or one of those French clowns. If I had put every dime I had on a long shot and the nag was dead last in the homestretch at Saratoga, it couldn't have equaled how bad I felt.

'Flat affect' the shrinks call it. The way she is. *Immoral* is the old-fashioned word. She's a taker, pure and simple.

Before I call the troopers, I put in a quick call to Duane. I take the Knicks and two and a half. 'The Foreman fight, you get him five-to-two. You want a piece of that?' Duane asks.

'Yeah. Give me Quarry. Foreman's got so much blubber on him he's liable to have a heart attack in the first.'

'Yeah, there's a lotta people wishing and hoping. I'll put you down.'

Then I fish for another quarter to call the troopers, but all I come up with is my keys and some fuzzy tissues. For ten minutes

I'm running up and down the hospital begging for change. You'd think some critter would have a quarter. Finally, I sell a buck for seventy-five cents. The lazy SOB's don't answer til I ring twenty times. Finally I get some bored woman dispatcher.

'Yes, sir, we received an all-points on him. We're aware of his condition. Our patrol cars have been advised.'

'You've got nothing? How hard can it be to find him on one road?'

'Sorry, sir, we're dealing with a number of accidents as well. You'll have to be patient.'

Patience is not what we need now. Maurice knows every back road in the hollows. It's only ten miles from here where we used to hunt turkeys. He bagged one when he was only ten. Damn thing was almost as big as him.

I taught him respect for firearms and how things work, everything from electric current to the sump pump, to the crystals that make up snow. Moira thinks snow is something to write a poem about, but I taught Maurice the hard realities, how moisture and temperature affect the shape of the flakes. You can sing songs about it, or complain about it, but the truth is it freezes hard for months and you have to respect that.

Outside in the parking lot, driven by a thirty mile an hour wind, the snow stings. I wonder what the poor kid had with him when he skipped. Thank God the Cherokee's got a blast furnace of a heater. But even a Cherokee's radio is useless in the mountains. All I can get is that idiotic WGY.

The problem with WGY is you can never get the scores.

Sometimes on a newscast they'll even tell you who won and who lost without saying by how much, so you can't even tell if you beat the spread. Why the hell do they think people want the scores for, fan loyalty? I keep thinking of getting one of those sports beepers at Radio Shack so at least I'll know what's going on in the world.

The road is glassy in patches, and I go through so many micro-skids I forget to breathe. But I've lived through this climate for so many years, I'm used to my heart clenching into a big hard fist. What bothers me is that I can't see more than a few feet ahead of me, and the tire tracks are half-filled in as if the last car passed an hour ago. I squint, looking for anybody, anything that will give me a clue. Who knows? Maybe I'll just run across him out of nowhere, it could happen. The wind whips up snow devils that make it hard to see. My jaw aches I'm grinding so hard. Half-blind, I think I see his shape a hundred times.

It takes me an hour to go thirty miles, and when I see the Quikway sign in Stick Willow, I turn in. Quikways are like the old stagecoach inns, the last thing to shut down, except the best you can get is a ham sandwich on white that a counter girl in clear plastic gloves takes ten minutes to put together. Every time I go into the Stick Willow Quikway, there's a different dimwit there, which means the turnover is every two weeks. Talk about a personnel nightmare. You'd have to hire an extra body just to take care of the W-2s.

This one is a needlenosed girl with glasses, some kind of albino or a mutation that came out of the hills. Of course, Moira thinks these Sloughters are the salt of the earth. She swears they're the ones who always stop when you've run out of gas or blown a tire. She's probably right, too. When they see the wreck she's driving, they think she's one of them.

This girl's got on a red Quikway apron and a paper hat. Her eyes are blinking like she's terrified. Maybe I'm the first customer she's ever served.

'Coffee and one of those twists, please.'

'Jelly or sugar?'

'Twist. The long yellow one that's like a braid.'

'Oh, yeah. You can fix the coffee yourself over there.'

'Right. I know. Have you been here the last few hours?'

'Since we opened?' She flinches and answers with a question.

'Have you seen a kid, around nineteen come in? He might have had on a black down jacket, one of those skiing things?'

Suddenly, in a jerky way, she comes alive.

'He sat right there for an hour and didn't say a word. He drank Snapple, coffee and ate Hostesses, chocolate frosted. I don't know whether the coffee did it to him, but I seen he was very nervous. He had on a black coat like you said, and he had his hair pasted down over his head like he was wearing his hood a long time. He was wearing low-cut duck boots, which I wondered about, not good for the snow, you know? But people are like that.

'My mother says, "They think if they pretend hard enough, the snow'll go away." Truth is, up here, the snow don't stop till the end of April a lot of times. Then try to take a tractor out when it melts, you can ruin your fields, or even get stuck like it's a swamp. That happened to my dad a couple of years ago, and we had to call the Whitackers to tow him out of there. Once the snow starts it's better to forget it, don't even look at it, and go about your business. Take care of chores.'

'So, did you see where he went when he left?' First she's a deaf mute, then she's a talking machine.

'No, I was stocking the chips. Later, though, I saw him get into a car with a man.'

That gives me a jolt. 'What kind of car? Did you see the man?'

Her frightened look returns. I try to restrain myself because I know this kind of girl, I've rejected her a thousand times for teller jobs at the bank. The second you ask them the simplest question, they go to pieces.

'I don't know, an old car. Just a man.'

'That's all?'

'Can't say. Man just looked like a regular man. He had on a hat.'

'What kind of hat? What kind of coat? Was he big, small, did he have a beard maybe?'

'Yeah, no, I'm not sure mister. I don't know mister. He could've.'

There's no point in going on. She really doesn't know because she's a dizzy idiot like the generations of dizzy idiots that came before her. When Maurice was in sixth grade a girl disappeared from class for a month, so they sent a social worker out there to find her, and some member of the clan, there were five men and two women, comes to the door of the trailer, and he says, 'Oh, yeah, Sarah died. We buried her over there.'

That's it, like a farm animal. Later, the county came out because the family hadn't gotten a death certificate, dug her up, and found out she'd died of diptheria. What a scare we had in the whole county. America in the 1990s. It might as well be Ethiopia in the Iroquois County hills and hollows.

Exhausted, I try anyway. 'You didn't see where they went?'

'Just up the road . . . Maybe they turned up Tatum Lake Road.'

Suddenly I get it. She knows exactly who it is, it could even be her father or her uncle or her brother or some combination of the three. Most of the houses on Tatum Lake Road are summer cottages, so any house with a light on could be the one. The road only runs about two miles all told. How hard could it be to track the man down? I try not to think about why he would pick Maurice up and take him home and just focus on the business at hand.

'Tatum Lake is the second right up this way?'

'Yeah, right after Vita's Auction.'

'Can I have some quarters for the phone?'

Nervous, she gives me change of a dollar. Blinking madly and licking her almost invisible lips, she seems to be screwing up her courage. 'You're not a detective, are you?'

'No, honey, I'm just looking for my son.'

Now she breaks out in a smile, showing wide-spaced teeth

but pretty good for around here. 'Oh, if that's all. Some of these guys around here, they got DWI warrants out.'

I head for the phone and call the troopers. But from the way the dispatcher is talking, I'm better off going after Maurice myself. Then before I leave, what the hell, what's the difference? I check the line on a few college games. UCLA's favored by nine. That's a lot of points. Washington's not bad this year. I take them and UNLV, too. Tarkanian is getting those kids out of phony prep schools and jails, probably, but they can run and gun.

Where's the action when you own a bank? You're the house. You can't lose.

My car is blanketed with a new layer of snow. Barely a light is on in the godforsaken town, which isn't much more than a single street with the Quikway, a gun shop and a hair salon. The big houses were put up in the late nineteen hundreds by railroad money. Smaller, older Greek Revivals, and a few Craftsmen from the 1930s make up the rest. One or two of the Victorian hulks burn down every year, but the insurance companies rarely pay off because it's always so easy to find the oil-soaked rag or the splash of gasoline in the ruins of the see-through stone foundations. Most of the people around here, they can't do a damn thing right.

A logging truck booms past, going way too fast, and then a milk tanker. These idiots will end up in a ditch if they don't watch out. In a minute they're disappearing in their own spray.

I let them get ahead of me before nosing out into the driving snow. When I think about the speech Maurice gave me under the bridge in Syracuse, I steel myself. Finding him may be the worst part.

# CHAPTER SIX: VINCE

## Sunday: February 28, 1990: 7:40 a.m.

'You've got to come, you've got no choice, Vince,' Mackey, the sheriff, says. He fills the scuzzy motel stairwell with his big, wide ass. Behind him the coffee and soup machine sounds like it has gas. Cream of mushroom coffee. I tried it last night before I remembered the wonders of botulism. An unscrewed bottle of Cremora, used plastic spoons, and torn packets of sugar cover the card table against the stucco wall.

Still half-asleep, I stamp my dead feet to keep them warm. Like my father, Joe the Barber, I don't have much sensation in them. Soft, surgical shoes he wore, with laces on the side. Joe the fucking Barber, he tried to ruin me. When I was sixteen he already wanted me to quit school. Cousin Vito needed me in his exterminating business, he said. Jesus, I can still feel the clouds of insecticide on my face, soaking my hands.

'Hey, Mack, how about lowering your voice? I've got Lonnie sacked out in there. I'm not risking my life for some psycho, so forget it. Anyway, nothing personal, but there's nothing in the law that compels me to go with you.'

'You know what I was doing when this thing blew up? I was screwing in a light bulb for Mrs Fabricant, who calls and says she's got a power failure. They won't leave me alone. They chase me around, they call me at my house.'

'You need this like a hole in the head, right?' I've known Mackey for a few years. More than once I've sat with him and a local judge in the back of the Hungry Heart Cafe and worked out an arrangement for some farm kid who burglarized a bottle of Seagram's and a deer rifle.

'Yeah, well, I'm used to dealing with the rear end of society. But Coleman's kid, shit . . . What a mess.' He shakes his head, his loose jowls wobbling. Mackey looks like a hunting dog.

A narrow window above the soda machine barely registers the early morning light. What the fuck time is it? I shiver, wishing I'd put my sneakers on. I need the padding. With my lousy circulation, the bottoms of both feet are dead. 'But you're willing to stick my ass out there? What're you, out of your fucking mind?'

How many times did I see Maurice over the years – a dozen? Crissie? Fewer. Just an ambiguous friend of the family. One day I was visiting from the city and Moira brought him along to go sailing on Tuscarora Lake. He must've been fourteen by then. At first he was telling us what to do with the tiller every five seconds, but then he lost interest and just trailed his hand in the water, staring at it like it wasn't his.

Moira whispered, 'Leave him alone, don't stare.' Arching her back and stretching those long legs, she acted like he wasn't there. Amazing how she could ignore the worst and act, no, *be* happy.

We didn't have sex that day without saying why. We even made noises about being friends. What bullshit. As if I hadn't once said, 'In a few days the license will run out. If you want to . . .'

In a *comidas criollas* we were. Not talking about getting married. Everything and anything else but. I was so nervous I poured half a bottle of green sauce on my *arroz con pollo*. Black beans and a shred of chicken stuck on my fork. Part of me was willing to take her kids on and shoulder the whole mess. I'd told her often enough, but she got that distant look in her green eyes like I was talking about plumbing fixtures.

'Aren't you the one who says everybody lies?'

'That's just in court, Moira,' I said. She didn't answer, she was letting me off the hook, and I was fucking levitating with relief.

'Look, Vince,' Mackey says, a lot softer. 'We've got carnage on our hands, real carnage. The kid says he wants you to negotiate for him. He thinks you're gonna be his fucking lawyer. I guarantee we won't put you in harm's way.'

'What time is it? I must've slept two hours. His fucking lawyer?'

'It's six-thirty. We can leave Summerville to keep an eye on your kid.'

'Summerville? The guy acts like he's twelve himself. He off the sauce?'

'Paulie's okay, you know that.'

'His fucking lawyer? How'd Maurice even know I was in town?'

Now he gives me that impassive cop look, and that classic flat delivery that says he's full of shit. I've cross-examined a thousand Mackeys.

'We don't know. But he must've seen your car or something. Can I get into the mind of a lunatic? Come on, we could use the help.' His eyelids blink rapidly, then settle down.

'So I stay behind the lines and talk through a bullhorn?'

'Something like that. Troopers got Crisis Intervention set up in the Gaiters' house. We don't want another casualty.'

'You gonna tell me what happened over at the camp? Anybody hurt? Moira?' Half-stuttering, I can barely get her name out. And I'm sinking all over again. The Longest Affair. We used to joke about it. In sickness, marriage to parties of the second part, and in health.

'Years ago, one time, you had a thing with her?'

How can he possibly know that? Twenty country miles apart, Moira and I hardly see each other. Sure, we're painfully polite, we're aware of each other's whereabouts, but we're definitely, finally finished.

Cops. Peeping Toms with badges. 'That's none of your fucking business. I moved up here because of Lonnie.' Immediately, I hear how phony these words sound. Why do I have to explain anything to this yokel? 'If I'm going out there, at least I get to know what the situation is.'

He hesitates, and in that short suck of breath I feel like I'm falling into a black hole. I once had a client who fell two stories down a shaft backstage at the New York State Theater. Shattered half her vertebrae. My knees turn to jello. Gripping the staircase railing, I take a shaky breath but keep on my poker face.

'I wasn't at the camp. I had my hands full cornering the little bastard.'

If she's dead, he's not going to tell me. He figures I'll lose my incentive to cooperate, and he's right. 'I'm not going near this sonofabitch, you understand? I'm not even going to show myself. That's your job.'

'Sure, sure. You want to wake up your son?'

I think for a second. To what purpose? It'll just freak him out before the fact. He'll sleep till noon if we leave him alone. 'Just leave Paulie, and get Lonnie whatever he wants. Breakfast when he wakes up. Two.'

'Sure, sure. We got this kid pinned down in Gaiter's barn. But better to talk him out,' he adds, distracted.

'I guess you didn't ask for this shit.'

'Friday, I got twenty years in. I was going to take my wife up to Maine to live.'

'You asshole, you're moving where it's even colder?'

'Funny, huh? But there's no people, no god damned people.'

'A man after my own heart.'

'People.'

The only thing moving in Accordia is the dirty orange snow plow. The Stewart's convenience store lot is full of emergency vehicles, cop cars, but the rest of the town is even quieter than usual. The Grand Union parking lot is vacant, Avenoso's Italian Cuisine is dark, Napa Auto Parts has got its steel gate down. For a few minutes the snow showers stop.

'Reporters!' Mackey spits.

Now I see the press packed together in front of Junk Heaven, held back by a thin line of troopers. We glide right past Tony Standa, who looks like a pink-faced baby, compliments of some Park Avenue plastic surgeon. In a three thousand dollar blue top coat, he's joking with a twenty-something camera woman, maybe hitting on her. Then I see Carol Tobias from the station in Kingston, and Louis Farburg, from down in the city, CBS, I think. Farburg's doing an interview with Martha, the fire-plug Gertrude Stein lookalike on the Town Council. The Toasty Tanning Tub's window is the backdrop.

Looming above Mt Sunayantha, the TV personalities look smaller than life, but the tube makes everything official. Without a good, healthy killing, there's no incentive for these media vultures. Why else would they be here? Sons of bitches ate me up on the Martini case.

Above Gaiter's dairy barn two helicopters vie for airspace. 'One's CBS, the other's ours,' Mackey says matter-of-factly.

All of a sudden fear gives me the water knees. I get that piercing hunger, the kind that makes me light-headed. I'm weak as a kitten. This is not my usual performance. In the Martini case I was the whole show. I was so sure of myself I didn't even put the kid on the stand. What an asshole I was, committing the cardinal sin, counting on a jury's ability to reason. Even these days, once I start thinking about the case it gives me acid in my throat.

Mackey pulls the cruiser up behind the Gaiters' rambling farm house, out of sight of the barn. We climb out into the icy muck. Wet snow oozes into my sneakers. Shit! Half-awake with Mackey driving me, I've forgotten my damn boots.

The elements have eaten the paint right off Gaiter's house. The siding is streaked with the remnants of a 1942 coat of white. Moira likes this 'distressed' look. She used to say decay was in fashion. The Gaiters, millionaires with a chemical business, are big taste-makers.

Captain Grimes spits out the situation in short bursts. 'Kid's getting more paranoid, and he's got a shitload of ordnance up there.'

A plain-looking guy, Grimes has one of those authoritative voices that sounds funny in real life. Like he's an announcer who escaped from the radio. Maybe I'm still not awake, but I have to bite the inside of my cheek to remind myself that the kid with the gun, the barn, the helicopter, the cop yakking in front of me are all real.

'They got these gun shows in Chenango County, you can buy anything,' Mackey adds. 'Conversion kits, silencers. We think he's got a Mac/10 or some piece of shit like that with him.'

'They're easy to modify. To fully auto,' Grimes comments. The two of them might as well be discussing mufflers.

Trying to keep my voice from shaking, I lay down my terms. 'I'm not going anywhere near this kid. You get him on a bullhorn or something, and I can talk to him behind the lines, fine. I got a son back there in the motel, I don't want this kid to know where I am, even vaguely. As far as I'm concerned, you can tell him you got me via satellite.'

Grimes lays a veiny hand on my wrist. 'No risks, Mr Vitale. We take the risks. We've got the CIU set up in the house here. You won't even look out the window.'

'Good. As long as we understand each other.' I start following him to the back door, sloshing through the heavy slush. 'You got some extra socks in there?' Fucking winter, fucking snow. You're freezing or wet and shivering all the time, and it never ends. Months and months of this shit. Behind Grimes the white fields roll on and on like a headache.

'What he wants is for you to finalize his will,' Grimes says as if we were in my office going over the minor details of an estate.

'His will? How am I supposed to do that?' The icy slush laps over my ankles.

'Just work with me. We've been talking. He says he can dictate it in a few minutes.'

'Then what?'

'Then we keep waiting. We wait til next summer if necessary.'

There's no transition between his soothing words and the explosions from Maurice's automatic. These aren't regular gunshots, they're quick, ear-splitting salvos that rattle every bone in my body. Panic slams me face down in the dirty snow. My heart is banging in my chest, I'm deaf from the shots, I've got a mouthful of crusty snow. Loud, sucking breathing fills my head. There's no way to hide it. I'm a total coward.

'That's all right,' Grimes says, yanking me to my feet. 'Just pissing in the wind. He's been doing that every once in a while.'

My coat, my pants are pasted with slush.

'Maybe he wants Wendy's, he don't like the Chicken McNuggets we give him.'

Embarrassed, hating their all-too-casual cop-talk, I brush myself off and head straight for the back door. Only when I get inside the mud room do I feel the chunk of snow stuck to my nose, and the warm, moist piss leaking down my leg. The inside of my thigh burns. At least I didn't shit myself. Somewhere I read it was normal for a World War I recruit to drop a load under his first barrage. Knowing this doesn't make me feel one fucking bit better.

Behind the storm door a trooper is staring stonefaced at Gaiter's barn. Unlike the house, this building's got a new roof and a fresh coat of paint. No cows though. I heard that inside the stalls you could eat off the floor.

The kitchen features a wood-framed oil of sheep grazing, a sleek refrigerator, a restaurant-quality stove on a cooking island. Money and the pretension to simplicity. I know the type.

Next to the trooper a red-faced man in a leather jacket speaks soothingly into a cellular phone. He has a large, flat, fighter's nose, and a fringe of red hair.

'Montgomery. Hostage negotiator,' Grimes whispers.

'Maurice, you still there? How's the food? Hot enough?

Yeah, we can call Avenoso's for a pizza for lunch, sure . . . yeah, yeah . . . no, I don't think so, now wait a second, I got somebody here you want to talk to, I got Mr Vitale with me.'

He reaches out and shakes my limp hand. The piss is burning all the way down my leg, and I'm trying to think of a graceful way to ask for some fresh underwear. 'You up to speed?'

Grimes intercedes. 'I don't think the sheriff told you, but he's got his mother in there. And the sister. We don't know what condition.'

Bang. Just like that. No warning. Probably they figured they'd just dump me in, and I'd have to swim. She's alive, she's alive I'm thinking, but then . . . if I say the wrong thing, I can get her killed for good. I'm fucking seasick. But I know I'll keep my balance out of professional habit. It's a useful, horrible gift.

'What condition?'

Covering the receiver, Montgomery says, 'He wants to talk to you. Be friendly, but don't make any promises. Don't confront him, just sympathize. You understand everything he's going through, or if you can't agree, say nothing at all.'

Taking the receiver from Montgomery I get confused, not knowing which button to push. Impatiently, he stabs at the phone with his index finger. Then Maurice's voice is inside my head, so distinct it hurts. 'You're the lawyer?'

'Yes.'

'I know who you are. I know all about you.'

I stand there speechless. Does he know about my fits?

# CHAPTER SEVEN: MAURICE

**Friday: February 26, 1990: 2:50 p.m.**

The Sloughter takes me to my father's bank in Accordia, but he stays back in his car while I run the cash machine. Now I'm sure he's reading my mind, but he's keeping it to himself, his yellow eyes like flat disks in their sockets. Sloughters have these Indian ancestors, so they hand down the recipes on how to see into your mind or poison you. And this isn't just superstition, it's scientifically based, otherwise I wouldn't even consider it. Look at how they found out that Haitian zombies were given some kind of herb or root-based drug, then they buried them alive, then they dug them up and put them to work on plantations. And they thought they were dead zombies themselves.

Even physicists believe there are other dimensions, anti-matter, superstrings. Just like there's left-handed sugar, there could be a mirror image of me doing the opposite, ghosting me.

Wish I knew dad's PIN number, but since the time in Syracuse when I emptied his checking account, he keeps that secret from me. But he always makes sure there's a thousand in my account, in case of an emergency. Now I have to concentrate on my own numbers, roll my eyes back to help dream them up again because if I go at them head-on they disappear. *2875. 2785.* The second time the machine gives it up, crispy, fresh bills I slap in the Sloughter's paw, which he sticks out of his window. Yellow eyes on me like he knows what I'm going to do before I do it myself. His bald tires spin on the icy road, his rusted-out hulk of a car swerving sideways.

Slinging my knapsack over my shoulder, I can feel the new weight of the Cobray. 'This is a spook gun,' the Sloughter said when I tried it out in his back field. When I pulled the trigger, even with both hands on the grip, the thing jerked and bucked real wild. 'You read about drive-by shootings, they always mention this weapon. Make a mess of a woodchuck.'

I figure nobody's out at Berry's shooting range, and they have this cool yellow gunk called ordnance jelly where you can dump your load right into it and it just goes thwack. Maybe I can find Jamie Whitaker and take him out there. He usually has acid or speed or something to keep him from going out of his mind in Accordia. I mean, in Accordia there isn't even a mall. The highlight here is watching the headwaters of the Van Deusen River trickle under a bridge behind the Grand Union parking lot.

What do they expect the youth of Accordia to do?

Jamie's father's a doctor, but since Jamie got busted for possession his old man keeps everything under lock and key. At the very least he'll have some hash or pot, and we can get off on some of his Nintendo games. (He's supposed to go to some crappy college like Tuscarora Tech, but I know he still likes to blast away with a joy stick in private. I know Jamie.) But all of a sudden I'm so cold and hungry I could die.

The Hungry Heart is deserted, except for Kiki sitting in the window doing her nails. Jet black polish. I've known her since kindergarten when she already had three boyfriends. In high school she didn't do too well, but she partied hardy. Her dad's a truck driver who's never home, so Kiki has to take care of the five other kids half the time since her mom's too fat to go to the store. I mean it. They'd need a derrick to hoist the woman out of the house. There was a TV movie about a mom like that, and Kiki told me it was so much like her mom it gave her major creeps.

How her father fucks the old lady is one of the biggest mysteries in Accordia. Jamie says he rolls her in flour and looks for the wet spot.

My meds kind of keep my sex drive down, but when I see Kiki doing her nails in black polish in the window seat, and she's got on black patterned stockings and a jean skirt four inches above her knees, I start getting these electric messages from her. Not words. Just this sizzling like a short in a wire, only the short's in my wetworks, I know that. So I keep a straight face and send her a sizzler right back. The way she flicks her nose ring tells me that she receives me loud and clear.

The meds must be wearing off.

On the wall behind her a cardboard Hungry Heart cheeseburger floats washed-out as the moon. It would be great if my meds started wearing off more because they make me feel like a wet wash in a washing machine.

'So what're you doing?' I ask her when she brings me the cheeseburger, seasoned fries and the hot chocolate. She's squirted a tower of Rediwhip on top like she likes me.

She can't possibly like me; she thinks I'm a freak. No, that's Black Thinking. Well, maybe, but usually Black Thinking is true.

'I got a job in Atlantic City.' Her skin is so white it's green. I don't think she eats a healthy diet.

'Yeah, doing what?'

'Maid.'

'Great.' I'm wracking my brains for something to say. 'You'll get out of town.'

'My fucking father.'

'Yeah.'

I duck my head and bite into the burger. It's a dry, over-cooked patty, and the cheese isn't even hot. Kiki isn't such a great cook. The seasoned fries taste great though. I wouldn't want to be somebody like Kiki because it must be so blank inside her head. I shoot her a sizzler, but she doesn't blink. Maybe she's not receiving.

'You got anything?'

'Na, I just got out. I got some money though.'

'I can get shit when I close up this hole.'

'When can you close up?' Just thinking about scoring gives me a rush, but to talk to Kiki you have to stay on one flat note otherwise she thinks you're not cool.

'Like now.'

I start to gobble the fries like a mad squirrel, half-chewed fries wriggling snakes in my throat.

'It's okay, slow down.'

A sliver of a smile breaks out on her face, and she puts her hand on my shoulder. Her tits are swinging free under her Hungry Heart t-shirt. I'm so hot and lonely I could howl like the coyotes near dad's cabin.

A skirt of dirt runs along the edge of her cheap blue parka. She swims in it. Maybe it's her brother's or something she just found. She walks right out into the snow in the same flats she was wearing in the restaurant, her feet almost disappearing in the fresh stuff. Maybe she's high already. I feel high just watching the snow drifting down over the houses with towers that run along Main. When I was a kid and my kindergarten teacher read us Rapunzel, I always thought of Crissie up in one of those towers and how I'd rescue her. Ricomocco. Mooccorico. Our secret names. She'd let down her hair and I'd be the one to climb up.

Tourists come up here in the summer and they think the whole town's a bed and breakfast and we're all the gnomy little innkeepers. My dad said that.

I don't know where she's going, but it can't be far because of her disappearing feet. It's like she doesn't have feet at all, just black-clad stick legs stuck in the snow. Along the curb hard, filthy mounds five feet high keep growing in the soft shower. I can't see her ass, but I see the slight swing of her parka, and I know it's under there, her small, hard Kiki ass. Then she turns in at the Top of the Mountain Motel.

There's three cars in front of rooms, probably skiers who couldn't get booked into the resort. The rest are empty. Outside the office she stops and waits for me. No gloves. No hat. Her hair crusted with snow. Kiki's hard core.

'You got twenty?'

'Yeah, sure.'

'Wait over there. Off the street.' In a minute she's out with a key. 'Room fourteen.'

Inside it smells like an ashtray mixed with mildew. Kiki switches on the TV before the lights. A mustard-colored, leatherette chair, a couple of end tables, a pole lamp, a painting of autumn leaves. On the bed a spread with ragged nubs like it was washed all wrong.

'Jessica's breaking up with Ron,' Kiki says. It takes me a second to realize she's talking about the soap.

'Ron's a geek.'

'So you ever try this, Maurice?' She pulls a glass pipe out of her bag.

'What, hash? Are you kidding. I used to get the best Moroccan.'

'No, no,' she says, producing a small pebble of shit. 'Rock cocaine.'

I can't believe what she's saying, I'm completely blown away. Maybe it's not such a good idea because it'll wipe out the last meds I took days ago or mix up with them in some kind of evil cocktail. But I only hold out for a heartbeat. I want it real bad, I want to suck on that pipe till the top of my head just pops off.

'One time I took acid I was quacking like a duck. Ask Jamie.'

'You never did this, right?'

'Sure. Before you were born. In my other life.'

She doesn't seem to hear this because her eyes are on the screen where Ron is shoving Jessica up against a bedroom wall A second later Kiki says, without looking at me, 'So you want to do it?'

'Shit, yeah.'

Pulling a lighter from her skirt pocket, and a crumpled pack of cheapo Bull's Eye cigs, she says, 'On this stuff you just go away.'

This suddenly seems brilliant to me. That's what you want every time you do some kind of dope. You just want to go away to another town or another country where you're anonymous. 'Take a Greyhound Bus.'

'And leave the driving to us.' She lights the rock and takes a long hit like she's trying to suck in every drop of smoke. Then she passes it to me, and after one long pull I'm atoms. Not even molecules. Lit up, vibrating atoms. A century later when words start coming out of our mouths, Kiki says, 'You got more money?'

And I say something I'd never have the nerve to say if I was on my meds. 'Yeah, but what're you going to do for me?'

I'm off on another rush, fainter than the last one. But still whirling.

'BJ?' She puts her hand right on my crotch like she's tweaking a little kid's nose. I go from curled-up soft to hard in a flash.

*BJ*. It takes me a shade too long to figure out what she means, but I cover it up with my face mask. Cool at all costs, keep every facial muscle dead. 'How much?'

'Twenty. That's the going rate.' I can see she's lying. Going rate's probably ten, or a dollar in Accordia.

'Okay.'

She disappears for a while, but I think it's just an illusion. Then the door flaps open and I see the scuzzy office with the peeling siding. Windy wild white world out there. Wooooooo. The door flaps closed.

She whips off her stained parka and throws it on the floor. 'Turn that chair over there. Sideways.'

I just do what she says. 'No, wait, stand up and pull down your pants. Now sit down.'

She goes down on her knees, brushes her moist hair off her forehead casually, and yanks my jockey shorts down to my knees.

'Could you . . . take your shirt off?' I ought to get my money's worth but I'm not sure she'll go for it. But she just whips the Hungry Heart t-shirt right over her head. Her tits are small with funny shaped, long nipples.

Not like Crissie's. She was behind the shower curtain with the floating penguins on it, and I was behind the hamper, pumping the bone. Then she came at me with the red plastic body brush. The bristles didn't hurt but the back of it cracked on my arm, the arm I put up over my face, and I thought she cracked my bones, too.

'Hello, puppy,' Kiki says, patting the head of my prick. She runs her tongue right under the rim where I can barely take it, then she gets down to business fast. I never really had a BJ except once almost and I don't know how it's supposed to feel but she just sucks it down whole, strokes me behind my balls in a place I didn't even know I had.

When I look down her eyes are open and she's watching the TV to see what Jessica says to Ron. Then I shoot to high heaven, and she spits me out, still slick and bobbing, and spits out the come into a tissue.

Screwing up her face, she says, 'You been saving that up for a long time I'll bet.'

I don't know what to say it's over so fast.

'You got forty?'

'Yeah.' I'm just limp, no bones. But that sounds like a lot for a thirty-second BJ, double what she told me. I don't want her to think I'm a total asshole. 'Not just for that though.'

She doesn't even flinch. 'Naa. Twenty for the BJ, and twenty for the second rock. That's fair.'

It seems fair to me. 'You can get anything in Accordia nowadays, huh?'

'Let's fire up,' she says, tilting the pointy butane flame to the coke.

Later we watch MTV, some shopping channel, a college basketball game, a Chuck Norris movie, CNN to find out what's going on in the world, and some nighttime Spanish soap that we can't understand but we make it up as it goes along. This goes on for hours or a second, the shows one long color smear, and from the vending machine outside, we eat at least six Snickers and bags and bags of onion garlic potato chips, too, and Sprite because that's all the soda machine has left. I try to get Kiki to fuck me, but she won't do it.

The best I ever had was by myself through dad's telescope.

'Just BJs. I'm going steady,' she says.

In a way I'm glad because I don't have to pretend I know how to do it. Who would do it with me anyway? But I'm mad, too. I mean, who is she doing it with anyway, some farm boy drug fiend or grease monkey with a 2 IQ?

'Yeah, with who?'

'Zack.'

'Zack Wheatley?' Mr Golden Shower. Drink it, he said. While it's warm. I'm down on my knees in the high school shower room like a dog, and they're squirting their wrinkled, fat hoses. Somebody needs to reform the American educational system.

'I've gotta go, Maurice.'

'Stay. I can go to the cash machine.' I grab to hold her back, but her puff coat is slippery and she gets away.

Now I can see I'm starting to annoy her, but I don't like the way she talks to me, like I'm an insect or something. Anyway, she doesn't have such a great body. One of her tits is bigger than the other. One of her nipples looks like an eye. Maybe she's got a tape deck behind it and she's recording everything I'm saying.

'You think I can stay all night?'

'I don't care.'

I beat her to the door and spread my arms out. 'Not yet!'

'Hey, I can come back in the morning.' She runs her fingers through my hair and it's the nicest thing anybody ever did for me. I feel so much love for her I've got to keep my mouth glued shut. But I can't let her go yet.

So that's when I decide to show her the Cobray. It's wrapped in an oily rag and under the table lamp it looks so cool. A dull black, not shiny and cheap.

But Kiki just shrugs and says, 'Everybody's got one of those.'

# CHAPTER EIGHT: MOIRA

## Saturday: February 27, 1990: 12:40 p.m.

The key clicks. Snow and sleet plaster the windshield and the passenger-side windows. As usual, I've left the window open a crack, so even the inside of the windshield is opaque with frost. Crissie is right. There is something wrong with me. It's as if I make things go wrong on purpose. A dead, wet cold fills into the car. I've been out in vicious cold, wrapped in sweaters and two coats, my face swathed in scarves, yet I could stand it. It's the creeping cold, the wet cold that frightens me.

Now I hear a sharp rapping on the window. I try to roll it down, but it's so frozen I'm afraid I'll snap the cheap plastic handle. Toyota charges two million dollars for these handles. Finally, it gives.

Crissie slides in on the passenger side. 'What're you sitting here for, mom? I was in the store for a century.'

'Oh, you love that store, Crissie.'

'What's the matter?'

I hate scenes so much. 'I think there's something wrong with the ignition.' I turn the key and demonstrate. Click. Silence.

'Oh, you probably left the lights on again. You're so damned scatter-brained. Try the radio. See if there's any juice.'

When I push the button a faint voice leaks out, '—a quarter pound of bacon, well-done, a cup of cream and fine spaghetti noodles. For free Grand Union groceries, call in and tell us what's cookin'!'

'Spaghetti noodles. God! Oh, let's try the lights.'

Crissie hauls herself out into the slanting snow, takes a sour look and shakes her head. 'Very weak. Your battery's dead. We have to get a jump. Does Julia have cables?'

'Why does the radio work then? Maurice is waiting for us.' She won't believe me, but I'm ready to see him now.

'I know, mom. It's on CNN.'

Ignoring her sarcasm, I let her take over in her capable way. Why not? Whatever she thinks, I've been working for her all these years. 'I've got to get inside for a minute. Let's have some tea. I'm frozen!'

'You don't have to sound so happy about it.'

'Happy?'

'You're . . . I don't know . . . all of a sudden you're in a good mood. Right in the middle of a big mess, especially.' This is her main theory, that I bring disaster on myself because then I'm in my element.

'Well, it's only a dead battery. Not the end of the world.' No doubt Maurice will be fine. He's probably got a knapsack full of Oreos.

It's an effort, but I hoist myself out of the icy cocoon and stamp my muck boots in the slushy street. Just then I see a familiar van, dirty white with a wooden rack on its roof, grinding up Main. Through its windshield I make out an impossibly narrow, long face and a crown of thick, curly gray hair. Weird Ben. Just who I need, he's a sweetheart. I start waving till the rusty hulk pulls over to the curb in front of us.

'Hi, Uncle Ben,' Crissie says. He's not really her uncle, but he and his wife, the beautiful, tiny Indira, like to pretend they're the kids' benevolent relatives.

'Hey, Moira, what's up?' Terribly tall and thin, he is wearing a stained jumpsuit the color of a used tea bag. His long, twisted-root hands brush together in a patty-cake gesture. Then his fingers start creeping through his wonderfully thick and tangled gray hair.

'Oh, Ben. Isn't this miserable? I'm supposed to meet Maurice.'

'Oh, yeah, O'Bannon said he was visiting.' Only Ben, with his perfect taste, could put it so delicately.

Up close the creases in his narrow, horse-shaped face look deeper than ever, the surprise lines in his forehead intricate webs.

'Her battery's dead,' Crissie says. I wonder if she thinks I'm so stupid I don't understand what that tone means.

'Oh, Indira left the lights on in the minivan this morning. I think this weather makes you dingy.' He has such a subtle, sympathetic smile you have to laugh. It seems to say, I'm over the edge, you're over the edge, but that's no big deal.

In a moment he has the old Dodge van nose to nose with the Toyota and the cables attached. Strangely enough, though, after the car starts, it immediately dies. We try it three times, but as soon as we disengage the cables the Toyota conks out with a human, hacking sound. Like mother, that pious beer keg, choking on her third pack of English Ovals.

After Vincent first met mom he said, 'You came from that?'

'Uh-oh. You've got problems, Moira. Unless it's just wet wires, your alternator is screwed up. Could be a bad cell in the battery, too. How old is the battery?'

He tries it one more time even though we both know it's useless. Now I have two dead cars at the worst time of the year. 'I don't know. Shit! We'll be stranded. Ben. Maurice is waiting for a sub.'

'He's eating meat?' Crissie interjects.

'Not to worry. I'll take you around. Indira's in the shop anyway,' he says, referring to their landmark octagonal barn, a cavernous space where they sell antiques in the summer.

'Oh, you couldn't. We've got to meet Maurice at the camp.' I haven't been in the camp for so many years. Even when I was married to Nathan I hated the place with the sad stuffed bear that his father, the great Jewish hunter, shot in the Adirondacks. Its fur always looked moldy to me.

But some of Nathan's background is so appealing, especially his great-grandfather, the tap-dancer who started Accordia National. In private, Nathan had always laughed and said, 'Nobody understands it, but banking is exactly like tap-dancing. You've got to improvise more than anybody knows.'

'Oh, I've got time. Don't worry.'

Crissie rolls her eyes now, as if I've given another man a hot fainting spell. What a laugh. When I look at myself with a hard eye, I see a slightly mad hag.

'You're so sweet, Ben.'

'Want to see what I picked up in Italy?'

Ben and Indira have dealt everything from nineteenth century iron lawn furniture to bakelite radios. Swinging the van's back doors open with glee, Ben plunges half his body inside, emerging with a crudely painted wagon wheel, snaky vines curled around its spokes.

Before I can ask, he explains, barely able to contain his excitement. 'Sicilian donkey cart. Turn of the century. You won't believe the other parts. We got all the panels and the bed. The painted fruit on it is unbelievable.'

I'd like to climb into the truck and examine everything in it, I could get lost back there, but I can hear Crissie's voice in my mind. Get going, you silly old bitch. Just get going.

'Well, let's go over to The Hungry Heart. I can call the mechanic, and we can get some food for Maurice. He said he was starving.' What luck! Only Ben, with his otherworldly aura, could understand what's happening.

'Maurice is where?'

'He said to meet him at the hunting camp. He was supposed to meet Nathan at Breitman, but there was some foul-up. That hospital. It costs a fortune, they're so full of themselves, and they don't even know where their patients are.'

'Oh, don't worry, he's probably just up the road. We just got back from Puglia. You should see some of the stuff we brought.

This art nouveau chandelier of all things, the guy who made it must've been on absinthe. We could fill up half the stores on Broome Street.'

'You saved my life again, Ben.'

Holding Ben's hand is the least sexual thing in the world. You might say he has worn, rugged good looks, but actually he's curiously neutral. Perhaps he's too tasteful to flirt. This both disturbs and comforts me.

'So how's the kid?'

'I don't know yet. I haven't seen him. He could be any way. Up. Down. Sideways.'

We load up on sandwiches and pumpkin pie.

The storm abates a bit when we set out, fishtailing in Ben's old van. Accordia never looks more beautiful than after a snowstorm. Its grand, seedy Queen Anne Victorians look fresh and cleansed. Lester skis down Main Street, his shaggy black dog in pursuit. Denise waves from the front door of the video store. Fire-engine red snow blowers line the sidewalk in front of Agway. Three boys toss snowballs that strike the side of the van with heavy thumps.

In the mountains, we take the beauty for granted, but when snow keeps falling on snow and then the sun comes out, the shock is thrilling. I love to go walking then in that intense light. The fresh snow is the most brilliant mirror in the world.

Ben is still in transports over his Sicilian donkey cart. 'The thing is, that level of ornamentation wasn't even unusual. When

I saw it at that dealer's in Lecce, I was willing to pay anything. Indira had to muzzle me, or I would have blown the whole deal. I think it's the vines. Some nameless peasant genius painted those vines. I had a dream about him the other night, he was painting vines on a TV screen.'

'You're weird, Ben.' After the word leaves my lips, I freeze.

'I'm comfortable with that,' he says, patting my hand. He crosses his eyes and sticks his tongue out, and I can't help laughing.

'Mom, it's late, you promised,' Crissie whines. In the back of my mind I've been hoping she'd come along to distract Maurice. They have that secret childhood language that goes back to when he was normal, even secret names, and at least she can connect to the part of his mind that isn't so tormented. When she was eleven Crissie paid a friend of hers $2.77 – she told me the exact amount – to kiss Maurice. And she was the one who found him with the push pins, but that was years later. By then she'd become the big sister, even though he was almost two years older.

What did she call him? Something like sirocco, the hot wind from Africa. She'd heard me say the word and changed it somehow. Chirroco. Kirroco. Moccoco. Something like that. When he started losing his friends he'd play with the Lesh boy, or stay in Crissie's room, drawing, listening to music, acting in little plays they made up together.

The selfish side of me wants her to come along. But why should I put her through this? It's better for her not to see . . .

on the off-chance. I don't want to think about what I don't want her to see.

'Oh, shit! I left the arrangements in the car.'

'Want to circle back?'

'That's all right, Ben. I'll send them tomorrow.'

Back at the hospital after the Syracuse episode, rocking and smoking, his fingers stained a filthy yellow, Maurice had looked up and at me and said, 'I got a faucet in my head, mom. Fear faucet. Fear faucet. Drip, drip, drip, drip.'

I didn't believe what the police said, either. Nathan was definitely right. That man under the bridge had been frozen for days.

At the bottom of his cycle, Maurice spoke in an underwater tone, thick and slow. His anti-psychotics were starting to take effect, but the bipolar medication hadn't quite kicked in. I just sat there in that barren, hospital green room and smoked Camels with him, smoked like I hadn't in years, letting the cigarettes sear my lungs just to feel one thing that he felt, but it was impossible. Just before I left he roused himself and smiled a pale imitation of the smile he used to have – I almost said, the smile he had when he was alive – and he said, 'You're afraid, but you don't know what you're afraid of. Eyes.'

We're Americans, we always think we can fix just about anything. Nathan always has a solution. The word *fate* isn't in his vocabulary.

I just sat there smoking until all those terrible unfiltered Camels were gone, and it was time to go.

'Are you listening to me?'

'Yes, Crissie. Ben, do you think you can drop her at the house?' Yes, let her go before I call her back again.

'Sure, why not?'

'You don't need me now.' I'm not sure what she means by this, but I'm certain she's desperate to get away and see Harry. 'Just drop me on the road. I want to walk.'

'I can drive you,' Ben says.

'It's only half a mile, Ben. Look how it's clearing up,' she insists.

She's right. Steep banked fields sail past, tilted at odd angles, the winter skeletons of maples and poplars marking the edges of farms. This particular light is subtle; it seems to come from inside things, making the snow glow without blinding you.

'How's business?' Ben asks.

It's such a relief to talk about business. 'I can hardly handle the catalogue orders, I had to hire two new girls. You know what's going like crazy? Those used maple buckets. I can get them for six dollars.' Nathan still doesn't believe that I can support myself. The banker in him wants to mystify making money into a male cult.

'That's great. We're just squeaking by, but we usually do okay in the spring.'

Ben pulls over on the shoulder of Bolivar Road, which is marked by a barely visible yellow sign tipped with a strip of tape that glows in the dark.

'Say hi to Maurice, tell him, uh, tell him I said hi.' Crissie leaps from the truck. I watch the boxy shape of her yellow Carhart coat bob up the white road.

'You know the doctors say it's all biochemical.'

'I think that's true,' Ben says. The last time I saw Indira she was taking some mood-elevating herb from the health food store that smelled like old socks.

'You think nothing you do matters. But look at Crissie. Didn't I do something right?'

'You did a great job. She's something else.'

'But don't you see? How can you take credit for the good ones and blame some nameless genes for your failures? Oh, never mind, Ben, I'm sorry.'

Only Julia knows about the trip. I was almost asleep when the rush hit me. Drifting off our bed, I looked out the window of our Berkeley house and saw a bear climbing over the moon. I felt transparent, amused, excited, frightened all at once. Then, without transition, we were in our 1957 Volvo, roaring around Tilden Park. Driving in reverse at a mad speed, sticking his head out of the window, Nathan barked, bayed at the brilliant moon to impress the tangled pile of bodies in the back seat. I took it for granted that I would die right then, in that instant.

Nathan, the prehistoric Nathan who has nothing to do with the Nathan of today, thought it was a big joke, slipping the acid into the punch. Was Maurice already a few hundred cells bathing in the LSD? A few nights from bursting out of nothing? Who can tell? This other Nathan will never admit these things. He'd rather accuse me of secret vices.

The driveway to the cabin is a quarter mile long, but Nathan has Hank Merwin plow it regularly. At the edge of the pond, entangled with waterweeds, ice flows bob. The tips of goldenrod stems and silvery gray milkweed pods poke out of the snow at the foot of the frozen sheet of water. I roll down the window to smell the air, heavy with moisture in my lungs. If the snow would only melt I could get my hands on a nice winter harvest, spiky Queen Anne's lace, spiny Yellow Rocket, Canadian Goldenrod with its silver onion in the middle of the stem. All you have to do is mix the pods with reed grass, red top, and accent with feather grass plumes and dried, russet-colored ferns. Actually, it's so ridiculously easy I'm embarrassed whenever Julia and her friends oooh and ahhh over what I make.

Nathan always called it 'the cabin,' but it's really a three bedroom Craftsman with a green-shingled roof and a covered porch held up by fieldstone pillars. A pair of cute dormers project out from the master bedroom. How many years has it been since I've even seen the place? A dozen? But every detail seems familiar, the peeling blue paint, the sagging roof, the roasting pan Nathan stuck on the chimney instead of a proper cap. Limbs sagging with snow, Norway pines form a wind break in the steep field behind the house. A single light burns in the kitchen.

'You want to have dinner later? Indira's making a *paella*. We picked up some fresh clams at that fish market in Tuscarora. You can see some of the new stuff.'

'I just made a fruit pie.' Who cares if I blow up like a balloon? Dinner by the wood stove, looking down at the fast stream under their window. Wood smoke and sea food and a couple of bottles of vino. Ahhhhh. And there's always the chance they've brought something back from Italy I won't be able to resist, some odd object, small picture, jewelry. Indira has such an unusual eye. I love the way she goes mad over something odd and beautiful.

When she starts raving about how much she loves Camille Paglia, I'll just close my ears. I love my friends. They're so talented and interesting it's almost a shock sometimes. We have such lovely times.

'Great. Indira would love to see you. Looks like somebody's home.'

I force myself to step down from the van. Under the surface of the snow my boot heel cracks ice.

# CHAPTER NINE: JULIA

## Monday: April 28, 1987: 1:10 pm

A spring afternoon, and Nathan's back is full of knots. I dig my thumbs into the notches of his spine, starting with the base of his neck, seeking the source. Every time I apply pressure he groans, emitting muffled cries, sharp outbursts.

The concept of *referred pain* mesmerizes me. Although every knuckle of his spinal column aches, I know each one may be far from the source of the spasm. His lower back may hurt because of gnarled muscles in his buttocks. Contractions between his shoulder blades may have nothing to do with their own muscles; they may be reflecting grief in the coccyx. Perversely, the source of the agony may be a torn muscle itself, a tiny rent in tissue that causes the surrounding muscle to seize up in warning. In other words, the back may hide its secrets in its surface; or it may not.

Nathan thinks Moira hides in the hollow of his lower back, pulling the strings of pain. There are many places in his spare six-foot-two-inch frame for her to hide, in his neck, behind his pointy knees, between his finger-like toes. I wish he'd stop talking about her, but he never does.

'She doesn't think there's anything wrong with it,' he mutters, face down, rocking between my naked legs. 'She' is always Moira.

'Well, I suppose ten o'clock is a bit late, but Crissie is in high school now. She can stay home alone.' I stroke his long, slender leg, hoping to change the subject, finding my way down to his calf, his elegant ankle. Then I dig into his arch with my knuckles.

'Stop! That feels like darts!' His face to the wall, he goes right back to worrying his obsession. 'Yeah, you can say she's in high school, but there's never a thing to eat in that house, and then she shows up at ten and the kid's famished.'

Spreading my legs, I let him roll over between them, his matted chest a soft, breathing pillow against my vagina. I rub myself on him, massaging lightly, searching for that elusive sensation that radiates from my clitoris. If I empty my mind, willing myself not to think about it, I find the exact place near the top . . . It's there, it disappears, I find it again. *Referred pleasure*. Why don't the orthopedists study that?

'I heard she might go into horticulture at the little school in Tuscarora.'

'No way. Why not computers, why not medicine? She's got a head on her shoulders. Keep doing that, *mmmmmmmm . . .*'

There are times when I think I am more than a simple anodyne for Moira's absence.

Through the eyebrow window I can see the creek twist and fall away into the valley. An enormous willow shades a fork in the stream where the water races over cream-colored boulders.

A red-tailed hawk rides high up in the drafts of wind, circling. Spring. A clever scrim that hides winter. Snow. All the forms of radiant frost.

Holding his erect penis lightly between my fingers, I can feel its pulse. It's like feeling the beating heart of a small bird. I brush against him some more in a gentle, circling motion, struggling to discover that faint, intangible stream of pleasure, agonizing behind closed eyes, finding it, nurturing it until it begins to radiate in luxurious pulses.

'Oh, shit!'

'What? Did I hurt you?'

'No, I forgot to call Carney.'

Carney, one of his bookies. Instantly, I lose it. And I was just getting there. He doesn't have the slightest understanding of the subtleties. Climbing off him, I try to cover my disappointment with sarcasm. 'Maybe you'll hit it big tonight.'

'Huh? Yeah,' he answers, so consumed with his calculations that he misses the irony.

Cupping the phone receiver, he says, 'Hey, Willy from Accordia here. Gimme the teaser.'

His pseudonyms are amusing. Even his speech pattern changes when he gambles. 'Last year you were Frankie, weren't you?'

Lost to my existence, he rattles off his picks, pacing up and back in his austere bedroom. Nathan is an ascetic. All he needs is a bed, a table and chairs, and long-distance service. It's ridiculous. He seems to be betting on every baseball game in both major leagues. I start to pick up my clothes.

'What're you doing?'

'Getting dressed. Why?' The line between insensitivity and blindness fascinates me. I can never tell on which side of the divide Nathan falls.

'Julia, I'm sorry, that was lousy of me. But I had to get the money down before game time.'

I shrug, let him peel off my blouse and jeans, but whatever he does now seems to take place far, far away. I wriggle and twist, offering him my sharp hips to make him get it over with. Sure enough he shudders, disgorges. I need a shower.

'I was reading to Mrs Orton yesterday.' Widowed, blind, retreated to a single room of her rambling farmhouse, Mrs Orton still retains all her faculties.

'Oh, yeah? I'll bet she likes tear-jerkers.' As if he doesn't know to what I am really referring.

He is right about her tastes, but I lie to get under his skin. 'Actually, she likes Tom Clancy. She had two sons in the navy. You know what she said? She said she was hiring her own accountant to look at her trust. She thinks you're doing something fishy.'

'You talk her out of it?' He's dressed in his suit pants and white shirt already, his black hair slicked back to show off his hard, even features. I used to think he looked like Paul Newman, but especially the Paul Newman of *Hud*. Deep creases that run from the base of his nostrils to the corners of his mouth give him a bit of a hound-like look now, but the symmetry of his face is still startling, especially his perfectly square chin.

'Are you?'

'That woman has nothing to worry about til the day she dies. And when she goes, the bank'll buy her the best casket Don Farley has in stock.' He flashes one of his sudden, shocking smiles, a smile that says, I may be doing wrong, but nobody will really get hurt. It is one of his most seductive routines.

Later, under the fine hot needles of water, I can barely hear them arguing. Maurice is supposed to be at school. In fact, I rarely see him because we organize my visits around his absences. If he does show up unexpectedly, I hide in Nathan's closet or the attic, waiting for the right moment to escape. More than once I have slipped out the back door and melted down Rose Lane. An invisible woman down an invisible path. Running a mile and a half to Accordia, past nothing but dead hunting cabins and the foundations of an old farmhouse, Rose Lane has fallen off the maps.

I don't resent our subterfuges. In fact I like the panic I feel when I almost get discovered.

Maurice doesn't know, no one is supposed to know I am in Nathan's bed at odd hours. In fact, no one in Accordia would believe it. My plain clothes from J.C. Penny and Spiegal's hang on me as if they're empty. I am a Pindar, tenth generation, from preachers and gentlemen farmers. Most were on the wrong side of the Rent Wars, preferring their help to remain in indentured servitude. A woman such as I can commit adultery in plain sight.

Instead of escaping as usual, I open the bathroom door a crack and listen to their angry voices.

A crashing sound. Dishes breaking? The thud of something

heavy against a wall. Nathan's sharp cry of pain. I slip into my jeans again and race down the stairs.

Nathan is crumpled against the wall, his dress shirt up. He gapes at a shredded wound in his blue-white side, just above his puffy love handles. His hand is smeared with his own blood. 'Oh, crap, look at this!'

'What?'

'No cops,' he says before I can get another word out of my mouth.

Before I call the ambulance I staunch the blood with a heavy bath towel, tying it around his back. Then I race to phone the Rescue Squad in Stick Willow.

'Give us five minutes,' Chad Hansen says. 'Sit tight.'

At least I have the forethought to put on my coat before they come, armoring myself against the obvious suppositions. But how can I leave? Later I will drop the casual remark about town business. It will be perfectly believable as I am the avatar of minor beautification and Nathan is the source of all loans.

Maurice gazes at the serrated bread knife in his hand, bits of red tissue in its teeth. For some reason I speak before I think. Otherwise, I would be paralyzed with terror. In my best, stern mother's voice I demand that he listen to me.

'Maurice, give that thing to me. Right now!'

And meek as you please, he hands the knife over. I surrender to one quick morbid glance at the weapon. Bits of skin and bloody muscle hang from the knife's teeth. I feel very, very ill.

'No cops,' Nathan repeats. 'He didn't mean it. He's just trying to protect me.'

'Protect you? Protect you from what?' But instinctively, I already know. Protect him from Her. Who else?

Cowering in the corner, his back to us, Maurice holds his head and shakes it violently, as if he could empty it of all its tormenting thoughts.

'It's not that bad,' Nathan says, detached, gazing down at the jagged wound. Lowering his voice, he whispers, 'He thinks she's destroying me a little at a time. Better to get it over with in one shot, he says.'

The logic is impeccable. 'Press on it or you'll bleed to death.'

Instead, Nathan starts crawling on all fours to Maurice. Holding the scrawny, twisted back of his son against him, he whispers soothing words in his ear. Slowly, Maurice stops rocking and muttering. Then I realize they are both singing softly:

> The teensy weensie spider
> Climbed up the water spout
> Down came the rain
> And washed the spider out

An odd, keening sound rises from them. Nathan hugs Maurice closer, kisses him on the head. Together they rock, in a trance, cooing to each other in a language that no one else, I sense, has ever heard. Or ever should. Not because it is sexual but because it is more private than that.

When Nathan faints I drag him onto my lap, his arms splayed over my thighs, his head, loose on its neck, dead weight against my stomach. Pressing the towel gently against the stab wound I wait in the cocoon of our breathing, my skinny legs spread on a field of black and white checked linoleum.

Inside the endless waiting I dream of everything I know, everything that will destroy and save Nathan all at once, and I wonder if I'll ever gather the courage or the rage to let it out. But I know this. Truth is the antidote to love.

# CHAPTER TEN: NATHAN

## Friday: February 26, 1990: 2:45 p.m.

Wallace Hill Road switches back, then heads straight up into nothing. I can barely see in front of me, so I focus my eyes on the right edge of the road. I can feel the Cherokee grab the road, slip back, then grab it again. The sand they throw on these back routes is useless. Tires just spit it out and find the underlying ice. Squinting, I search for the fork at Tatum Lake Road. First I roll past the beaver pond with its skinny, dead black trees. Right after that the road plunges straight down, and when I hit bottom it's glass. The Cherokee glides, drifts sideways, bites, and starts clawing up again.

Through a veil of snow I see a complicated compound of trailers, campers, small outbuildings. A sagging power line, probably illegal, runs to a green cabin that nests in the center of the warren. Stealing electricity is like breathing to these people.

If Maurice is out in this squall, he could easily get turned around and lose his bearings. Half of the landmarks are buried in snow, or changed into shapeless mounds. Where is the small horse barn that says JES S IS L RD? The Pindar family plot with the obelisk? What did Julia call it? Her exclusive boneyard? I crawl past Merwin's car and truck graveyard, which we've been trying to zone out for years. The dead tractors, the hump-backed sedans, the step vans, the pick-ups, the broken down garbage truck, the things you can't even name anymore are all buried in snow. Like old tanks covered by sand dunes.

In this weather Maurice could freeze to death overnight or get stuck in a snow bank in the middle of nowhere. I'm trying to think positive, but it's hard to keep the fear away. He gets stuck, his temperature starts falling and he gets sleepy. You can't fight off the urge no matter how tough you are once your body temperature falls below ninety-five. Ten years ago Matt Zebriski went looking for some stranded Holsteins, and he got stranded himself. Right in sight of his own barn. When they tried to warm him up too fast, his heart blew up. Crap, don't think about it.

Half-blind, I still find the fork and head up Tatum Lake Road. A lifetime of negotiating these back routes has stamped them in my mind. Automatically, I switch on the radio. A man is shouting.

'Let's get this straight. I never owned any slaves, okay? None of the white people alive owned any slaves, okay? So if I want to criticize the behavior of Troy teenagers who happen to be black because they're scum who throw beer bottles at cars at three in the morning, I'm going to do it. You tell me, does that make me a racist? I'm Mark Moranus, give me a call.'

When I push the seek button every number on the dial flashes past. Finally, the radio settles back at WGY.

'Hey Mark, it's getting so I'm starting to hate black people.'

'Why would you say a thing like that, Frank?'

I used to like listening to this garbage, just to hear how sick people are, but now it just bores me. Moira still goes crazy about stuff like this. When she'll grow up, I don't know. That's the way people are. Big news.

Peering through the misty windshield I try to locate Maurice. But it's the moon up here. The wind takes no prisoners. If he's tramping around he'll lose his feet, they'll turn into blocks of ice in his low-cut duck boots. In the warm blast of the Cherokee's heater my feet are so hot they're sweating. When I think of my poor, freezing son, freezing to death, I hate my feet.

Better to think of the action while I cruise. If Foreman goes down on his fat face I'll get back $2,500, which'll put me on a small roll. With the gut on him, he could have a coronary in the first round. The chumps are the ones who don't know you can win, too, if you know what you're doing. One time in Atlantic City I was up thirty-five grand after six hours. Another time I had a trifecta worth $17,686.22. Then there was my big streak. Baseball. Only the National League because I despise the designated hitter. Over forty thousand in the first two weeks of July, enough to pay off the bookies and then some.

Anyway, with the weekend coming, I can always slip into the bank and cover the losses by Monday morning. I could give myself a home equity loan or a new line of credit on another invented house. The bank doesn't give a damn if they exist or not, as long as you pay the mortgage. Right now there's a Colonial in Summit and a pair of three bedroom Trident trailers in Angel Heights that I filled out the forms on. Who's going to find out, some four-eyed auditor?

I drive by a shabby Cape, not a single light burning, the driveway covered with unmarked drifts. It's a decent piece of property, sixty acres with some creekside, shaped like a wedge. If you get lucky you can sell that to some bozo from downstate who doesn't know that land can go as cheap as five hundred an acre if you know where to look in Iroquois County.

Near the bottom of Tatum Lake Rd there's a raised ranch with a driveway scraped down to black muck. I slow and try to make out signs of life. No smoke from the chimney, no lights. The sky is a few feet above me, pressing down.

Could be that the Quikway girl with the paper hat had things screwed up. Not could be. Definitely. But how far could Maurice have gone? Anyplace if he got a ride . . . My heart sinks. What else can I do but drive? At Simic Road I have a choice. Left or right. Right runs to Accordia, so I head that way doing twenty until a pick-up with a cap tailgates me, and I pull over to let the imbecile pass.

I glide past the Vendlers' dairy farm, a whole wall of pink insulation still exposed on the north side of their house. A pair of log chalets – half-finished, harebrained speculation – cling to a hillside. Finally, I crawl onto County Eight.

The black-top is thick with slush. The uselessness of my search takes hold of me. Trying to find a single boy in a universe of snow. Acid rises to the back of my throat. My left leg twitches. It takes me forty minutes to go fifteen miles.

Now I start breaking down, imagining every stage of Maurice's descent into hypothermia. He walks for miles on some back road, maybe drinking some cheap beer. Nothing makes you more vulnerable. And his sickness keeps him from feeling the way the snow is getting into his shoes or inside his gloves. Maybe he's left his coat open a little. The snow leaks down onto his shirt. He's having fun after a quart of Colt 45. He falls down in the deep stuff and starts laughing. The first time he gets up.

With an exercise of will, I jerk myself off this line of thinking. What good does it do to think negative?

At the Stewart's Shop in Accordia I stamp my boots on the rubber mat and head for the pay phone. In rapid succession I call the cops, Dr Greenberg, the sheriff. But I don't have the energy to take their heads off when they make their pitiful excuses. When I try to reach Moira, I get her machine. Even her recorded voice makes me grind my teeth.

Focusing again, thinking positive, I drive through town, then out Hegan's Rd, cutting back onto Bowser, cruising Van Deusen down by the old train station. Nice building. Worthless. I drive past Keene Lake, skirting the hunting camp. I drive in loops, tricking myself by making sudden turns I don't expect, as if right around the next bend I'll find Maurice. Two or three times I do. But he's just an old road sign, a shed at the top of a hill, a spinning snow devil. It gets darker, and I lose track of time, but I squeeze any negative thoughts out of my mind.

Dead tired, I crawl home. The snow thickens in my brights, and I have to go to low beams, but then I can only see a few feet in front of me. Moving in slow motion I feel as if I'm not moving at all. I bite my lip to keep awake.

Across the road from my place, Moira's house is pitch black. No point in even ringing the bell. My place is dead quiet, and I have to jack up the heat to seventy-five. I can keep an eye out for Moira from my bathroom. The rest of my windows look out over the valley. All my friends who said I should have moved away instead of renovating the barn across from Moira never understood how I had to keep an eye on her to protect the kids. They thought I was exaggerating, but they weren't the ones who snuck into the house to find a refrigerator with a single container of juice, or discovered Crissie all alone while her mother was sleeping one off on the couch till eleven in the morning. If I didn't keep track of the stream of Tuscarora hippies with pony tails and black portfolios who spent the night with Moira, how would I know who my children were being exposed to?

I pour a Heineken and make another round of useless calls. Nobody knows anything. 'Maurice is a survivor, just like you said, Nat,' Greenberg says through a hail of static. Piece of crap.

'Yeah, well, call me.'

His legs are getting weak, it's dark, he loses his sense of direction, the last sleepy surge is getting to him. We find him buried in the snow, we're scraping ice off his blue face, carrying his stiff corpse to the Cherokee. When I put the seats down, he fits right into the back. Oh, crap, I'm deep in the negative groove. I'll have to go out again, right away, find him in the dark.

But I tilt the Lazy Boy back just for a minute, and the next thing I know it's morning. I can tell because my jaw aches, and I've got fur in my mouth. Just by listing the scores, Sports Phone tells me I'm a chump. And Foreman won by a knockout. This blimp's resurrection has to be fixed.

There's nothing in the fridge but two day-old Arby's. As if no time passed at all, I'm back at the Stewart's Shop at nine in the morning, eating a chocolate covered donut and reading *The Wall Street Journal*. SemTech is just laying there like a dead fish. Dazed, I eat another chocolate one with frosting and stare at the S&P 500 graph like it's an Egyptian hieroglyphic.

Finally, I gas up and start driving because I can't stomach calling the police or Mark yet. If they'd found Maurice, they would have called anyway. In loops I drive over freshly scraped roads. At least our tax money is going someplace. Sedgwick Road. The usual warrens. Simmonetti Drive of all things. The county is swarming with Italians who came up in the twenties and thirties. LaVergne Hollow Road. Two miserable skinny cows getting whipped by the elements. At LaVergne Corners I practically run Maurice over. There he is, trudging up the street in his uncoordinated gait with an overstuffed knapsack on his back.

Unbelievable. I feel like I've been holding my breath for days. He's alive. A minor miracle. 'God damn!' I hear myself say, my hand pounding the wheel. Slowing down, I think for a second. Calm down. Don't startle him.

Shuffling along in front of me, he looks so ordinary, it's as if nothing has happened at all, but I'd like to hug him or strangle him or do something I'm not allowed to do. But maybe I'm losing it, and it's not him at all. Tapping the accelerator, I squint through the dense flurries. These kids all look the same from the back with their baggy pants and back packs, so when I pull up alongside him, as slowly as possible, I take in every inch of him, and it is Maurice all right, looking none the worse for wear. Flustered, at first I'm talking to him through the closed window, and I forget to release the door lock. I hate feeling incompetent, but that's how far gone I am.

When he hops in he doesn't look too much the worse for wear either, just slightly disheveled. He's combed his hair, or at least run a pair of fingers through it.

'I thought I lost you, kiddo.' Reaching across the seat, I cuff him on the head. But I have to watch myself and not get too demonstrative, or he'll pick up on it.

'Did you misplace me, dad?' He sounds so normal it hurts.

'Hope not. How about some breakfast and a hot shower?' Keep it upbeat. Ask no questions. That always triggers his paranoia.

'Sounds cool.'

But somehow, against my will, the words pop out. 'So where were you last night?'

'You know I was thinking, how come it makes so much difference if a girl is good looking or not, the way they affect you? I mean with a good looking girl, you can't stop staring at her and you want to eat her up, too. Why not the uglies?'

I'm not sure where this is going. 'Guess it's biology. Put on your seat belt, okay?'

'Yeah, you're right, dad. It's biology. I met this girl last night, I think it's serious.'

I don't like the sound of this, but at least he buckles up.

'No kidding. That's nice.' At least he's alive. I feel the strangest, fluttering sensation in my chest.

Deceptive, Whiskey Hollow Road twists and switches back so you never see a long, straight distance. But the climb is wickedly steep, so I'm always careful to shift all the way down to first gear. Up above, near the peak of the hill, an old, wide-bodied American car hangs stock-still. Winter cars they call them. Fifty dollars cash. First I wonder if it's climbing inch by inch to the top. Then I start to change my mind. The junker looks as if it's creeping up and falling simultaneously.

Maurice's legs bolt straight out, his palms pressing the dash.

'Hang on, it'll be okay.'

'No it won't, it won't!' He's panicking, and there's nothing I can do about it.

'Grab the grip!' Oddly enough, he listens to me.

Then there's no doubt. The old bomb is picking up speed, skidding backwards down the narrow incline, one red tail light flashing. Desperately, I try to decide what to do. Hit the brakes and slide back down, too? But the road is too treacherous, in reverse I could lose control entirely and smash into a tree or flip over on the icy surface. Avoid the sliding bomb? But now it's turning sideways, almost filling the entire width of the road.

Paralyzed, unable to decide whether to gun it or hit the brake, I start to lose momentum.

The old tub keeps coming, flat-out sideways. Now, imperceptibly, we're falling, too. I'm mesmerized. It's so much like one of my nightmares about driving I shake my head and blink to wake up. It doesn't work.

'Look out! It's coming, dad! Look out!'

'Shut up! I see it!' I regret the words as soon as they leave my lips.

'Turn! Turn!' He's in full-blown hysteria now.

There is no place to turn. The rusty bomb fills my windshield.

Instinctively, I jerk towards the shoulder and stomp on the accelerator, my chains chopping ice, our descent slowing. No time to worry about taking a hit. If I keep skidding backwards, in a flash I'll be doing sixty in the wrong direction. And what if there's somebody behind me, just around the bend? Oh, Jesusjesusjesusjesus.

Somehow the junker throws a hard right and plunges past us, but not before clipping our front bumper and ticking my side door. The collision snaps my head back against the head rest, knocking my hands from the wheel. We start to swerve and spin, mountains, trees, road a blur. Dazed, I grab at the steering column, clutch the wheel again, but it's not connected to anything but black ice. Nothing at all. Hydroplaning, we go round in a sickening dream, and I wait for another car to smash into us from around the bend. Turn in the direction of the skid. Turn what? There's no tension in the wheel. No traction. No brakes. That's it . . .

'Nononononono!!!' Maurice shouts. 'We're gonna die!'

I'd like to slap him hard, but I couldn't if I tried. Anyway, I'm limp with terror. The wipeout goes on forever, til we whip into a 180 and snowblind I wait for the Cherokee to smash through the guard rail, flip and roll over down the slope, tearing through the four foot drifts.

We complete a 360 and then another 180, slowing down, merrygoround, almost to a stop, and I can't hold back anymore. I've got the chains, so I give the brakes a small tap and pray. Stupid. We fishtail out of control again. Losing my nerve I yank the wheel against the skid, but nothing can stop the spin-out anyway. We're sailing off the side of the mountain. It's the last time I'll ever see Maurice, so I stare hard at him one more time. To remember him after we're dead. He looks like a wax dummy.

Then suddenly we slam into a snowbank. The hard jolt knocks the wind out of me, like a shot to the solar plexus. The rest of my body feels as if it's still sailing forward. Stunned, we both sit there gasping for breath, looking at each other like strangers. I can't swallow. Aftershocks race through me. I can't stop vibrating. Still, I have to say something to calm him down.

'Jesus, that was lucky. Amazing. You okay?'

His right hand still up on the grip, Maurice nods. But he's not going to say a word. He's punishing me.

'Good thing we were strapped in. We could've gone through the glass. Okay. Nothing happened. We're in one piece. Okay?'

Still, he won't talk to me. I don't like the rigid way he's sitting or the way he stares straight ahead.

Tentatively, I throw the car in reverse and to my surprise it bolts backwards, right onto the road.

Under my parka I'm sweating bullets. My mouth is wide open, sucking air. The windshield fogs up, so I blast the defrost. Rattled, I can hardly bear the noise, but I don't think I'm in shock. But what about the other driver? He could be pinned in a wreck three hundred yards below, bleeding to death, and I'm sitting here, letting my mind drift.

'I'll pull over and just go down and take a look, okay?'

'Sure.' The Sphinx speaks.

Ever so carefully I guide the Cherokee onto the shoulder of the road. A scrap of shoulder.

'He could be hurt.' I don't say 'dead,' editing every single word that comes out of my mouth. 'Just wait, okay?'

'Sure.'

'You'll be safe here.' I shouldn't have even mentioned how safe he would be. I know he'll take it the wrong way.

Then I'm walking out in the storm. The wind changes direction every six seconds. The snow slashes at me from the east, swirls, and slashes me from the west. Then it's parallel to the ground, getting right under my collar. I sure as hell am not going to drive down that hill. Safer to walk.

Nose in a ditch, its massive trunk pointing up at a crazy angle, the old Bonneville looks totally wrecked. The snow is so deep in the trench the driver probably can't open the door. Even if he's alive. I start to run, but instantly I'm flat on my back, sliding like a sled. Lucky I don't break my neck. Painfully careful, I pick myself up and practically tip toe down the hill.

I don't look over my shoulder, hoping Maurice didn't see me take the fall. He'll lose confidence in me if I don't handle this right. It's so quiet my breathing sounds like the ocean. I smell the stink of oil and burnt rubber.

The Bonneville's back window is already covered completely with a thin layer of snow. I brace myself, sure I'll be confronted with a gory mess. People in these junkers never use seatbelts. In fact, the cars don't even have seatbelts. I edge up along the driver's side, knee-deep in the ditch. I was right. No way he can open his doors.

Then George Antonelli's head pops out of the window like a jack-in-the-box. His face is flaming red. His white beard goes all the way down his chest. And he's laughing his head off.

He thinks this is funny. For some reason I hope Maurice doesn't see him laughing.

'Shit! We almost bought it this time, Nat. I saw you . . . you were shitting a brick!' Flinging his head back, he howls.

'You're laughing?'

'I'm up to my nuts in this shit!' Now he's got me laughing, too.

'Damn, now that I know you're alive, screw you. You can stay there till the spring.'

Without a word he turns and starts rummaging around in the back of the Bonneville, which, I notice, lacks a seat. Then he shoves a rusty spade through the window. 'You don't want me on your conscience, do you?'

I try to figure out if George has been drinking but decide he's just being George. There's not much choice. I start digging.

'I'll bet you don't have any insurance.'

'You selling insurance now?'

I dig for a while till my head starts spinning, then go for the door handle. That's when I notice it's been sheared off in the accident. I was so out of it I didn't even check the Cherokee when I staggered out into the storm, but I can imagine the wicked tear in the Jeep's skin. When I remember the deductible on my policy, I start to lose my sense of humor.

'Wait a second, will you?' I climb onto the glassy road and walk part of the way up the hill to see how Maurice is doing. He's still as a statue in the front seat. On the way down I fall flat on my back again. This one hurts, and I'm getting more and more pissed off.

'George, how old are the tires on this thing?'

'Pretty good. Plenty of tread last time I looked.'

'When was that, in '78?'

'About then.'

'You lost your handle.'

'Yeah, I noticed. I'll just push her open.'

Putting his shoulder down, he explodes out of the car, practically knocking me down with the door. Now we're both wedged into the snow-filled trench. Until George puts his hands on my waist and easily lifts me up to the road, scrambling up behind me.

The wind kicks up, blowing needle-like particles horizontal to the ground. In the sharp gusts, showers of snow shake free from blue-green spruce. Whiskey Hollow Road might as well be a highway in Siberia.

Gasping, we tramp up the hill to the Cherokee perched on the crest.

'Guess you'll have to drop me off.'

'What's the matter with that heap of yours? Why couldn't you make the hill?'

'Since they took lead out of the gas, it runs like shit.'

'Tell me the truth. You have insurance?' Now that I'm coming back to my senses, I'm getting incensed. Who knows? I could have five thousand dollars worth of damage.

'I know a guy does beautiful body work. It's on me.'

'George, you can't pay for body work. You don't have a pot to piss in.'

'He's a customer of mine. I'll pay him with goat cheese. He's a Greek.' Goats keep George alive. Goats and bees. Otherwise, he's got a small disability check and around $157 in the bank, tops.

'Listen, I have Maurice with me. Let's keep it light,' I say as we approach the Jeep.

'No you don't,' he answers, flinging open the passenger's side door. 'Less he's hiding.'

# CHAPTER ELEVEN: CRISSIE

## Saturday: February 27, 1990: 1:20 p.m.

I slam the truck door. Yeah, well, she's got Ben now.

Blowing cold flurries melt on my face. I stick out my tongue like I used to when I was a little girl because the snow tastes so clean. Then I start to run up the powdery road, past the Samuels' house and barn. You know they're downstaters because their barn was just fixed up and painted. I run a few yards and slide my feet sideways, turning them into skis. The packed snow squeaks. If I make it all the way to our lower field without stopping, maybe I'll knock off a whole pound.

Oh, God, I can breathe now that I'm away from them. Another minute and I would have died with that walking corpse Ben cackling like an old lady at everything mom said, like he's one of the old bags in her reading group she's so proud of. Most of the women don't really read the books, they talk about them for six seconds and then pounce on the chocolate eclairs and the pies that they swear have hardly any sugar in them.

I hear them talking in this heated way about boarding their

horses and restaurants they stuffed their faces in. Ooooo, Helen, those sea urchin ravioli with garlic and lemon . . . the fried artichokes . . . the grilled endive . . . Oooooo, I came right in my scabby old long johns . . .

Like everybody else, they love mom, they seem to worship her. And half of it doesn't make any sense. They're all these big environmentalists, but they love to talk about the time mom borrowed a rifle and shot the woodchuck that was making this big racket under the house six years ago. Like everything mom does, they turn this into evidence that she's 'such a free spirit.' I mean all she did was blow a poor woodchuck's brains out. On top of that, she's the one who's always giving money to the Save a Crippled Puppy Foundation. She's worried dolphins are getting too many colds. She makes absolutely no sense.

I hear all these stories about her being so 'full of life' and 'real' and 'honest', but they're not the ones who had to wait up for her when they were ten years old while she was driving some back road, wasted, on her way home from some 'new friend's' place. One thing though, after the silly bitch flipped our old Saab skidding downhill past Pindar's old building and supply and ended up with five broken ribs and a nice scratch on her lung, she started behaving better. She's not stupid. Self-preservation's her middle name.

When I found out when I was a Freshman how much she wasted on Baltasar, I had a total hissy fit. She sees a video about these horses and goes out and spends a million dollars on one and I'm supposed to go to college in a few years. And she defends herself, too. She says when the horse does a tolt gait it's so smooth you're in a dream. She says she'll make the money back on stud fees. Meanwhile, I end up combing the nits out of Baltasar's mane.

All day long I've been trying to tell her about the creepshow at school today, because one thing about mom, you can say anything, and I mean *anything* to her, but as soon as the call from Maurice came, all she could think about was herself. 'Come to town with me, Crissie, I'm uncomfortable Crissie, just stop by the camp for a little while, I'll give you a ride.' So how come her car breaks down every time?

But who else can understand me? Mom has this way of facing certain things that's impossible for other people. Parents. It's sort of upside down. The forbidden subjects are mom's specialties. She's so cool about things you can't upset her.

That's why I wanted to tell her what happened at school. It started today with that pinhead Jerry and his slave Monty hanging out in the lobby in front of the trophy case. I was late for class, talking to Dolores. So Jerry said, just loud enough for me to hear, 'Hey, Monty, she's wack, yo?'

'Dime piece.'

These pathetic fifteen-year-old farm boys with their hats on backwards are talking MTV black talk. And they've got their eyes pasted all over me, it gives me the sicklies.

'Yo, Crissie, meet us after school. We'll vogue in The Van.'

I give Dolores the look so she knows what I'm doing.

The Van is Jerry's. Supposedly it has a thick carpet, a futon, a refrigerator and a TV. He's always inviting me to see it. 'Just say when and where, Jerry. I'm into it.'

He blushes like a baby, but he tries to cover it up with his usual, dumb wisecrack. 'What happened to Space Happy?' That's the jocks' snide name for Harry. Space Happy Harry. Because he can understand what NASA is doing, and he just goes off into these fantastic, totally absorbed speeches about it.

'Cut out now. We'll meet you over by the courts,' Dolores puts in. In warmer weather the smokers, the trailer trash and free agents like me hang out there.

'Really?' Monty gags.

'Sure,' Jerry says, trying to act cool. Nobody's around so they head for the side exit.

Without saying a word to each other, Dolores and I race in the opposite direction and down the stairwell, but it's hard to run because we can't stop laughing. There aren't any monitors around, so we cut gym and hide out in the storeroom in the basement and smoke a roach Dolores has. It doesn't do much to me, I can still read and do math and everything when I smoke, but Dolores, it makes her ditzy. She blinks her big false lashes and crosses her eyes and looks like a demented Barbie.

So we're in the storeroom sitting on a metal desk with a giggly kind of buzz on, not a wipeout or anything, and Dolores takes this package of condoms our of her bag and reads off it, really serious. 'A rainbow of colors!'

'Oh, shit! A big green one!'

'How about hot pink!'

I'm falling into one of those laughing fits I'm afraid won't stop, but I want to make it worse. 'A . . . nice fire engine red . . . for his little . . . fireman's hat!' It's stupid, I know, but it practically makes her wet her pants, and she's begging me to stop.

Only with Dolores with her I-don't-give-a-shit attitude can I be this way. Gwen, who's in the Honor Society with me, freaks out when she sees me with Dolores. If you ask me it's just snobbery and hairdos. Dolores has her blonde hair cut short on the sides, but the back is long and she's always snapping it in her face like a horse tail.

So we're laughing so hard we're crying, and all of a sudden the door to the room flies open and Ronnie, the custodian, who is about fifty with tattoos on his thick forearms, bursts in and slams the door behind him. He sniffs with his snout and laughs.

'Smells like good shit, girls.'

Dolores isn't afraid of him, though. 'Oh, give it a rest, Ronnie. My dad told me you and him used to sniff carbona when you were in high school.'

This absolutely grotesque expression comes over his face, I can't describe it except to say that it's like a smile and a grimace at the same time, and he says, 'Yeah, wadda you girls thinka this?'

And he just pulls his thing out right there in the dim, dusty storeroom. I don't want to look at it, but I can't help it – twisted curiosity, I guess. It's way bigger than Harry's with veins and even warts on it, and he's squeezing it and petting it and talking to it like it's his pet dog or something. It's the most disgusting thing I ever saw, and Dolores, who is so cool, says, 'You can lose your job for that, Ronnie. C'mon, Crissie.'

But he grabs her by the throat and slams her flat on her back on the desk. I'm so afraid I almost faint. 'Say anything I'll slit your throats, the both of you. You ain't seen nothing, right?'

Dolores sits up and straightens her little black skirt, and she still doesn't look scared, she's unbelievable. I'm so frightened I'm biting my lip and trying not to cry, but Dolores says, 'Yeah, right, we ain't seen *nothing*.'

Then I have to go straight to Mr Weiss' class and study permutations and combinations. I keep looking at him and thinking it's like he's speaking Chinese or something. I don't understand a word he's saying, and I'm doing great in his class. I think Ronnie's warty thing put me in a state of shock. I'm sitting there thinking, I hope they all don't look like that when they get old.

Then I start thinking about the time in the shower and how mad I got at him. Who else? It's not that I didn't have a right, look at what he was doing, but after I did what I did, I think he got worse. Or I thought he got worse til I got older and started reading that everybody in a family with a kid like Maurice feels like it's their fault. That made me feel better, but not entirely. Because he really did get worse after I caught him, and I suppose I lost it with mom's body brush, but he was really being disgusting. I was right, I was definitely right, but at the same time I went too far.

So Mr Weiss is talking about permutations and combinations and my mind is snapping up and back between Maurice and his skinny little thing and Ronnie's grotesque hose. Finally, I have to excuse myself and go to the nurse for a Midol, even though I don't need it.

And all day after school I'm thinking about telling my mother the Ronnie story, and getting her to go to the principal, even if I have to admit I was cutting classes, and even though Dolores thought it was a big joke, but mom's all freaked out about who else. He can be in a hospital or an institution for six months, but it's like he's always around, the thing we don't mention that we're always thinking about. So who cares if a janitor exposed himself to me when Maurice has got bigger problems than I could ever have, right?

I don't try out of spite. But like always I start thinking of little Moccorico and how he looked the day Maxie was crushed on the road. I tried to give him Maxie's collar, but he wouldn't take it, he was all curled up in the corner of his room with his back to me and I was petting his head, poor Moccorico, poor Moccorico, and when he showed me his face finally he had a single push pin stuck in the middle of his forehead. A clear plastic push pin. Mom was the last person in the world I could tell.

That's the way it works. I'm taking a nice walk in the cold to cleanse myself of all of mom's B.S. and forget everything, and he comes back into my head. So I try an act of will, as my dad would say. I'm going to puuusssshhh him completely out of my thoughts and concentrate on choosing a college. One, it has to be two thousand miles away from home. Two, it has to be in a better climate. If I can get away from snow, I can get away from home completely. Mom's always saying how beautiful the snow is, and dad will give me a lecture on all the different crystals, but snow makes me think of them. It's like snow is mom and dad's natural element.

And Mr Winston, the part-time Guidance Counselor, said, 'You got almost thirteen hundred boards. What about a small liberal arts school?'

He's right, but I have to laugh. I mean I grew up in a small liberal arts college, Moira State. Art books and novels and poetry were stacked in piles every place. Incense. Great music, I have to admit. When my friends say John Coltrane sounds so grating, I can't even begin to explain how beautiful it is. I mean, I just grew up with jazz. There were also roaches you could smoke and she'd never know, plus towers of dishes and greasy pans in the double sink. There was a whole room set aside just for dirty laundry, and the room was usually half full. And don't forget the back porch full of wine bottles and beer bottles from her last drunken mess. Moira State.

In my dorm room I won't have any dead weeds or cow jaw bones on the kitchen table, and there won't be any grizzly hippies getting wasted and stuffing their faces while mom looks on with that expression, that smiling, stupidly self-satisfied face of hers. I'll be two thousand miles away.

And before I know it I'll be on the phone to her every other day, and then I'll be putting her up and getting into bed with her with a bowl of popcorn to watch a stupid sitcom and tell her what an asshole my boyfriend is, and she'll tell me what to do. Because she knows. It's the most humiliating thing to love your mother.

* * *

I'm almost up to the house now when the Cherokee pulls up alongside of me. Right away I see the gash in the side, so I assume it isn't dad's because his Cherokee is so perfect and shiny that they could put it back in a showroom and nobody would know the difference. I mean, how did these people, my so-called parents, ever get together, and why, and how could they do it with each other? This is like the Mystery of my life, like the Mysteries the Greeks had in their plays or the mystery of Christ being three people and one simultaneously or who Jack the Ripper was.

At first when the Jeep slows down and glides alongside me my heart starts to beat fast, and I get drenched in sweat. I'm sure it's Ronnie, and he's going to grab me and slit my throat. Well, not exactly. I've known Ronnie for years from Stick Willow, but I'm afraid to turn and see if it's him. Then dad rolls down the window and shouts at me, 'Hey, Crissie, what're you doing?'

'Going home.'

'Well, come on, get in.' When he swings the door open I smell the oiled leather seats. Dad always rubs down the seats and cleans off the dashboard, and he has a custom wood steering wheel. It's funny because in these old snapshots mom has he's in a beat-up Volvo that looks like a bug, he's got this bushy hair and he's even skinnier than he is now. Actually, he looks like a cartoon character. It's as if he was another person, which I suppose maybe is possible. Mom is the one who never changes, and that's why her friends think she's so great.

'You haven't by any chance heard anything about your brother, have you?'

He doesn't even say, Hi, how are you, do you have a life? 'Actually, yeah.'

Dad has this hard, thin face that goes dark when he's worried. It's dark now, and I can see the bags under his eyes. Tea bags, he calls them. I'll kill myself before I get those. 'What? Where is he?'

'He called mom hours ago. He's down at the camp.'

Dad pulls the Cherokee into mom's driveway and starts yelling. 'I've been driving all over creation, and he's at the camp?' It's like, why does he have to act like that?

'What happened to the Cherokee?'

'I had him, then I lost him.'

'What?'

I know he's really upset because he just shrugs, and that Cherokee is like his biggest thing. 'Accident. So when did he call?'

'I don't know, hours ago?' I'm getting ready to get out. 'Later, dad.'

'You know how long he's been out there? All night wandering around? He probably stopped taking his pills, too.'

'Unsupervised?' If Maurice gets into one of his states, he doesn't even feel the cold. I remember one time when he was about sixteen and it was raining ice balls, he started running up and down the driveway in his t-shirt to prove he was a yogi or something. I just prayed none of my friends would drive by.

'Can you believe these assholes? You pay them a fortune and

they can't even keep track of their patients. At least I've got some anti-psychotics on me.' He flips open the glove compartment, and inside there's a sealed, Tupperware bowl full of drugs. 'Once he goes off them, it's good-bye, Charlie.'

'Yeah, well, he'll be okay, dad.' I push open the door, but he takes my sleeve. This is not normal for him. He's usually Mr Calm and Collected.

'You've got the best touch with him, Crissie, why don't you come along? Just to talk him into taking his pills.'

I feel like saying, Thanks a lot, dad, but a janitor showed me his warty pewee today, and I'd like to go inside and throw up in private, but he's acting really super-strange, so I get back in. 'I can't, I've got something to do.'

'What? I'll drive you. With your mom there and everything, it would change the dynamic.'

This is so complicated because what he says is true. If Maurice is there with both of them he'll really start to act out. He's always saying mom is a scum bitch if dad is around, maybe to prove his loyalty, or because he just hates her, you never can tell, maybe both. And I know dad wants me there so he won't go off on mom because she once told me he'd never act a certain way if I was around, and maybe he wants to protect himself against himself. (I think that makes sense.) Also, it's true I have a way of talking to Maurice, but the problem is I start to think maybe if I talk to him just right, say the perfect magical incantation like the Good Witch of the East, all of a sudden he'll be miraculously cured, which I know is a pathetic fantasy.

When mom wasn't paying enough attention to him – three

quarters of the time – he used to cling to me. Everything was backwards, I was the younger sister, five maybe, but he hung onto me and made believe I was a kangaroo. He'd read about kangaroos and their pouches, and he liked to make believe I had a pouch, too. 'Slip me in your pouch, Ricomocco,' he'd say. Oh, God, that was repulsive.

I have to say something to dad.

So I try to sort it all out, and think, What if I forget me for a second? What if I think about whether I really can help the situation? The truth is I can smooth things out to some extent, as long as Maurice isn't totally wigged out. All I need is one look in his eyes. If he's gone, I'll know it right away.

'How long has he been out of the hospital?'

'Since yesterday.'

'Well, what are the chances he stopped taking his meds?' Meds. When did I adopt Maurice's way of saying it? It gives me the chills, as if he's a ghost under my skin.

'I'd say a hundred per cent. He always says he wants to be himself. Sometimes he tries to half-swallow them or hide them under his tongue in the hospital. I thought you knew that. I keep thinking with all the biotechnology there'll be a new treatment, and he'll get better. Somewhat.'

I look at dad, and this is the most amazing thing, he's crying, and in my whole life I never saw him crying. It's sort of more like choking and sniffling actually because he probably doesn't know how to do it. Probably this is an Oprah Moment, but he's making me feel really uncomfortable.

'You never know. We had a wicked fender bender on Whiskey Hollow, and then he just, he just disappeared.' He snorkles up some snot and reaches across the seat to tussle my hair. This also blows me away, I mean it's not exactly his usual behavior. 'At least you're okay, huh?'

'Yeah, great.' He misses my sarcasm completely. He takes out a pressed white handkerchief and blows his nose. This is not dad, and it scares me.

'We almost . . . bought it back there.'

'What?'

'Oh, well, it was more of a fender crash really. Why not give me a hand, Cris?'

I don't know how to say no now. I even touch the sleeve of his black coat, but I don't touch him.

Dad isn't afraid to drive the Cherokee fast, even on the icy roads. Maybe that's how he got into the accident, but I don't want to open that can of worms. He puts on one of his boring Van Morrison tapes. On this one Van's singing about being Irish is so cool, which is funny because mom is always calling her family shanty Irish. Van Morrison is the only music dad listens to, over and over, one of his definite peculiarities, and I think maybe mom's right about how rigid he is, but one thing about dad, if he says he's going to pick you up at eight, he's there every time.

Before I know it we're heading up the driveway to the camp, and I see smoke coming out of the chimney and the kitchen light on like this is the most normal place in the world. We don't say anything now, we just get out of the car and march to the front door, but then dad says, 'No big deal. Let me handle him.'

I'm wondering why he made me come, and I'm mad all over again. One thing though, I won't go out for pizza with them.

# CHAPTER TWELVE: VINCE

**Sunday: February 28, 1990: 8:45: a.m.**

The ghost of a fit flits through me. Even though medication controls most of my seizures, I still feel them the way an amputee senses a missing arm. I get quick leg jerks at dawn, flashes of black in between stabs at a sunnyside-up egg. Once in a while a coffee cup flies from my hand. Always, I get intensely hungry on the rare instances when I do black-out, but there's not a fucking thing wrong with my blood sugar. Did Maurice ever hear my one-liners to Moira about face-dancing, or my explanations about why auras weren't all they were cracked up to be? Pretty unlikely.

One thing for sure, I keep the pure fear to myself. I stay conscious just long enough to know I'm helpless. Long enough to hear the noise coming out of me. I could have made a living as a human siren. One or two whole-body twitches, and then it's going, going, gone. Still, I never get a cold, I'm never sick at all. Just a *gran mal* every two or three years, nothing serious.

'Do I have to pay?'

'It's on the house. I heard you wanted to talk to me.'

'My legal affairs aren't in order.'

It's mind-bending the way he can put things. 'Ah.'

Before blacking out on the deck I saw the hummingbird sucking at the feeder and Moira's naked feet with their candy apple red nails.

I bolted up because standing was as far away from losing consciousness as I could get, but Moira was far down at the end of a tube. A rolling power failure grabbed me, and I spasmed to my knees, my body snapping like a whip, the world blinking on and off, on and off.

'I'm here to help you.'

'I know who you are. That's why I called you.'

A sickening chill takes hold of me. He knows. He doesn't know. He knows.

Odd joints ached, knuckles and elbows and hips. Moira brought me crushed ice for my bitten tongue, and we sat there watching the fog curl into the San Francisco Bay. 'It's like smoke in a bowl,' she said.

'Who do you think I am?'

Montgomery seizes my wrist and starts shaking his head.

'I remember in the boat. You stuck your hand right up her dress.'

'No, I don't think so—'

'If you didn't stick your hand up her dress, I don't want to talk to you! Who are you. Are you the lawyer or what?'

'I am.'

'I know who you are.'

Moira wanted to know if I saw auras or had second sight.

What a fucking laugh. I told her the truth. It was like dying in flashes.

'Do you know who Freeman Dyson is? Do you know who Stephen Hawking is?

'They're physicists, right?'

'Fucking right! All the suns are going to turn into dwarves. You're a son. Do you want to turn into a dwarf? Nobody does. It's going to happen to everybody in a hundred trillion years. Neutrinos. Positrons. Got a pencil?'

A few weeks after mom died, Joe the Barber snapped head-first into his bottles of hair preparations, shattering a commercial-sized bottle of Vitalis, cracking the barbershop mirror with his skull. He left behind six pairs of surgical shoes shaped like his flat feet.

'Gimme a second.'

Montgomery, on the other line, nods.

'First suns explode, then they implode, then they die. Do you want to explode? Do you want to die? Just leak away.'

'I got a pencil, Maurice.'

My eyes flick to Montgomery's impassive face.

'You want to say something for me to write down?' I avoid the word 'will' to keep from agitating him.

'I was never interested in things. I don't need anything.'

'Yeah . . .'

'So I want to give everything away, all of it, but not to the wrong people. Some people would like to get it for purposes . . . I can't say exactly what . . .'

'Just tell me. I'll write it down. You can give it to whoever you want.'

'I want it to go to an international consortium of scientists . . . yeah . . . do it through the UN. How do I know you're writing this down? You're not doing it, I know!'

'I'll show you a copy.'

'Yeah, send it FedEx.'

Montgomery shakes his head. 'I'll have to check on that for you, Maurice.'

'That's it, I got to see it, you bring it to me after you write it down.'

From somewhere Montgomery produces a pad and pencil and nods. 'I'll write down every word. Whatever you want. We'll send over a copy some way or other.'

'You know what entropy is? Can't be my lawyer otherwise.'

'Uh, it's when energy becomes disorganized, isn't it?'

'Great! Terrific! You're the man!'

'He's bipolar and manic,' Montgomery whispers, jabbing his thumb skyward.

If Maurice's mania gets any worse, he might explode, just like his suns. In a funny way he understands exactly what is happening to him.

'Anytime you want to start dictating—'

'Okay, okay . . . lemme start . . . Do I have to say "Being of sound mind?"' Getting the irony, he laughs. His gruesome awareness is the worst part. It would be easier if he made no sense at all.

'I'll put it in . . .'

'Okay, okay, being of sound mind I leave my house to Columbia University Medical Center for the study of . . . Does that sound okay?'

'Very good.'

'Cosmography . . . cosmology . . . and genetic disorders. Because I'm the first person to think about the DNA in suns. That's why they blow up.'

'Is that it?'

'No! No! There's a lot of other stuff. The bank accounts. The cars. The. . the. . the . . . insurance money. They get it if you don't kill yourself, right?'

'Right.'

As I talk to him he becomes more incoherent. I try to follow his disconnected thinking. The tail of a Felix the Cat clock over the counter flicks up and back. Shooting a glance at Montgomery, I try to catch his eye.

Cradling his phone under his chin, Montgomery interrupts suddenly. 'Maurice. You still hungry? You need anything else?'

This practical question seems to focus Maurice. 'Uh, yeah, fine. Who's this?'

'This is Frank, we talked before, remember? How about some more drinks? Blankets? You warm enough in there?'

'She's drinking everything you give me. Eating, too.' This is another voice, cunning and angry. And why does he only refer to 'she?' Is one of them already dead? I try to kill these questions, but they shoot through my mind against my will.

'Why don't you just let us see her, just so we know she's okay,' Montgomery says calmly.

Why does he say 'she,' also? Am I making too much of every word? How can I stop interpreting every remark? It's impossible.

To my complete shock, Maurice agrees. 'I'll show her if you send over some V-8. It doesn't have so much sugar.'

'Okay, fine. You're right, it's the best juice on the market. Give me a few minutes, I'll send one of my men over to the store. We'll call you back.'

Without warning he shuts the phones off. 'You think there's any V-8 in this shitburg?'

'You cut him off?'

Montgomery looks at me blandly. Now I know where I've seen his face, in a print Moira used to have over her dresser, a detail of some Dutch farmer. His eyes were small, blue and shrewd.

'Let's see how he handles the silence.'

Suddenly I'm pissed as hell at his whole self-assured bit. 'Don't you think that's dangerous? Aren't we supposed to keep him talking?'

'I've been consulting with the kid's shrink. He's schizzy and bipolar. A real witch's brew. The thing is, when they peak, they want company, they want somebody to talk to. Let's just sit tight awhile.'

'This is completely irresponsible. Who elected you God? Is Moira in there? Is she alive?'

Montgomery's voice falls to a low, hard note. 'Nobody. I'm

not even an archangel. I've negotiated a couple of dozen of these things. How many have you done, Mr Vitale?'

'You're not going to answer me?'

'Wish I could.'

There's nothing to say. The trooper shows me the john. It's one of those overdone ye olde antique jobs with a polished wood water cabinet and a pull chain. In a distant way I become aware of my soaked feet and my moist pants leg again. Inside, the pounding I feel is similar to the sensation I get before a closing argument, anxiety I know how to handle. And that's exactly what bothers me. Is it possible that Moira won't exist in a second and I'll find a professional way to minimize her murder? Or if I look it in the face, instead of with my habitual, sidelong glance, will I be totally wiped out? That's what I think I think anyway. There's no way I could let grief loose. Worse still, I'm starting to feel as numb as my fucking feet.

I felt like that after I lost the Martini case. How could you fail in a case like that? An EMS worker pushes open an apartment door and discovers a two-hundred-and-fifty pound woman slamming her six-month old daughter against the wall.

Martini lands one punch to the mother's head, she hits the wall and dies of an aneurysm. But the baby died, too. If it had lived, everything would have looked different to that jury, Martini would have been a hero. Instead, they convict him of manslaughter. Of course, I figure it's an open and shut case, and I'll keep him off the stand in case he makes a mistake, or the jury doesn't like him. What did I do, what did I say, what did I miss to get on the wrong side of that jury?

'She nearly ripped that baby's arm off,' the poor kid told me. And she had. How could I possibly lose? Maybe I should've cried my eyes out before that jury. There's a Tennessee Supreme Court ruling that says if it'll help your client, you have a duty to bawl. No shit.

I'd wake up day after day, so fucking ashamed. Before my first cigarette I'd be running the case through my mind again. It was funny because like every other jerk who passed the bar on his second try, I'd lost plenty of cases. I did my best, and if I lost I blamed the DA for cheating me on discovery, or the judge for giving misleading instructions, or my beloved client, who was almost always guilty. Maybe I had too high a regard for my own cynicism, but that fucking case just blindsided me. I hit a breaking point, and I hadn't even noticed I was bending.

I wander to the living room where a smokie is watching the barn through a pair of binoculars. For the first time I see the sharpshooters crouched on the front porch, not moving a muscle.

On the lawn a rickety gazebo tilts downhill, half-collapsing. The three-story dairy barn with its fancy Dutch roof blots out the rolling, snow-covered hills. 'See anything? Any movement in there?'

The trooper lowers the binoculars for a second and gives me a stony look.

'I know this kid a little. I don't think he has it in him. He's really a little pussy.'

'Are you authorized to be in here, sir?'

'Yeah, yeah, I'm fully authorized.'

* * *

When she came to my room in Berkeley a few months after marrying Nathan, in his Buddhist period back then, I didn't ask her any questions, and she never explained why. It was as if nothing had happened, our break-up, her marriage, we just picked up again, and I was too lonely and too happy to say a word. Later on we talked about how we were such good friends, we were so used to each other, we could only talk to each other, but that was a bunch of phony crap. When we *weren't* talking, when we *weren't* trying to understand how we felt about each other, then we were really together.

In April we drove down to Stinson Beach and when the mescaline hit we both saw a whole hillside packed solid with wild flowers. Moira said the entire hill was breathing, and then I saw it too. We stayed all day, running in and out of the long cold waves and later trying to fuck in a dark cove. But our bodies got too sandy, and we both started laughing so hard we had to give up and just watch the ocean breathe.

'Meditating is so boring, and it makes my ass sore anyway,' she said.

Either Nathan the Buddhist had entered Nirvana, or Moira was too cunning, but he never found out.

What Maurice is doing in there I don't want to know, but I wish something, almost anything would happen. No, not anything. The torture of nothing at all is better.

Nobody stops me, so I climb the stairs to the master bedroom and rummage through the dresser drawers and the closet. In a blind rush I peel off my pants and underwear. Mr Gaiter favors boxer shorts and wide-wale corduroys two sizes too big for me. In these ballooning pants I look like a corduroy clown. Even in the days when I was riding a hot streak of negligence cases, when I was knocking those juicy little legal stenographers of Court Street down like nine-pins, even then I was rehearsing for this role. All I need is a nose that lights up.

I can't sit still. The kid's voice is in my head, that strangled voice that sounds like it's put on. I meant what I said, though. I can't imagine him really going through with this. He'll crack and start whining is more like it.

When I make my appearance downstairs in my clown suit, nobody notices.

Montgomery peers out the kitchen window at the barn. We've been out of contact with Maurice for almost twenty minutes. Now I notice another perimeter of state troopers crouched behind emergency vehicles with their rifles aimed at the barn door.

'Isn't there some back way to get in there?' I ask Montgomery.

'No.' He presses his lips together and gives me a hard look.

'Sorry. Mind if I walk around a little more?'

'Stay down here. I might need you.'

I go take a look at the Vermont Castings stove. The old monster I've got doesn't even have a catalytic converter. I could fire up this baby, open the door to my stairs and heat the whole upstairs. I walk all around the living room, trying to drum up some interest in the Gaiters' things, but it's too much like a museum for me. The walls are sheetrocked and the floors are scraped and some genius they hired figured out how to make right angles in corners.

A series of dull shots explodes inside the barn, every one a fist digging deep into my chest. I'm shouting, 'You asshole! He killed her! Them . . .' I race back to the kitchen to choke Montgomery to death, but then I think better of it.

Ignoring me, Montgomery rushes to the porch and grabs a bull horn. 'Hold fire! Hold fire!'

The shock of cold air tells me I'm outside too, standing on steps.

Blinking at the blinding white hills, my eyes can't focus. The SWAT team stays crouched, the troopers on the porch completely still, their faces impassive. A burst of gunfire, confusing, explosive sounds. They're so unreal I'm not sure where they're coming from or whether they're shots at all.

Montgomery's roaring through the bull horn. 'Hold fire! Hold fire!'

Every cop I see is frozen in place, but the fusillade continues over Montgomery's screams.

Then I make out Maurice running in an odd, uncoordinated way, and I understand why I couldn't locate him at first. Against the snow his naked body is hard to pick out, his bare arms and legs churning as he heads for the pasture. When he turns away from us, I can see his skeletal back.

Bending down, he grabs his leg, awkwardly ducking under the barbed wire.

Suddenly, the shooting stops, but the hidden marksmen don't reveal themselves.

Nobody makes a move yet as Maurice staggers and limps another hundred yards. All of a sudden he lunges head first into a snow bank, the damn thing must be four feet deep, and he's digging. He gets his head and shoulders in there, but you can still see the rest of his scrawny body.

I plunge out onto the porch, I've got to get to the barn now, but strong hands grab my shoulders.

# CHAPTER THIRTEEN: MAURICE

## Saturday: February 27, 1990: 6:30 a.m.

I must've slept a minute, but it's morning on TV. Kiki's probably coming back later, but I can't wait. I'm too hungry. There's a new Stewart's in town next to the Magic Carpet Motel, so I walk over there and get a large hazel nut coffee and two cheese buns and read the papers. This old bag French actress Brigitte Bardot castrated her neighbor's donkey, but I can't figure out why. Then there's this one about is Miles on *Thirtysomething* like a real ad executive or not. I mean real ad men are just like anteaters for money. Talk about stupid to the *n*th degree. The black letters on the page won't stay still, it's like they're in three-D, floating on the paper, and I can push them around with my finger. I do that for a while when nobody is watching. I get all charged up on two more giant coffees. It gets lighter.

So I walk over to Jamie's place on Hanford Street where there are all these old mansions. A few of the houses have pillars like Greek temples, but most of them, they've closed off half the rooms or more cause it's too expensive to heat. Or they've got a crazy old lady living in a kitchen alone in a house with twenty rooms. The economy of Accordia isn't what it used to be. That's what dad is always saying. His father owned the Mountain Star and the Winsota. Big hotels. They're just brown pictures now. I'm going to inherit them.

I wonder if Jamie's got any new computer games.

There's this one I read about called *Dreamscape,* you get to control your own dreams, which sounds cool. But if you make a mistake the dream starts turning into a nightmare and you have to know which doors to go through to get back to the good dream or something. That's what I read anyway. That could be a lot scarier than cartoons jumping around shooting at you.

All I do is climb the back staircase onto the second story porch and look in Jamie's window and there he is, sleeping on the floor in his sleeping bag just like he did when he was ten, and his room looks like a bomb hit it. I don't think he works or anything.

So I let myself in and stand there over him. His head is shaped like a football. He's got a harelip but most of it's gone after the operations. Maybe that's why he ended up at BOCES, the extension school. And he really can't read too well, I mean, especially for a doctor's son. I give the football a soft kick.

'What the fuck?' He scrambles up onto his bed and tries to get a look at me. 'Maurice, when'd they let you out?'

'You got anything, Jamie?'

He rubs his eyes and laughs. 'Same old Maurice. Over there, in the pocket of my jacket there's joints. Breakfast for your head.'

Jamie sits with his legs crossed, lights a cig and blows a

cloud of smoke full of blue snakes. Do you know the difference between an illusion, a delusion and a hallucination? I do. If you study the differences you can get off on your hallucinations and still remind yourself they're not real. Smoky blue snakes. It's easier when you're on your meds though. Smoky blue snakes. Whooaaaa.

'Gimme one here.'

He tosses me the pack. After a few hits of the Marlboro, I torch up a jay and pass it to Jamie. Now we're both smoking cigs and joints at the same time, which strikes me as funny. But I don't want to laugh too hard because there's a danger zone inside laughing which, if you cross it, you might keep laughing forever.

Me and Jamie had good times together. 'Remember in the sixth grade when we ran away?'

'We woulda got away if you didn't start shooting your mouth off.'

He says it like he really means it and I feel real bad. Maybe we could've gotten away when we were twelve and none of this would have happened. I don't believe in fate, I believe in naked singularities. Events inside black holes that nobody can see.

'Remember when we tried to use the gasoline card at the Quikway to buy food?' Now he laughs and I feel better. He remembers the good times, too.

'We had a stack of shit. Baloney and donuts and chocolate milk and the woman looks at us and says, "And how much in gas?"'

'And you took her serious!'

'Did not!' Actually, he's right. To my surprise she'd already called the troopers. You'd never think anybody working at the Quikway would be that smart.

'So how'd you get out?' Jamie asks, passing the roach.

Now I'm lifting off like the space shuttle. 'Hopped like a rabbit.'

For some reason this cracks him up and I start laughing too until I'm inside the hall of laughing, mirrors of my own laughing, and I get this panicky feeling like I'll lose my way out and Jamie is shaking me to stop. I stop.

Now I try to be real straight and sober. 'So what are you doing with your life, Jamie?'

'Same as you, hopping like a rabbit . . .'

This time he goes way around the bend and I have to snap him out of it. If getting high weren't so scary, it would be great to be high all the time. 'You want to see something?'

'Yeah, what?' Jamie says, throwing a flannel shirt over his shoulders. Then he jumps into his black jeans. He's got legs like a spider.

I go and get my knapsack. I take out the Cobray and unwrap it. Shining in its grease it looks so cool laying there on Jamie's bed. Then I toss some of the clips next to it, the black night operations mask and a couple of boxes of cartridges. The Sloughter had an arsenal back at his place. I think I could've bought anti-tank weapons.

When I look up at Jamie I'm surprised. He lets go with a nervous laugh. 'You think that's a good idea, Mo?'

'What?'

'I mean, are you on your meds and everything? That's a lot of firepower.'

'You think I don't know how to handle a firearm? I've been handling firearms since I was a kid. You used to hunt with me and my dad. What's your problem?'

'No problem. How much ammo you got there?'

'Six clips and five boxes of extra cartridges. You got any dental floss?' An idea is taking shape but I leave it alone. Better to let it grow on its own.

'Sure, uh, you wanna go out for breakfast? I could go for some French toast and bacon myself. We could drive over to the Greek diner in Tuscarora.'

'Cool, just lend me the dental floss. I wanna do something on the way. You still got the jeep?' Jamie's got this army surplus jeep his dad bought him at an auction years ago.

'The Green Horse? Sure, it's around back. Wait for me on the front porch, and I'll pull it out.'

Creeping through the living room I get the feeling I'm in a funeral home. The drapes are drawn and the furniture's this heavy, dark, old-fashioned stuff, highly polished. There's an empty cut glass bowl on an end table, I remember. It used to be filled with Hershey's Kisses. I think of the great times me and Jamie had as kids running in and out of this tomb, hiding under the oak table with the clawed feet, hiding in closets and leaping out, screaming at his ghost of a mother. I used to bring over my books about the constellations and take Jamie out on his front lawn to see Orion and show him how the whole sky revolves around the north star. Inside, I can feel myself, the boy inside the polo shirt, the boy with the stick arms, and how carefree he was, another person, and I wonder if he's still in me somewhere, some kind of homunculus.

But that boy died. It was like a heavy snow started inside my head when I was around thirteen or fourteen and kids I used to blow away with my brain power, slow kids like Jamie, caught up with me. I was standing still, my thinking got so cloudy and streaked with pain. The pain was like lines in my head, wires of shooting pains.

That's how much thinking hurts. And I'm getting zapped with other people's thoughts, too, otherwise why the shooting electric currents? Cell phones for ears. Did I pay my ears bills? EEEEEEEE. Black Thoughts you have to smother with reason.

I'm on the porch.

The snow is falling and it reminds me of snow on TV when the dish blows out and that reminds me of the snow in my head. Electronic pixels.

I'm on the porch and the jeep comes roaring out of the driveway. Jamie jams on the brakes, rolls down the window and tosses the dental floss at me. I miss it and it rattles onto the wide planks. 'Gotta go, Mo! Gotta go!' he shouts, flooring it.

He doesn't really like me.

Yeah, well, it's not like I'm not used to it. And I start to think of all the other cretins who used to say, 'Lookit the geek, lookit the freak, lookit the creep,' when I'd just be minding my own business, practically trying to be invisible, in the classroom or the schoolyard.

They'd make noises like animals, spit on my shoes, stick sharp things, a hairpin once, in my back. They'd howl like they were howling at the moon. Then my dad complained and the principal must've said something because after that it got quiet, I moved in a bubble of silence wherever I went, and in a way that was even harder to take, like they didn't see me at all. And I'm watching them in the halls wondering how they do it, how they smile and poke each other, and walk around happy as clams when entropy will get them, just like everybody else someday. Nasty turds.

I pick up the dental floss and put it in my pocket. Now all I need is some tape, which I get at the Quikway.

The train station's been abandoned since 1952 when the resort hotels shut down and they stopped running the passenger train through Accordia. The windows have been boarded up and there's a padlock on one door but I force the baggage door and I'm inside in a cloud of dust and mouse shit. There's black magic graffiti on the walls, heavy metal satanic shit, pentagrams with an extra side but there are also things nobody's touched in forty years. An old schedule on the wall. A calendar showing a little blonde girl drinking Coke. A wall of pigeon holes without the pigeons. (Joke.)

In a way it's colder inside the old station than it is outside, like the coldest air in the world leaked into the building and died there, but at least I'm out of the wind. That's when I sit down on the old chair with one wheel, wheeee, and roll up and back, and that's when I get out the dental floss and the tape. When the Sloughter took me to his place, he showed me how to do this shit. Dental floss and tape.

Then I remembered this was something I learned years ago in the Boy Scouts, too. Ronnie Garzella's father had been in Nam and he said he shouldn't've been teaching us this, but you never knew, it might help one day if somebody took your mother hostage, or your sister, what would you do then? He showed us how to do it with his old M-16. Ronnie said using this trick he could shoot so fast he could hold off a whole army. I think I also read about the same thing in *Guns and Ammo*, it all comes back to me. It's simple.

First you take two clips and jungle tape them together. That way when you empty one magazine, you just flip it over and jam in the other one. Instead of thirty-two rounds of constant fire, now you've got sixty-four. A dimwit could do that. Also, with a rag I found in the motel and some tape, I add on a brass catcher. That way you don't spray the spent cartridges all over the ground wherever you are, you take them with you. The Sloughter said he could get a silencer from Ingram, they sell them in two separate pieces so it's legal, but it was too bad, he didn't have one on hand. Still, he sold me a sling, which was like the ones they use on Uzis.

Then I get out the dental floss and stick it through the base of each magazine. Presto! A homemade speed loader. This way you stand on the string and hold back the spring inside the magazine making it easy to snap in cartridges when you're reloading.

I wonder who else is home. It's time to go walking to see what I can see.

In a second or an hour the Cherokee pulls up and all of a sudden I'm inside where it's so warm I could choke and dad is being so careful and so nice I can't breathe. I'm dripping, melting away, turning into fog. Dad wants to feed me, clean me up, take care of me the rest of my life. That's the way he is. After Syracuse, he saved my life. They could have hooked me up to an electric generator after Syracuse. But dad makes me so uncomfortable, he wants to help me so much he's like a piano wire. Strung too tight. I didn't say that, Crissie did a century ago. When Crissie talks to me in the old way, it's like my favorite song from 1983. I sing back.

That's why I was so surprised when she came out from behind the penguins with the body brush. The back of the red brush hit the front of my teeth, but I kept my eyes open and saw the mole. It was right next to her nipple, like she had two nipples. I was caught, so I thought, I might as well see what I can see. Plastic hurts more than you think.

The Cherokee climbs straight into the clouds. Then it just hangs there while I start to fall. Inside the Cherokee but outside the Cherokee. But how can that be?

# CHAPTER FOURTEEN: MOIRA

**Saturday: February 27, 1990: 1:50 p.m.**

Then I think better of it. I just need to sit and collect my thoughts before going in. 'Ben, wait just a second, okay?'

I climb back into the truck, breathe the moist, hot air. It smells of wet wool. Ben's been wearing his dead patrician father's 1950s wardrobe for years, tweed jackets, Irish wool sweaters, plaid caps that balance like colorful pancakes on his curly gray hair. He puts his heavy hand with its long fingers and red arthritic knuckles on my shoulder, pulls me to him, and kisses me on top of my head.

'It must be hard,' he says. Probably without knowing it, Ben has mastered perfect love without sex. Or is that just the way I want to see him, a friend and not a lover? The rarest of all men.

'What's hard is remembering what he was like when he was small. I remember the first time he climbed the stairs, he was like a puppy, on all fours. When he got to the top he stood there, so unsure of himself, with a mystified look on his face. My heart was in my mouth the way he was teetering around up there, but he didn't fall.'

'I suppose he was okay then, he didn't have the disease.'

Sweet Weird Ben, why can't I just run away with him? But the time for that sort of thing is over now, at least that's what I keep telling myself. Then I start drifting away, imagining a sudden, new life. I'll find a small apartment in the Trastevere and start a new business in Rome exporting to New York. Take one of those theatrical Roman men for a lover. God, how disgusting I am now, even to myself.

'Oh, he was beautiful, he was the Monkey Boy. That's what we used to call him. The Monkey Boy. Nathan thinks I'm a terrible person, really, you can't even conceive of it.'

'Oh, c'mon, Moira.'

'No, no, it's true. He thinks he's the king of the Puritans or something.' Even when he was pretending to be a hippie, Nathan was conventional. Maybe that's what really attracted me. I knew I could count on him in a way I never could with Vincent. The worst part was that without knowing it I was doing just what my mother told me.

'You get one of those Jewish fellas, they take care of their wives like queens,' she said more than once.

I pretended to myself that I'd never take that kind of pathetic, materialistic advice. Especially from a woman who lived on cigarettes and beer.

'He's got his own problems,' Ben says, the peacemaker to a fault. A man who never takes sides out of impeccable taste. How suffocating.

'The worst part is, once he starts lining up his little arguments in neat little rows he starts convincing me I'm a monster.'

But I know, as logical as Nathan is, there is that undertone of hatred that distorts everything he says. Really, I can't stand the way he talks to me. Sometimes just the sound of his voice makes me want to run out of the room. Yet even now, sitting here in Ben's van, I'm hoping Nathan will show up to shield me.

'Well, I suppose we should go in,' I say, but I notice that I don't move a muscle.

Anyway, Nathan doesn't know a fraction of what I did, especially weeks after our San Francisco City Hall wedding. Just lunch with Vincent to keep up our new, Platonic friendship, lunch at the house in the Berkeley hills Vincent had kept when I left. A truly terrible cook, but enthusiastic, he tried to cover his mistakes by pouring gobs of *chili verde* all over everything. Actually, he didn't even seem to notice that he'd burnt the canned refried beans, or that the cheese-stuffed *chilies* were soaked in grease, tepid and underdone.

Sucking on a joint, he poured out a bag of white tortilla chips with the abandon of a great chef.

'Okay, let's do it,' Ben says.

But I'm rooted to my seat. Perhaps Maurice just left the light on, perhaps he's gone. I listen for the sound of Nathan's Jeep, but there is nothing but the squeaking of Ben's high rubber boots against each other.

'Let me just get my things. He's probably fine.' My lips are so dry. Where is that lip balm?

When Vincent and I broke up he was controlled, but sad, I thought, but when I saw him again his animal spirits had already gotten the upper hand. In my heart of hearts I was offended that he didn't miss me more, but I also realized something else when I stood in the kitchen watching him cook, naked to the waist in his cut-off jeans, his muscular chest sworled with black hair. I realized I shouldn't get too close to him. So I backed away while he talked a mile a minute, waving his spatula like a wand and spattering grease on the wall.

On the verandah Vincent had set places on an industrial cable spool, on either side red sling chairs on black frames. We had to balance the plates on our knees. How long had it been since he slammed face down on these gray boards? I picked three soft splinters from his bruised cheek, holding his head in my lap and praying he would come back to life. Yet he had shrugged it all off as if he were more than normal, more than healthy. That was the strange thing about Vincent. Despite, or maybe because of his seizures, he seemed more vital than a normal person, as if he could barely contain the wild energy in his body, as if its only outlet was an electrical storm in his brain.

'Pretty good, huh?' he grinned, swigging a Dos Equis.

'So how's law school going?' I didn't have the slightest interest in this subject; I just wanted to keep at least three or four feet away from his electric aura.

'Oh, it's bullshit a lot of it. But the First Amendment law is fun. You know what I do? I bought a hundred fifty watt bulb, and I sit right under it when I read case law. It's the only thing that keeps me awake. So how's married life?'

I could feel myself blush, not just my face but my throat, sweat breaking out between my breasts. 'Oh, you're not interested in that.' Then I became aware that with the plate balanced on my knees, every inch of the underside of my thighs was exposed.

'You're right! You want another relleno?'

Flustered, I suddenly dropped my legs to the redwood deck, barely catching the plate before it fell. 'I don't think so.' Standing up, I turned my back to him and grasped the rail. I was thinking what I didn't want to think; that I knew already that Nathan was too soft, too eager to please, too full of a mania for fairness. And in that game, he was the fairest of them all.

The light in the cabin window flickers off and on, off and on. Is it a power failure or Maurice sitting there, obsessively clicking the switch? My heart sinks. I dig in my bag for the elusive lip gloss. Finally, I fish it out. This weather always dries out my lips, no matter what I do. In my compact mirror they look swollen. I smear the waxy stuff into the fissures.

'If you weren't here, Ben, I'd drive away right now. Can we drive away?'

'I don't think you want to do that. Let's go see him.'

'We're on rural electric here.'

'What?'

'There are power outages all the time.' But the flickering has stopped.

From the balcony a slice of the San Francisco Bay was visible, an impossible post-card blue. California was like that, too beautiful, too much. I loved to sit on that balcony till twilight when wisps of fog blew under the Golden Gate Bridge, slowly filling the bay with wet smoke.

Even two or three hits of the Panama Red had made me feel

giddy. Everything was warm and buzzing, the hummingbirds, the bottle-green flies circling and diving down to my greasy plate. I could smell the eucalyptus trees in the yard. When I turned he had broken my invisible, protective shell, and I was buzzing too, like everything around me. His arm slipped around the small of my back, his fingers hardening on my spine, and I lifted myself up to him without thinking.

On the bed he put his head between my legs and sucked me so slowly, so delicately, my whole body became a charge on the tip of his tongue. Fucking him then seemed too mild. I could have swallowed his body whole, and even afterwards I didn't feel anything but shock and awe at what we had unleashed. I had been married three weeks.

'You're about the farthest thing from a monster I could imagine,' Ben says. 'We should go in. He's probably starving.'

I look at the smoke pouring from the chimney, and the light in the kitchen, and I think, yes, Ben is right. This won't be so hard. 'You know, the Freudians used to have this thing about the mothers of schizophrenics. They were supposed to be so cold they made their children psychotic. Now you know what they say?'

'No?'

'Something like, "Nobody's to blame, it's just people who blame each other."'

'That sounds sensible.' Ben puts his raw-knuckled fingers on the truck's door handle.

'What keeps you two together?' I don't know I am going to ask this, and I can't put it the way I really want to – How do you live together for years without sex? Because dear, elegant, austere Indira is only interested in antiques, though she seems to love Ben in her own, private way.

Ben is quiet for a moment, and I'm afraid he's read my mind and is offended. But finally he says, 'Tin picnic baskets.'

I can't help laughing, though I know Ben is probably half-serious. 'That's what makes your relationship work?'

'The variety is unbelievable. Didn't you see the one we had with the art nouveau leaves on the lid? But it can be anything. Watering cans. Nineteenth century irons. Corning made a glass iron in the forties, I think, red glass. We once saw a plastic pen, the kind filled with liquid, at a flea market. It had the whole Last Supper in there, and when you moved the pen the bread and wine moved up and down. We had to buy it. It's like a fever.'

'You always want the same things?'

'No, of course not, but we know how to compromise. There's a kind of scale. If one of us wants something really bad, we always give in to each other. And after a while, you have this huge, this monster collection of things, things you don't even know you owned, so when you love the same things so much, you can't help loving each other. The things are the love.'

'Like children who never leave home.'

'Yeah, sort of, but I suppose children are a lot more complicated.'

'I may have been exaggerating. He didn't sound that bad on the phone.'

'He may grow out of it. I think he has a real creative side.'

I can barely keep from laughing at that one, it's so Benish.

A month after I was married and because I didn't feel I was doing anything wrong, and I felt guilty for not feeling guilty, I mentioned it at my women's group. In an instant I knew that Fran and Deborah, who were usually more feminist than thou, thought I should be shot, even if they didn't say anything like that. I could just tell by the way Fran sucked her lips until they disappeared, and the way Deborah started twining her kinky black hair in that maddening, nervous way. But Zena, who had married her boyfriend as a freshman and had two kids, the only one of us who was truly monogamous, had a different take.

'Every fifteen seconds they do it to us. So why shouldn't we do it to them?'

'I'm not trying to do anything to anybody,' I swore. As long as Nathan never found out – he'd never believe it anyway – nothing had happened at all. 'What's wrong with pleasure without pain for a change?'

'Sounds like you're doing everything to everybody,' Deborah said sourly.

We were talking in her flat in a dark, Victorian house above Golden Gate Park's 'panhandle' – a moody, treeless neighborhood close to the Haight. On her walls she had the predictable Frieda Kahlo prints. As I recalled, she had fucked at least two men in that room other than her husband.

'That's not fair! Who elected you mother superior?' I shot back. 'When you do it it's always, "Oh, but it didn't mean anything." But if I do it, that's another story, right?'

'That's right! Because you used to be in love with Vincent! It is different!' Her voice cracking, Deborah flushed under her graduate student pallor. 'You're taking some sort of revenge, if you ask me.'

I felt hurt, confused and angry all at once. All I could think about was something so small and ridiculous I couldn't say it out loud. I couldn't stand the way Nathan patted me on the head sometimes. It was so condescending. 'Oh, fuck you, Deborah . . .'

Then it got so quiet. I think we were all too embarrassed to talk. We'd never had a fight like that before. Finally, Zena passed the baklava plate around and started pouring more tea. 'Let's get fat and lose our teeth, girls,' she said. But nobody laughed.

After that I never went back. When Zena called I promised to show up, but I couldn't. Finally, they gave me up for dead. What a relief. If they wanted to be bound by all these rules, conventional or anti-conventional, I didn't want any part of it. As long as I was discreet, as long as no one got hurt, why should it matter? It wasn't as if I were wildly promiscuous, either. It was just the Longest Affair with my Pompeii-eyed Vincent, beautiful as a Roman wall painting.

'I can do it now, Ben.'

'Good, good.'

Determined, I make everything look normal. The house is the house. The stairs are the stairs. The door is the door.

Stamping my boots, I touch the rust-pitted brass knob and catch my breath. I can feel the security of Ben looming behind me as I yank the door open, a blast of over-heated air rushing out, that mildewed stink of the unlived-in house enveloping me. This is definitely a Man's Place. No curtains. A vintage license plate is nailed to the wall. That wretched moldy bear leans in a corner, the poor thing. A few rickety wooden chairs are jammed under the battered, graceless table. You have to work at making a place this stark and charmless. Are men born with this aesthetic, or are they taught it at their fathers' knees?

Hunching over the table, Maurice throws a pair of dice, picks a card and thinks for a second. 'Hey, mom, what comedy show had the most spin-offs in history? And name them.'

His voice has a brassy, excited quality, but otherwise he looks all right. A bit thin maybe, and he could use a shave, but nothing like the condition he's been in before. Now that I'm finally facing him, I can breathe again. Love him again.

'Trivial Pursuit? Are you hungry, honey?' I walk over and tousle his hair. The ordinary hair of a teenager.

'Uh-huh.'

'How about "All in the Family?"'

'Right! What about the spin-offs? Can you name them?'

'"The Jeffersons?"' Ben offers.

'Right!'

I notice that Maurice doesn't acknowledge Ben's presence; instead, he keeps staring at me with those shining black eyes of his. The Monkey Boy's shining eyes.

'Maude?' I guess.

'Cor-rect!' He holds the card away from his face, waving it theatrically.

'I brought lunch, Maurice. Sandwiches. And pumpkin pie.'

'Wait! Wait! Two more, can you get them?' he insists.

'Gee, I don't know,' Ben says. 'Maybe we ought to eat and think about it.'

'Think, think,' he persists. 'If you don't get it, you'll kick yourself later!'

# CHAPTER FIFTEEN: JULIA

## Tuesday: May 20, 1987: 10 a.m.

Five of us work at Moira's during her rush periods, arranging, wrapping orders, keeping track of invoices, postage, faxes, a rough, imitation Edo Period pot of Red Zinger steeping on a tray. Cynthia, the part-time jeweler; Gwendolyn, the caterer; Mona, the graphic designer; Julia, the pharmacist's wife and Moira herself. We talk about our families, listen to Jao Gilberto sambas, rock, Glenn Gould and Marion McPartland's Piano Jazz on NPR, the work passing in a pleasant dream.

At first, when her business was just starting, Nathan said Moira was just a dilettante, a hobbyist with two rich friends who pitied her and gave her orders. Now, in bursts, she hires four or five of us to meet the demand for her creations, and Nathan says nothing at all.

Moira is too practical to put it this way, but she hasn't just succeeded in business. She has connected Accordia to time again.

When the train from New York City died in 1952 the summer people stopped filling the last, crumbling hotels. Even

The Sayerville, Queen of the Catskills, closed off its upper floors and eventually turned into a social service agency. The Accordia Hotel, once a stage coach inn during the days of planked roads, shut up in 1972.

We once had a gyroscope factory, of all things, a milk plant, and a lumber mill. And further back, before I was born, at Vidalia Lake we charged for bright red row boats in which men in celluloid collars rowed their wives, actresses and paramours in sedate circles.

After the trains stopped, time moved slower and slower. Without jobs, marginal families that had first gotten electricity in the late forties, slid back. Their refrigerators died, their ancient ice boxes reappeared. Without power their paintless houses no longer pumped water; new furnaces fell into comas, and the nostalgic stink of burning wood grew denser in the hollows. When leech fields jammed up with waste, and the poorest of the poor couldn't afford to have them pumped out, many families quietly resurrected collapsing outhouses. In the hills, time flowed backward.

Moira is energy, energy without strain. She doesn't have a minute to cut her grass or take care of her horses, so she hires local farm boys. She doesn't have the inclination to wash windows and sweep floors, so she hires the boys' mothers. When a rotting maple splits in a storm and falls onto her barn, she hires a local contractor to fix it. There is no altruism in this. She thinks she's barely keeping her head above water. But she is really dragging dusty Accordia, weighed down and stunned, back into the flow of time.

Unlike Julia, who had everything and does nothing much except fill up notebooks and drift past the Lasters' abandoned stone cottage, Doroski's pale green hunting trailer, and over the ruins of stone walls that once marked fields of hops to Rose Lane, so perfectly hidden, and into the bed of Nathan Coleman, who took up with her a few years after his wife locked the door on him in a single, spontaneous rage.

After all the orders are filled and the other women pack up, Moira asks me to stay. Much to my surprise, Maurice wanders in, looking perfectly well-appointed and in control of himself. Nathan dresses him in preppy attire, and Maurice doesn't seem to notice one way or another. He kisses Moira on the cheek and casts himself down, awkwardly draping his knees across the sprung, stuffing-leaking easy chair.

'Hi, Julia,' he says. 'I like your hair.'

He has Nathan's shining black eyes, his face reflecting Moira's fine bone structure. I haven't changed my hairstyle in twenty years, but I thank him. In deceptive moments like these, you can see the ghost of the person he might have been. Charming. Charismatic. Two weeks ago he stabbed his father with a serrated kitchen knife. But Nathan, who knew better than the psychiatrists, didn't see this as a cause for alarm.

'I'm not saying I'm not concerned,' he said to me the day after on the phone. Nathan, who pretends to himself that he doesn't need me, who calls discreetly when O'Bannon is at the store. 'I'm just not hysterical. Greenberg's got a new cocktail for him, it's really tamping down the hallucinations.' He sounds rather hysterical to me.

'So you think ten days inside is enough?'

'We don't want him to get institutionalized. He'll lose his independence. He won't be able to function at all. You should see him. He's perfectly okay, as far as it goes, I mean.' The note of uncertainty is new for Nathan. It might be good for him to admit he is human now and then.

'How is your astronomy going?' I ask Maurice.

'Oh, I'm past that. I just do thought experiments.' If you knew nothing about him, you would take him at face value he sounds so confident.

'You don't use the telescope anymore?'

He giggles briefly, inappropriately. 'Dad's the astronomer now.'

Immediately, I know who the object of his astronomy is, but I push the thought out of my mind. Eventually, mercifully, Maurice saunters upstairs to listen to music.

'Did you see Baltasar when you came in?'

'Oh, I meant to tell you. I saw him when I was driving up. Is he the Icelandic? He's gorgeous.'

'I wanted to thank you for taking care of that . . . situation . . .'

'It was such a coincidence I stopped by.' There had been no way of hiding my presence from the Rescue Squad, but I had wondered whether it had gotten back to Moira. Maybe Maurice or Nathan mentioned it in passing.

In her unconscious arrogance, she seems to accept this bald lie completely. I clutch my secret tighter, for only in hiding the truth can I gain any real pleasure. In this way I protect myself from the worst response of all, her congratulations for entangling my body with her ex-husband's. She would probably be sincerely happy for me – it being an honor to pick over her leavings – and that I couldn't bear. This is the dark side of Moira's serenity.

'Do you think he would have stabbed him again. I mean if you didn't come in?'

'Oh, no, Maurice was horrified at what he had done, he was all balled up in a corner. By the time it was over Nathan was comforting him.' Now I am on true ground, perhaps better to hurt her. 'Are you nervous having him around?'

'No. Yes . . . But Greenberg, Nathan swears he's not . . . You know, a long time ago, when we were just married in California and Nathan was so different, the times and everything . . . I've never told anybody this, Julia, so promise not to repeat it. Please.'

'Of course not.' Maybe yes, maybe no.

'Well, this could have caused it, who knows. Nathan was throwing a party in that shake house we had in Berkeley. And he spiked this punch with acid, I couldn't believe he'd do something like that, and I had two cups.'

She cries briefly, but with Moiraesque astringency. One tissue.

'The trip was awful, the only bad one I ever had. I was sure my face was disintegrating. I was afraid and I didn't even know what I was afraid of. Anyway, I was almost sure that I was already pregnant. Every time I look at Maurice I think of it, I can't help it. But Nathan didn't know I was pregnant, even if he did do something unbelievably stupid. And I didn't know what was in it.'

I can't fathom what to say. 'Oh, Moira—'

'Or maybe it had nothing to do with it. My friend Jackie took acid when she was two months pregnant, and I just heard her son has a coffee business in San Francisco. He roasts the beans.'

'It's impossible to tell.'

'You think it's something you did, you think it's everything you did, but who knows? Look at Nathan's great-grandfather.'

'The tap dancer?'

'Yeah. One day, after he'd had the bank for ten years or so, they found him doing his old soft shoe routine in the vault one morning, all made up for a performance and everything. He couldn't stop dancing.'

'What do you mean?'

'I mean he was tap dancing like mad in there, and they couldn't stop him until the doctor came and they poured a bottle of whiskey down his throat. They said it was senility, but he was only fifty-four. Or could it be because I left? The way I left?'

'It could be anything.' Now I am lost, too. A multiplicity of causes, an infinite number of effects. No one considers chance or fate anymore, as if with our petty flaws we could preordain ourselves.

* * *

'No, not anything, not anything.'

Face down, naked on his clean white sheets, Nathan guides me. 'There, no there, yes, yes, there! There!'

In my hand I hold a rubber mallet which I use to strike, ever so gently, the bone xylophone of his back. Each blow makes a faint pink orb in his skin. I worry about disturbing the wound in his side, but he swears that underneath the small, neat bandage he feels little pain.

'Lower, try the small, you know where,' he gasps.

'I was talking to Moira . . .'

'Mmmmm . . .'

'She told me an interesting story. About when you lived together in Berkeley.'

'Yeah?' He stops breathing, tensing his back muscles between my legs.

'She said you spiked some punch with acid. I find that hard to believe.' I wait to hear the noises he makes, not the words, but the quality of his sounds. Constricted? Guttural? Angry?

'She'll say anything to get off the hook.' He twists beneath me in a slow, awkward maneuver, his rage held back in his throat. A throat cramped with words. 'Could you imagine me ever doing something like that?'

'No,' I say honestly. 'Not now.'

'What's that supposed to mean?'

'I read somewhere that we replace our cells so fast that every few years we're somebody else.'

Nathan's face burns, a dark, black fire. 'If you mean we're

Nathan's face burns, a dark, black fire. 'If you mean we're not the same people we were, that's a bunch of bullshit. I've always been the same person.'

'I believe you believe that.' No one is more solid, more monolithic than Nathan. Or, rather, no one is more convinced that he is.

# CHAPTER SIXTEEN: CRISSIE

## Saturday: February 27, 1990: 1:40 p.m.

Boring fields of snow, one after the other, so even if you live here you don't know where you are. Sagging black electric wires whip past. I used to be ashamed of these wires. You'd never see old poles and droopy wires in the suburbs.

'So, um, how're the classes going, Crissie?' His voice gets this 'I really care' tone.

It's like when mom ignores me it's real, but when he pays attention to me it's fake. It's like he knows what paying attention is supposed to look and sound like because he read it in a psychiatry book, so he does a good imitation of it, but he's really someplace else. But then I wonder if I'm being fair. I mean, why am I mad at him when he's acting perfectly nice? Maybe it's the opposite of that slick thing about mom, how she always gets away with things because, 'Oh, that's just Moira.'

Dad's profile looks sharp, just like Maurice's. He's really good-looking, dad, almost too good looking. Maurice once said, 'Dad looks geometric.' That cracked me up so much. In a warped way he can be really funny.

'Fine, I guess. You know that school.'

'What about it?'

'It's just so easy, I mean *A Tale of Two Cities*? God! I read that when I was ten. Calc's good, though. I'm the only girl in the class.' He may know this, but I can't remember.

'I used to love math. Making the problems work out.'

See, this is typical of him. I tell him something significant about my life, like I'm the only girl in a class of geeky boy geniuses, and he tells me something about himself. But I love math, too, maybe for different reasons. It makes me forget I'm a girl, I'm not this slab of meat anymore, I'm pure thinking. Of course, Glenn with his attaché case, and Samuel, with the sewer breath whose father teaches math at Tuscarora Tech, they're constantly trying to get next to me, but if I contribute something and Mr Weiss compliments me, they're *so* condescending.

Harry, on the other hand, gets this glazed look on his face when I solve a problem, and he'll say things like 'Isn't that formula beautiful?' Which to me makes him so attractive because he's not even trying. He's in Harryworld.

'You know they just let Maurice jump the fence. Just like that.'

That was a record for talking about me. 'Yeah?'

'I wonder if it would be better if I just took him home again. The way he goes in and out all the time can't be helping him. If I keep him on his medication he could get a little job and get something out of life.'

This is why he makes me suspicious. He says he's going to do these great, self-sacrificing things, like he's looking for approval, but they always turn out to be smaller than he's pretending. 'I don't think that's very practical, dad.'

'No?'

'Look what happened after he stabbed you.' I like to say this out loud because mom and dad never say it. 'You took him home, and he was back inside of a month.'

'Yeah, but I think we've adjusted his dosages better now. You know it's tricky because of the manic depression.'

'Unless you get somebody to follow him around all day to force him to take his pills. Besides, he likes the way it feels when he gets off the drugs, you don't understand.'

Nobody could really understand how we were friends, and even now, if I catch Maurice looking at me sideways and I shoot him the same look back it's like we're on the floor in front of the TV making complicated castles out of those blocks mom got at the auction, traces of red and blue paint almost worn away on them. Once we read the myth of the Minotaur in a children's book and when mom came home we showed her the labyrinth we'd made, a wind-up Godzilla hidden in the heart of the maze, and she fell down on the floor laughing. In her raggedy jeans, on all fours, she tried to trace her way to the Godzilla-Minotaur, but she kept pretending it was too hard for her, and we were the greatest architects in the world. Even Maurice liked her then. How old was he? Seven? Eight? Disgusting. All I can think about is him, too.

He'd beg me to do it over and over, put my hands up like paws and hop around the room while he sang, 'Kangaroo, kangaroo! Kangaroo with your pouch!' And he'd crawl under me, wriggling and laughing. 'Kangaroo, kangaroo! Kangaroo with your pouch!' I never knew what was so funny.

Even when I think about myself I think about him. But I suppose that's normal. Anybody who had Maurice for a brother would watch their own thoughts like I do, always searching for some faint sign that they were getting out of order. Paranoid of going paranoid?

A flashing yellow light swings on a thick wire. Thane Corners. When I was a kid the post office was just down the road in Jerry Bond's saggy house. Through one door on the porch you went into a complete post office with wooden safety deposit boxes with little glass inserts, and counters with those miniature sponges for stamps, and through the door right next to it you went into Jerry's living room. When we dropped off the mail, we could see his horse-faced mother staring at us through the browned lace curtains. Mom used to say those curtains were as old as The Shroud of Turin. Just the sight of Jerry's mother made me want to vomit.

A left at Thane Corners and in a few minutes you're in the backwoods. The road narrows to a strip of solid ice. It's funny, but I always feel as if the winter is dirty despite all the clean snow surrounding you. Maybe it's because you see so many of the encampments that are hidden when the trees are in bloom. People live in sheds and tin shacks with satellite dishes. In elementary school I tried to be friends with this girl Cora, who lived in Merwin Hollow, but she couldn't even figure out why I was trying to talk to her. It was like she thought of herself as an outcast and didn't deserve to have any friends.

We're climbing up where you can see hilltop after hilltop. Harry says around here it's like one of those moons around Saturn, dead since the beginning of time, just frozen.

Dad's still going on and on. 'But he'll talk to you more. Remember when Max got killed by the logger? You ran out on the road and got his collar, you couldn't have been more than nine.'

'What?'

I was so confused. I didn't know who to feel sorry for first, Maurice, who was crying in his corner like his whole body was coming apart in pieces, or poor Maxie, his head crushed, flattened and oozing blood and brains on the hot asphalt. I was looking for his soul, but I didn't see it. Why did they send me to get his collar? But I didn't argue, I just wandered out in the middle of Stone Valley Road in a daze, my hands getting warm in Max's thick, matted fur, searching for the hook to get his tags.

'You sent me out on the road.'

'No, you were in shock, you probably don't remember. I ran out there and carried you back.'

Now I'm not sure. Dad does that all the time to me.

'Maurice wouldn't come out of his room for a whole day.'

'Till you talked him into it. Right?'

'Honestly, I don't remember.' Even now, all these years later I feel funny talking about the clear plastic tack. I remember thinking, If I don't say anything, he never did it. But if I betray him, then he'll go to some kind of jail. At the same time I wondered how far had he pressed the push pin into his skin. Not far, it was drooping, it barely broke the skin, and that made it better. Or not as bad somehow.

Then I think, this may be the last time I ever see him because nobody can make me come back. Instead of coming home for breaks I'll stay in my dorm, or during the year I'll get a work-study, save up and go to Europe. The idea of leaving the mountains and the endless snow makes my heart pound. I'll do whatever I want. I'll live my life in perfect climates.

'Isn't that Ben's van?'

'Yeah, I just told you, dad. Ben took mom here.'

'Oh, right. Well, we'll just say hello, and I'll take him back to my place.'

The muscles in his neck stiffen, and his voice sort of cracks. He always gets this way around mom, like he's afraid of her. Which is a joke because he's the one with the money and the golfing buddies who are judges and lawyers, and mom is always terrified he'll put her out of the house like he threatened to do two or three times when he didn't approve of the way she was living. (Of course, she was so ditzy she let him keep the papers on the house when they split, it was all too much for her.)

'Self-centered, domineering fart,' she called him once, and we both couldn't stop laughing. It was like a girlfriend telling you a joke that's so right you want to die.

'Knock, knock!' dad shouts, pushing the door open. I'm kind of hiding behind him, so I don't see what's going on right away.

But I recognize Maurice's voice. 'Whose first album was

called *Dream of the Blue Turtles*? Peter Gabriel? Prince? Sting? Blondie?'

Sitting at the old table, mom and Ben are facing us with pinched, funny expressions on their faces. Mom is good on Natural History. But she used to spend all those afternoons playing Trivial Pursuit with Julia, the two of them giggling like they were teenagers when they got one right. Maybe she knows this one. Every inch of Ben's brain is filled with antiques and collectibles.

'Tick tock, tick tock,' Maurice says in that grating way of his. His back to us, he's wearing some kind of tight black hood, thin, like one of those expensive skiing things. Why is he wearing it inside? It's always a bad sign when he keeps extra clothes on. Hunks from a hero sandwich are scattered on the table.

'Can I help?' Dad asks.

'No, that's not fair,' Maurice says without turning around. 'We're playing a game, aren't we, mom?'

'Peter Gabriel?' Something is really wrong, the air smells bad, mom looks stunned, Ben's eyes are too wide open. Unnatural.

'Wrong! Thought you'd get that one, momsie,' Maurice says, dragging out the last syllable in that obnoxious way of his. I wish he'd turn around. I can't see his face. He can say 'mom' and make it sound like a curse word. I know he stabbed dad because he was afraid to stab mom. Or me. I'm sure he remembers, but what was I supposed to do?

* * *

I'm trying to wash my hair because it's so oily it's sticking to my head, very attractive, and I find him yanking away behind the hamper. Repulsive. Naked, I grab mom's body brush in my hand, and I don't know what I'm doing, I'm just going like totally off, and I smack him so hard, all over his head, so hard, flush in his mouth, in his forehead, the top of his skull, and he's crying, 'Don't tell! Don't tell!'

All of a sudden I'm looking at a broken stick of red plastic. I can hardly tell what it is, I'm so mad. 'Don't tell! Don't tell!' he keeps crying, but I keep wondering, Who's worse? Me or him?

The next day on the way home from school, opposite the Tastee Freeze, he gets stuck trying to decide which way to cross Kilmer Street. Straight or diagonally? There I am pretending everything's okay and talking to him and waving to my friends Noreen and Frieda, but I can't get him to move for ten minutes because he keeps saying he has to cross in the exact, right way or something really bad is going to happen to him. He swears he can't make the wrong decision, it could be fatal.

Then he says, 'Hey, Cris, I'm frozen at the Tastee Freeze!' I laughed, but I wasn't sure he meant to be funny.

'Here's another one! What city was Harrison Salisbury writing about in his book *Nine Hundred Days*? Berlin? Paris? Prague? Leningrad?'

'What about Stalingrad?' Ben asks and for the first time

Maurice turns around to look at us. Now I see that the hood he's wearing is actually a black face mask with his eyes only visible in narrow slashes. A thin slit at his mouth and small nose holes. He can't be serious. It must be some kind of role-playing game. I'm so nervous I start cracking up for a second, but I keep it in. He looks like the Black Flash or something.

'It doesn't say Stalingrad, does it? Hey, the whole family can play.'

Just when I'm trying to figure out how to back out of the cabin and disappear forever, Maurice pulls this clunky black gun from under the table. With two hands he lifts it and aims it at mom's face. 'We did extensive surveillance on you, mom, didn't we dad?'

Mom flinches, but she just stares back, looking super-aware of what's happening. Her eyes are wide like she can't believe what she's seeing. She blinks. Her eyeliner is smudged under her eyes. Was she crying? Maybe he's been doing this to her for the last hour.

I'm thinking, he's so close he can't miss, I'm thinking so fast, I'm thinking we should all jump on him at once. But at the same time I'm sure he won't hurt me. Then I'm certain he would because it would be the last thing in the world he would do. How could he? We played together a million hours. But he could be holding a grudge, I always worried about that. In my crazy, racing mind this makes sense. It's horrible, but in a certain place in my mind I'm calculating how to let mom die just so I can get out alive.

Why doesn't Ben do something? He could reach over and

knock the gun out of Maurice's hands with one swipe. But Ben is leaning back, chewing on his lip, his long face expressionless. He looks like he's carved out of soap. Mom used to give me and Maurice bars of Ivory to work on.

A hand is pressing car keys into my palm, I'm almost too stupid to grasp them, and then two hands are pushing me back and I realize dad is pushing me one way while he goes the other, he's guiding me towards the door while with every step he moves around the table, edging closer to Maurice.

Counter clock-wise he moves around the table, unbelievably slow, he's not saying a word. We all watch him edge behind Ben's chair, then stop. Maurice's eyes, all we can see of his face in that silly, scary black silk mask, dart from mom's frozen face to dad. Hands behind me, I grope for the doorknob, I feel its smooth roundness in my left hand. Turn it a centimeter at a time, I must be brave, I must be brave, if I don't take a chance he could turn the gun on me.

'Maurice, let's calm down. Put the gun down, it's dangerous,' dad says in the softest voice in the world. Oh God, dad wants me to live.

One last notch and the doorknob turns in my hand. I don't know what comes first, the explosions, unbelievably, deafeningly loud and fast, or my lunging and running. I stay low, running with everything I have. I'm a blur, my mind's a blur. My boots slip, I almost fall down. My boots slide like glass on the ice. My heart's racing so fast it's insane. For a split second the Cherokee's door handle looks like it's a puzzle from another planet, but then I grab it, do something with it, and scramble into the front seat, ducking my head under the dashboard. My hands are jerking so bad I can't get the key in. Once, twice, I'm jabbing it in, and for some mysterious reason it fits. I turn it.

The motor whispers on.

# CHAPTER SEVENTEEN: NATHAN

## Saturday: February 27, 1990: 2:15 p.m.

After the burst of shots, I don't dare move a muscle, but I sense the empty space behind me. Has Crissie slipped away? I start praying inside my head, Iroquois County's leading, hard-headed atheist is praying to the Great God of Nothing to let her live. Slowly, the plaster dust starts to settle, and I can see Maurice staring up at the holes in the ceiling. Eyeing the barrel of the black semi-automatic, he looks more curious than frightened at what he's done.

Flakes of plaster stick to Moira's reddish hair, but she doesn't make a move to touch them. Her green eyes are bugging out. People used to ask her if she wore tinted contacts. Ben stares at his big, bony hands.

*Don't insist, don't argue, don't confront*. All the literature says you shouldn't try to argue with a schizophrenic about voices or broadcasts they're hearing through their fillings. You shouldn't argue if they swear you're reading their thoughts or the smell of burning flesh is filling the room. *Change the subject, but be firm about disruptive behavior. Don't tolerate acting out*. You wonder who writes these things. What's the etiquette if your flipped-out son is waving a cheap machine pistol in your face? But I know, like no one else, how to calm him down without drugs. But you have to descend slowly into Unconditional Love, you don't fling yourself into it without a slow, careful transition.

If Moira finally understood what I have been doing for Maurice all these years, she might forgive and forget. Anyway, if she hadn't been so stubborn it never would have gone on this long. I was always ready to compromise. All I wanted was a *written agreement* that she wouldn't put the kids in danger, and that she'd make sure there was food in the house, for godsakes. How many times did I go over there and find one scabby package of lunch meat in the fridge and nothing else?

But they're all looking to me, waiting for me to soothe him. 'Hey, bud, you're making your mother a little nervous with that thing. How bout you pop out that clip?'

His mouth twitches, a tic from the drugs. Side effects of the psychotropics that can only get worse with time. By now Crissie is definitely outside, but no one says a word, and Maurice doesn't seem to notice.

'No way, dad. You like this? It's wack, isn't it? The Cobray. No way. You're just thinking if you can get your hands on it, then it's a cold meat party for Maurice. I read that in a detective book. Cold meat party. Wack, huh? Don't try to figure out what I'm thinking cause I'm purposely thinking different things on the surface. Then I'm doing subterranean thinking. Under the lobes. Camouflage thinking. I could be thinking about the opposite of what I'm going to do, it could be the same, it could be something different. What's he doing here?'

Turning, he points the crude semi at Ben's head.

'Careful Maurice,' I whisper. 'Ben isn't involved.'

Moira's voice cracks. 'No accidents, honey.'

Ben pulls his head back, keeping his eye on the gun barrel. His pupils dilate, his lips turn white. Yet he seems to sense that any sudden movement could set Maurice off.

Outside, the Cherokee cranks, starts with a quiet woosh. Studiously avoiding the sound, I stare at the wall.

'No! No! I'm sick of it! Don't tell! Don't tell!' Stepping back from us, his stride herky-jerky, Maurice hunches his shoulders and turns his face away. Warding off voices. I try to judge the distance between us and whether I should lunge over the table or keep edging closer. In this state he'll be powerful, as thin as he is. When he stabbed me, I saw the blade's quick arc, I grabbed at his arm, but he threw his whole weight behind it. When you get stabbed very hard and clean, you don't even feel it at first. Later he told me he wasn't stabbing me at all, but I already knew who he was sticking the knife into.

'It's not you, Moira, it's not you,' I say. It's important to keep everybody dead calm, and I'm the only one who can do it.

'Is so! Who does she care about, the little bitch? Nobody but herself! Look at how she treated you, parading around. Ha!' He spits on the floor, then jumps back in fear. If I could only get him out of the room I could put my arms around him, whisper all the right things, soothe him limp. Now he's out of reach of a sudden move.

'Maurice?' Ben's voice is barely audible, and I see he's crying. Pathetic teardrops run down his creased face. What a weak suck. 'Don't hurt me, please. Wasn't I always nice to you?'

'Nice is cheap. Nice to the geek. Nice to the creep. Wait a second, I'll go forge you a medal.' The mouth spits out words through a slit in the mask. Unnerving.

'Maurice, let's go outside, you and me, and leave them alone. We can talk. You can tell me what's bothering you. In private.'

'Don't talk out of both sides of your mouth, dad. I don't know what I want to do. I can do anything, you know that? Steven Hawking called me this morning. He has a cell phone on his wheelchair.'

With a slow pivot, as if he's testing the possibilities, he rotates towards me and takes aim at my head.

A wave of fear breaks over me now, and I go under. It takes me completely by surprise, almost knocking me to my knees. The room is out of air. No one speaks. A burst of sweat pours out under my arms. My shirt is soaked in a second. My stomach turns hard as a baseball. To my shock, I am struck dumb, my tongue a numb piece of meat in my mouth. In a panic I try to think of something to say, but I'm hypnotized by the two-inch gun barrel, the plain grip rammed right in the center of the pistol's bottom face.

'Maurice, honey, that's your father. You don't want to hurt

him. Are you feeling bad, honey? Let's sit down and talk, we all love you. Your father loves you, Ben loves you. We know you're suffering.' Moira's voice flows out, just right, casting a protective blanket over all of us. Through the corner of my eye I can see how composed her features are, and the set of her full, beautiful mouth. I'm more ashamed than ever.

Ben makes no attempt to hide his weeping, my stomach turning at the sight of it. Still, I can't seem to get another word out of my mouth. The cabin's plasterboard walls press in, the whole room contracts, and I'm filled with a terror I can hardly control.

'We've got . . . nice lives,' Ben whispers, making no sense whatsoever.

'Please, sweetie, put the gun down and we'll all talk. We'll have some tea,' Moira keeps on, never taking her eyes off him.

'Shut up! Shut up!' he bursts out again. 'Too much yakyakyakyak! I can't hear myself. Yakakakakakakakaka!' As he shouts the snout of the pistol bobs up and down, and I can feel myself fainting, going down in stages, fighting it, clinging to the lip of the table. I see the last things I'm going to see. The license plate nailed over the sink that reads NY 1929. Cobwebs in thick clumps in the corners of the ceiling. Cobwebs everywhere. A calendar from Pindar's General Motors featuring an Oldsmobile with Dynaflow.

Julia's body feels like a brand new bow. Smooth as plastic lacquer. Bow hunting. That takes a lot of skill.

'Why don't we go outside?' Moira says, getting up from the table as casual as you please and heading for the door.

I wait for the bullets to rip through her, but Maurice simply stops ranting and gapes at her. Maurice. It isn't even Maurice, just a bunch of raging, diseased neurons. X-rays show shadows in schizophrenics' brains, empty spaces between the cortex and the skull. He's not a person anymore, just sick cells. I'll be murdered by bad chemistry after trying so hard. Giving more than I had. It's almost funny. I won't have to cover my overdraft, I won't have to pay off the bookies. The Knicks could win, the Knicks could lose.

Moira slides to the door and opens it. A rush of cold air pours in and I gulp it in, starving for oxygen. As she descends the stairs, I see the snowy fields and hills rising above her, filling the doorway. I squint. She's going to get away.

Into the vacant space where she stood a second ago the pistol spits fourfivesix deafening rounds. The roar makes my ears ring. I'm totally deaf. This is the last noise I'll hear. Moira's body is warm nooks and crannies. You can lose yourself in her. Julia's is one muscle. You stay on the surface.

'Get out, go after her,' Maurice says from far away, the ringing in my head almost wiping out his words.

Ben and I practically knock each other over trying to leap outside. I stumble, catching my balance half way down the steps. The cold blasts my dripping face, the shock reviving me. My mouth falls open, sucking icy air. Another second inside and I would have suffocated.

At the foot of the stairs Moira turns towards us, showing us her palm, wounded and seeping with blood. A look of wonder on her face. Then she starts walking back towards us.

'Do you have a handkerchief, Nathan?'

'Yes, yes I do,'

'Tie it tight.' She may be in a state of shock, but the force of her concentration is amazing.

Wrapping her hand brings me back to myself. I'd forgotten how long her fingers are and her skin, how tough and dry it is. Hands that strip dry weeds, rip them in half. Hands that can clip hedges forever. I never told her that I really liked the Giant Turtle she made at Zelakowski's hobby farm. I was always too pissed off at her to say something like that. Her blood flowing under my handkerchief looks black.

Ben comes closer, tearing the tail of his work shirt. 'Here, let's use this.'

But I don't need it. After knotting the bandage around her wrist, I can see a second stain seeping to the surface of the cloth, but slower, less in a gush.

'Down to the pond,' Maurice says, lower, more threatening. 'C'mon.'

Canny, he keeps his distance, herding us with the pistol. But the pond is across the meadow, my feet sinking into a foot of dense snow. Wet, it acts like cement. Every step is a struggle, but that seems merciful. We have more time to survive. Plastered with snow, a spruce tree bends in the wind, a heavy limb springing up as it loses its white load. Freezing sweat drips down my spine. As we climb, the wind kicks up. A little wind can cut through you in this weather.

Next to me, Ben shambles, his boots making sucking sounds

as he pulls them from their fresh holes. Barely audible, he mutters, 'Maybe we can rush him.'

I'm glad to see he's got a grip on himself finally. But our chances are worse out in the field, we'd be lumbering towards Maurice, easy targets. 'We've got to get closer.'

'God, it's cold,' Moira says, hugging herself.

Keeping my voice as low as possible, I say, 'Maybe Crissie'll get help.'

'She's alive.' Moira exhales the secret we've all been keeping.

Ben reaches for her, hooking his arm around her waist. But she pushes him off, turns and plants herself. 'Maurice, that's enough. You're frightening us. Look what you did.' Raising her arm like a traffic cop, she shows him her clotted palm. Only shock could protect her from the pain of the gun shot. Yet she's standing up to him as if she's in a perfectly normal state, and not in danger of bleeding to death.

Twisting back, I gaze at the hooded figure, another burst of sweat pouring out of me. I'm shivering, and shaking like an alkie with the DTs, but I get the words out. 'Aren't you cold, Maurice? We could go back to the cabin and make a fire.'

'Take off that mask, honey. Let me see you.'

'Then you'll know who I am.'

He means this, I know, but Moira persists before I can tell her to stop. 'But we know who you are, honey. Maurice.'

Without a word, he whirls and rakes the tree line with thunderous, rapid-fire rounds. Sheets of snow cascade off the pines. The quiet afterwards is almost as bad as the noise from the gun. I wonder if he's depleting his ammo, but before we start up again he slaps in another clip. Now he just motions with the weapon and we obey.

We march through the woods, rows of red pine marking clear paths. Years ago they were laid out as a plantation, but when the property changed hands a few times in the 70s, they were never harvested. Red pine is worth garbage in today's market. They'll pay you pulp prices. What I should do is clear-cut the whole lot and plant some decent hard wood.

'Hurry! Hurry!' A few yards from us, Maurice squeezes off a few rounds in the air. The echoes seem to take a century to die down.

'Maybe we should just stop,' Ben says. 'Make him come to us. Otherwise, he's going to shoot us, Nathan.'

I don't know what to say. What's happening can't really be happening, but I do my best to believe it.

'I'm so tired,' Moira says faintly, leaning on Ben now as we climb a stone fence and begin sloshing through the next field.

'If we can get close enough, we can take him from different directions,' Ben insists.

But I'm not so sure. 'Maybe I can talk him down. If we make a move, he'll shoot us for sure. Crissie could bring help.'

As if in answer to our questions, Maurice shouts, 'To the boathouse. That way.'

Our eyes turn to the open shed with the tin roof that we use as a dressing room and for picnics. On the right I see the long, narrow dock, the weathered, unpainted outbuildings clustered near the pond, the horse barn where we used to keep Bobby, the chestnut mare, and Dusty, the mean crossbreed who would bite Bobby's ass if she even got near his oats.

'We can grab him in the boathouse,' I add, sure of myself now. Inside the shed it's a tight space. If we can just coordinate our attack. 'We'll time it.'

Moira says, 'It wasn't such a bad winter.'

'Nathan's right. Let's just work together,' Ben agrees eagerly. Ben was always malleable. It's Moira I'm worried about, and the panic inside me that contracts and expands against my will.

'To the water!' Maurice says, pointing his weapon. He's herding us now with more confidence.

At the pond the ice has retreated around the edges. If you walked on it you might go right through. Jutting out into the frozen surface, the old dock itself is piled with a foot of snow. As we close in on the boathouse, I wonder if I could take off and hide behind it, or get to the old barn and climb up to the loft somehow. Cowardly, fleeting thoughts I can't control. Anyway, my knees say I don't have the nerve, buckling in every new surge of fear. Every thought I ever had will die inside my head. My ideas for jump-starting the local economy. My plans for zoning in light manufacturing. My analysis of Maurice. But how much has that helped? I'll die in the middle of talking to myself about him without resolving a thing. Or am I being too hard on myself?

I never thought about dying. There's always another game tomorrow, another fight I can get on cable, another teaser from my bookie, Duane. Michael Milken. He never thinks about dying, I'll bet.

When we reach the boathouse's covered porch, Maurice shouts, 'Stop there. Wait!'

Ben and I exchange glances, each of us waiting for the other to make the first move as Maurice approaches. He comes stumbling forward in his uncoordinated, pigeon-toed gait, again stopping far out of reach. It would be suicide to attack him. Running at him would definitely set him off.

'Okay, dad, now this is what I want you to do,' he barks, his high pitched laugh making my skin crawl. 'I want you to . . . to go jump in the lake. Go jump in the lake, dad.'

'C'mon, Maurice, I can't,' I start to argue, but my words come out like a whimper. I reel towards him, falling against my will on all fours. I'm crazy to live. I'll do anything to live. But what can it be?

'Maurice, tell us, honey, why are you doing this? You don't want to hurt us, think of how you'll feel later on,' Moira says.

'You made me out of nothing, right? Send me back there.'

'What can I do, Maurice, what do you want me to do?' My breath smokes. My voice is a croak. On my numb knees, I suck snot. I disgust myself.

'We're sorry, whatever we did. But we can't change things, sweetie. We have to live with you.'

'Go jump in the lake, dad. Go 'head. Hop hop!'

'And he's not your father.' Planted, her feet wide apart, she says these words with conviction. Defiance.

Under me the cold ground stays solid, but her words are a body blow, and I recoil. Immediately I believe what she is saying, then immediately, I don't. It's ridiculous. Accepting what she's saying is too hard and way too complicated. I believe her, I don't, I believe her, I don't. Everything I ever said, everything I ever did is suddenly completely misguided. Completely meaningless. A few words and my whole life is undermined. Unconditional Love for no reason at all.

'You're just saying that.' In the slit of his silk-like mask, he squints against the light.

Yes, yes, this must be true. How could I know absolutely nothing? Have no inkling? And Maurice bears such an eerie resemblance to me, his voice has that same carping quality I take on when I'm irritated. Moira must be maneuvering to distract him and break his compulsive train of thought. A good idea, too.

Struggling to my feet, I watch her performance with fear and admiration. I think she always frightened me.

'No, Crissie is his, but you're not. I'm sorry. I could never tell anybody. But I'm telling you so you won't hurt him. And I have to pee now.'

'Well, you can't pee in front of us.'

'I might have to.' Devious. Clever. She's saving her own skin now.

'I don't know. You two made me out of nothing . . .'

'Maurice, this is a family thing. I shouldn't be here,' Ben says, sensing an opening, taking a gingerly step back. Moira has set the tone. Any pretense that we'll work together falls away. Typical. She's angling to save her own skin. I brush myself off and eye the pond, wondering if I could swim under its thin crust to the far side. But the simple shock of the icy water would knock me cold, my waterlogged clothes would drag me to the bottom. I'd die of shock. Or maybe not. I never thought about dying. But I can't, not until I transfer some funds. I'll die overdrawn. Against my principles.

'I could go behind the boathouse,' Moira suggests.

Ben retreats further, a single giant step. Moira always said his white hair looked like a dandelion puffball. It does. My mind is swirling, it's so hard to breathe. Maurice looks up and back, from Ben to Moira, seemingly unsure of his next move. After another step back, Ben turns sideways, making his six-foot five inch frame a narrower target.

'If it's all right with you?' Moira begins trekking through the drifts, teetering in her weakness.

'Go 'head, dad. Go, go,' Maurice's mouth says. 'Hop hop. In the lake. Whoever you are.' It's his barking laughter that sets me running, running like a crazy animal. If I stand there another second he'll spray holes the size of quarters in me. Crouching, I run low to the ground, serpentine like you see in the movies, the pond with its black edges tilting up towards me. My feet are dead in my boots, blocks of ice, my arthritic hip aches, but I run faster than it's possible to run. Gasping, I can't clear the bile from my throat.

Loaded down with two sweaters and a coat, I can't dive, so I wade in, flapping my arms when the shock of the frigid water hits me. Every bone in my body aches. Shooting pains and then a kind of spreading numbness. Wobbling, off-balance, I wade out, wondering if I can go on. Running flush into the frozen surface I stagger, flail in the other direction. My legs up to my calves are no longer a part of me, but somehow I keep going, instinctively heading for the dock.

Behind me the black gun spits, its fire reverberating in the indifferent hollow. Round after roaring round. But nothing hits me. He hasn't sighted in yet. Now I'm pure panic, scrambling up, crawling on hands and knees, straightening, slipping, walking on ice.

# CHAPTER EIGHTEEN: MOIRA

### Saturday: February 27, 1990: 2:35 p.m.

I've been holding it in so long I'm going to explode.

Behind the boathouse I squat, hearing voices. Whose? Ben's? Maurice's? Finally, I let go, the piss steaming under me, the hot yellow liquid melting the snow. A beaver climbs out of the pond and stares, trying to decide whether I am a danger. Sniffing, he stiffens at the shouts behind us and dives in an eye-blink into the dark water, his tail slapping behind him on the edge of the pond. How funny. I'm pissing my life away.

The rapid, flat explosions make me jerk, and for a moment I can't figure out how to pull my pants up. Imagine bleeding to death with your pants down. Finally, I yank my jeans over my paunch. No use calling it anything else. Is he really shooting Nathan or Ben or just firing into the sky? In my pocket I grope for my bloody utility knife. If I have to cut myself again to get mercy, I will. Only I wish I hadn't dug out such a deep wound in my palm. Still, it seemed to stun him. With trembling hands I open the blade of the tool I use for cutting and trimming on the fly. You never know when you're going to find some interesting weed on the side of the road, or clumps of winter-weed skeletons in someone's yard.

The fire from this single gun is so loud, so rapid I'm afraid the noise alone will kill me.

The knife open in my wrapped palm, I start to run, faster than I ever thought I could, but not exactly like a deer. To the far side of the small pond, near the dock. But I'm out of shape, winded in a minute or two. I stop, my chest heaving, start again, manage another fifteen yards. Disorienting, blinding, the white landscape expands and contracts with every suck of my breath. Another burst of sputtering gunfire shakes me to the core. If I can't run, I have to walk. Anything to get away from this brain-aching din. If I live, I'll worship silence.

Mercifully close by, the horse barn is my haven. Leaning all my weight on the door, I open it a crack. Out in the open I'll be a perfect, gross target, but in the barn I'll be trapped. Burrowing comes back to me. Perhaps there is a rotten bale of hay left there, or I could cover myself with a horse blanket. Years ago I had a lovely red blanket I put on Bobby when it got really bitter and the wind tore through spaces in the slats. Something will cover me, I'll survive like a mole, a woodchuck. But I look over my shoulder and Nathan distracts me. He is walking on ice.

Shoulders hunched, his whole body tilted forward, his head down, he walks furiously, blindly. In the mouth of the barn, I can't tear myself away from the curious sight. Where is Maurice? Suddenly, the quiet presses down. Dizzy, I can't seem to drink in enough of the heavy, moist air.

One of Nathan's legs disappears. Straight through the ice. For a heartbeat the leg is severed at the knee, but in his fury he yanks it out and keeps boring towards the dock. In his black parka with the hood up, and his black jeans, he is distilled Nathan, pure rage. I hold my breath, waiting for him to crack the surface and go straight down, but he keeps stalking across the frozen pond till he reaches one of the dock's snow-capped pylons. Then without warning the ice opens, and he plunges straight down.

He goes down like a black stake. So unreal. He's completely gone. Where he disappears dark ripples of water hit the iceless shore. A few feet away bullets fracture the frozen pond, peppering the air where Nathan had been. The din is unbearable. I have not doubt he is dying down there, the freezing water stunning his brain, but then his hooded head bobs up on the far side of the dock. I can't let it happen, I don't know what to do. Such a coward I am. I loved him and I'm letting him die.

I rush a few feet back in the direction of the pond and shout at the top of my lungs. 'Maurice, we want to help you! Don't, please! Don't! Don't! Don't!'

But where is he? I spin around and around but the landscape is blank. So blank I'm even more terrified.

Loving Nathan comes in between heartbeats. No memories. Flashes of the feeling in racing blood. How awful. There's nothing I can do. Fear drives me, an animal force I can't resist.

Whirling, I scan the inside of the small barn. Nothing, not a scrap of cloth, not a clump of hay is there to cover me. Just like Nathan. He swept it out and left it neat as a pin. If I'm cornered in here, I'll be slaughtered. No doubt, no doubt. When the next eruption of gunfire rings in my ears I slip out, edging away, pressing myself against the rough, unpainted planks. Nathan goes under again, Maurice racing to the dock, kicking madly at the snow.

Holding his pistol with two hands, he starts shooting down straight through the snowy boards. When I watch him moving methodically, horribly methodically up and down the length of the dock, his whole body jerking with every new blast, my will evaporates. I'm paralyzed. Where can I run? Into the treeless meadow, my stick-legs barely moving me across the open field? If he'll shoot his own father this way, what will he do with me who avoided him, hid from him at every turn?

One more time Nathan rises, pulling himself up onto the ice on all fours like a dog, a poor black dog streaming with pond muck. Oh my God, but at least he's still alive, even fighting his way to his feet. Oh, Nathan, I did love you once, it's not true that I never cared. I can't watch, I can't listen. I start stabbing my palm again.

I dig in, turning the knife. Through the bandages. Under the wrappings the blood flowers again, hot and wet. Are there arteries in the hand? I don't think so. It would be amusing if I accidentally killed myself trying to stay alive, wouldn't it? Because watching Nathan turn into a thing, inanimate, Nathan who I loved so long ago, I start to wail inside.

But I can't listen to this sound, won't, I refuse.

Almost as an afterthought, the boy in the black hood lets off his shooting and turns to me. Before he can say a word, I come out, holding my bloody hand high. 'Maurice, I need a doctor, look, honey.'

Casually, he slaps another clip of bullets into the vicious little weapon. I wait for the hot tearing, the searing bullets and the flash of darkness, I wait to crumple. I go weightless in the silence. But nothing happens, an endless, terrible lack of anything at all. Suspended in this absence I wonder if I am already dead. But he trots towards me, the squeak and crunch of his boots painfully loud. Cutting through me.

'Sorry, mom. I didn't mean to scare you. You just got in the way.' His tone is sarcastic, but completely reasonable. He just wanted to scare me to death. He's acting so matter-of-fact I know he could shoot me and just shrug, as if I were a thing like Nathan. His own father, who he loved more than anyone. 'My learner's permit ran out, mom. You think you can drive?'

'If I can stop the bleeding.' My voice is soaked with panic, but he doesn't seem to notice. 'Do you have a handkerchief or a rag?'

I see both of us from a great distance, me rewrapping my hand with his red neckerchief, Maurice leaning over in a deeply concerned way. The devoted son. Somehow, I staunch the blood again, or slow it down anyway. The thickening, moist stain stops spreading under the mass of cloth.

We are standing over Ben, but I can't say how we got there.

'Get his keys, mom.'

I hadn't thought of Ben's keys. Squatting by the boathouse, I didn't see him cut down by the stream of bullets or fall, one leg bent unnaturally beneath him. Flat on his back, the tucked leg makes him look like he's doing a stretching exercise in the snow. He has no nose, just a fleshy red hole in the center of his face. His puffball of white hair is spattered with blood.

Kneeling over Ben's corpse, yet watching from a high, unnamed place, I marvel at my coolness. I start to dig in his pockets when I discover the other wounds. Part of Ben's groin is shot away, the head of his sad white worm of a cock poking through the blood-soaked cloth of his fly. Convulsively, I retch over his body, on him, unable to control the spasms. Speckled with bits of undigested zucchini, the bile stinks to high heaven. My last meal. Zucchini and brown rice. I shudder, heave again, helpless to stop it. Yet, at the same time, in between spasms, I search feverishly for his keys, in one wet pocket then the other, then in his antique army jacket. I can do anything to stay alive.

Crammed in a nest of used tissues and roasted peanuts, the keys are hidden deep in a flapped pocket.

Maurice hasn't said a word about my puking. Slowly rising, I brush snow and vomit off myself with the big ski glove on my left hand.

'Just feather it,' he says when the van won't turn over. Oblivious to what he's just done, he sounds like Nathan in his usual morning mood.

But there is no Nathan. How can that be? Or is there? He was crawling, lifting himself off the ice. I wouldn't, couldn't look.

In a gush of fear, I floor the pedal, the starter whining, the old engine coughing, sputtering. If I can't get the truck started, will he kill me right here? I focus, baby the pedal now, trying not to flood it, keeping the rough rumble going. And it catches. Now I gun it in neutral, the motor banging and missing, but running, thank God. Thank God.

Without the slightest idea where we're going, I slam the clutch into first and start climbing the icy driveway.

Bouncing and skidding down the narrow, glassy road in Ben's van, I spot a police car light flashing and spinning up ahead. Maurice doesn't notice it till the trooper's car makes a hard turn up the drive and races straight at us, blocking the way. I have to slam on the brakes, but Ben's tires are bald, so we keep going for a few yards in that heart-sinking way you can sail, helpless on black ice. When the van's bumper knocks into the cop car's, we lurch to a stop.

Baby-faced, the trooper has a wisp of a red mustache.

Next to him on the front seat, her mouth moving behind the sealed window, Crissie shouts soundlessly to me. Hat flying off, the trooper bounds out, his gun drawn. Crissie stays fixed in the front seat. We are too far up the drive for them to see Ben's long, crumpled body or Nathan willing himself across the ice.

For some odd reason, Crissie keeps pointing down her throat. I wonder if her stomach is upset.

'Watcha got there, son?' the trooper asks, at the driver's side window now.

This happens so fast I barely see it. Before the pale-faced

cop can get another word out, or raise his gun properly, his forehead shatters, becoming a knob of bloody meat, wormy brain, the top of his head disappearing like magic. The spitting shots seem to come afterward, the way you hear the boom of the broken sound barrier moments after a jet passes overhead.

As the trooper's body vanishes, Crissie's gaping face appears in the cruiser's window, her jaw locked open, her palms pressed against the autoglass.

## CHAPTER NINETEEN: NATHAN

### Saturday: February 27, 1990: 2:38 p.m.

I'm walking on ice, but it's not solid, it's not deep winter ice. Lapping over with black water, its edges are already melted. There are small puddles on its surface, visible cracks that start to give way under my weight. Every new step makes a maze of new cracks. Maybe he's shooting in the air. Not a single bullet comes near me. I can barely breathe, I can barely think. White fields rise and fall. My heart bangs hard in my chest. Fear fills me up. I head for the dock. Slipping, sliding on legs without feeling. I'm getting away, I'm going to live.

There is nothing but this raging will to live. It almost lifts me off the ice with its power. Every terrified step I take is driven by it. I am living, going to live, survive. The dock, piled with snow, sticks out into the black water, almost touching the frozen surface of the pond. The dock, the dock. Summer sunlight on the dock. Searing. My back on the wet slats, I roast on the dock like a chicken on a spit. I rush towards it.

But I am hardly moving, staggering on the slushy surface, weighed down by my hundred pound clothes. I'd like to strip them off and lie on the summer dock, burn in the sunlight, burn, scorch. Then I lose my leg. It goes right through the ice, and instantly my leg bones, my knee, my foot freeze solid to the core.

I know I have to retrieve this frozen thing or it will die. I am yanking at this thing that is part of me but not part of me, lunging forward, driven by this frenzy to live. And all of a sudden the black thing connected to me pops out. It's made of stone, but I drag it with me. But the dead feeling rises up to my hip and starts spreading and I'm afraid that all of a sudden my organs will freeze, my intestines will stop churning, my stomach will turn hard and solid, my lungs will harden, my heart will stop pumping blood that's turning to icy slush. I'm totally exposed on the sheet of ice.

There's nowhere to hide. There's no shelter, really. The boathouse is paper-thin. The hills beyond are studded with a few scrub bushes and naked maples, a perfect background to sight-in on a crawling, fat target. All the air goes out of me. My surging will grows less and less powerful until it is just a faint pulse. What is the point? I am being killed by my son or my non-son, and I can't figure out which is worse or more meaningless. Is there a half second left to stop lying to myself? When I kept Syracuse quiet, it was for my own benefit, wasn't it? When I kept taking him out of the hospital, it was for my own benefit, wasn't it? I could have done more, far more, or maybe less. Or was there something real in every phony word that came out of my mouth? Is there any way to tell?

Terrible, stinging shots. Smacking into the ice. Whizzing

over my head. I'm afraid to turn and see him because if I do I'll lose my last shred of resistance. Instead, another bolt of energy blasts through me, and I start running somehow, or pieces of me run just to escape the deafening gunfire.

I'm running in the air, I'm running in the black water. The world disappears. I freeze, sink, shudder, choke on my heart. Drowning. I weigh a thousand pounds. But somehow I'm climbing an invisible ladder in the darkness, I'm a blind mole that knows its way. In shock, I keep on living. I know I'm in shock because I watch my head break the surface of the water, I watch my mouth suck air, I watch my shoulders, spattered with pond scum, rise up. My feet touch bottom and I'm walking out, choking on muck, bits of ice and grit in my mouth. I want to throw up, but when I get to the shore another shot tears past my head. I'm dead, I should be dead. I'm immortal.

There is a humming, a singing outside my head. I try to make out the tune. It's a singsong, squeaky thing sung by an idiot. 'Tan Shoes and Pink Shoelaces.' My requiem mass. A piston slams into my shoulder and I fall to my knees. All fours. Under me a spattering of red drops on the snow. The animal that is me staggers to its feet baying like a deer in terror. An eerie sound, part honking, part cry. This thing that is me is running again. They said he used a shrimp fork in Syracuse under the bridge, but they couldn't prove it. My lawyer said.

Under the dock. No one will see me. I'll stay there forever. Hidden perfectly. I can't believe how clever I am. I'll make myself disappear where everybody else is exposed. I was always resourceful, I could always solve problems, I was always good under pressure. I stumble, crawl, dig like a woodchuck til I make a hollow for myself under the boards. Concealed forever. Safe. Losing it, growing faint, I can't feel my body at all. Or just bits of it. My fingertips, my lips, the tip of my nose. It's funny actually, to be reduced to these shreds. Boots tramping. Boots squeaking in the snow, on the boards over my head. Boots kicking away the bullet-proof snow. My son is walking on my head.

Laying off the bets. Tyson and Douglas. Long reach. Overnight deposits. That bitch Moira. Kissing Moira on the dunes of Stinson Beach. Lost in her mouth. Moiramoiramoiramoira. Scraping over my head. Stamping. Muffled shots. Louder, hotter, flushing me from my cave. Bullets in water are soft. Deep, deep I sink back into the freezing darkness. I float. I drown. I roll, thrashing on my back. Nothing can kill me. I claw my way back onto the ice. Straight above me my son glares.

# CHAPTER TWENTY: MAURICE

**Saturday: February 27, 1990: 2:32 p.m.**

My father turns himself into a tall black bird. The tall bird sails across the ice, but it can't fly. He thinks he's hiding inside the bird while he gets away, like I wouldn't know the bird is him. I step on the string of dental floss and the Cobray jerks and jolts in my hands. The speed loader works all by itself. The Cobray knows where to shoot and what it wants. It has a brain inside its handle. A primitive reptilian brain. I flip the magazine and fly across the snow. Eeeeeeeeeeee! My feet don't even touch the ground.

Now he loses a leg, it just sinks right into the ice, and he's clawing at it and I'm running towards him because he needs help. Whenever I see somebody in pain I feel it in the same place in my body. It's like I'm losing my leg and I have to help him get his leg back to keep from losing my own. Then he grows another leg and starts to stagger away again. The Cobray is sniffing and thinking. It starts barking all over again, shooting black holes all around the black bird.

Crack. Pistol shot from the woods. I spin and the Cobray

sprays like it's an extension of my arm. Slowly a red pine comes down like it's a big match stick. Slow crash. Red pines have no needles, except near the top. Mom says after an ice storm their heads look like frozen hairdos. The hairdo crashes through the crusty snow. The wind blows snow crystals sharp as darts. Their points stick in my face.

Icy trees snap all winter. Like pistol shots.

But the shots keep coming. They're not pine trees snapping, they're shots snapping. Slow shots. I go down and bury myself like an Eskimo and watch but first I hear a high-pitched whining, mixed with grunts and snorts. Right out of the woods behind the horse barn a big doe staggers. She looks around like, What am I doing here? She's deep above her knees in the snow, trying to drag herself forward. A small wound in her side doesn't look like much, just a little stain on her dark winter coat, but she doesn't have much energy left. She stumbles and takes another bullet, smack, right in her throat.

Her front legs buckle and when she goes down she looks right at me like I'm the last thing in the world she sees and can I help her. Whimpering, she falls over on her side, her legs twitching. Out of her mouth this gunk starts pouring. Dad would be really pissed off. It's off season and they're poaching on our land. And it's not fair, I mean, in the deep snow a whitetail can't run hardly at all. It's like these guys who sit up in tree stands and shoot down at the bucks.

From my burrow I see a blue snowmobile come out of the woods. A guy with a fur hat is driving with one hand and holding his rifle with the other. Snowmobiles are cool, but this is like a drive-by shooting. When he gets closer, I recognize him. It's our neighbor, Harlan. Dad calls him HoHo Harlan cause he's always laughing at his own jokes. Brushing myself off, I get up and aim the Cobray right at him.

He can't see around the barn to dad on the pond. Lucky for HoHo.

'Hey, Maurice, I heard shots. I thought somebody was shooting targets. Auto, huh? Got a taste for venison, you know.' His fur ear laps stick up like a cartoon character. His chinky, flat face is snow-burnt. 'Well, I'll just throw her in . . .'

But after I squeeze off a couple of rounds, he dives down into his snowmobile. I know what the Cobray wants to do but I'm the boss. This time I shoot high. 'Leave her, Harlan. That's poaching. Dad's gonna have a shit fit.'

Then I wonder if maybe dad sent Harlan, like secretly Harlan's his bodyguard.

'Well, he gave me permission, but sure, sure, anything you say, Maurice. I'll be going.' While I'm still wondering, Harlan crouches over the steering wheel and floors it, heading back into the red pines. He drives ducking down. That proves dad sent him. Maybe it's a black bag operation they do with snowmobiles.

Even if he's not working for dad, Harlan doesn't really need the venison. He's just doing it for fun. That's the worst. Maybe I'll give the carcass to charity later.

I know what the Cobray wants to do but what about me?

I fly across the snow in two places at once. Back to dad and the pond.

When I blink dad's gone. The pond is a plate of ice with black edges. The edges are water. I fly across the snow, the Cobray growing onto my arm, getting veins. My blood flows through the Cobray. I'm playing hide and seek with dad but it's serious. Suppose he lived and he had to see how I turned out? I mean his whole life is getting Maurice to straighten up and fly right and he finds out mom's been lying all these years. I mean, who is he, anyway? He could still be my father in a parallel universe, but not this one.

But the opposite of everything mom says is true so he could be my father. Or my anti-father like anti-matter, which is just as real as matter. Unless you weigh the anti-matter, most of the universe is empty.

So the opposite of what dad says is true, too. Like dad thinks he's the only one who knows how I feel but I'm the only one who knows how he feels. I'm dad's shrink but he doesn't know it. And when mom says he isn't my father he is.

The dock sticks out into the pond. The tip of it's in the ice. I bank like a plane coming in for a landing. It's easy to see where dad's tracks lead but he could be a magician. He could have made himself invisible. I could be looking right at him but all I see is the ice plate on the pond, the boat house, and the fields. Driving around those fields you can get snowburn like Harlan. Dad sent him. The woods could be full of a snowmobile army. Dad's the general.

The snow on the dock is like a pillow, all fresh and soft

and white. I kick it off and stop to listen. There's something breathing under there, dad or maybe a beaver. I start stamping to flush it out but it makes believe it doesn't exist.

That's how I know it's dad even though I don't see him. He likes to make believe he's interested in the stars, but he isn't at all. I don't think he could tell the Crab Nebula from the Milky Way. When I found him using my telescope, his pants tangled around his knees, I didn't know what to say. I was too young to understand.

'It's another kind of love, Maurice, don't worry,' he told me, buckling his belt, tilting the scope back up towards the dark sky. Later, I found out how to use the telescope, too.

The Cobray sniffs up and down the icy boards, spitting bullets. Guess who crawls out?

Dad stands up flapping like a penguin, slapping at the snow that sticks to his coat. His face is interesting, he's making noises, but they don't make sense. It's like he's choking but I can't tell why. He slaps his chest, wobbles, then wades backwards again into the black water. Two long snotty streams of blood pour out of his nostrils. I get such bad nosebleeds I could die, so I dig in my pockets for a handkerchief to make dad's stop, but he trips and falls into the water. Splashes. Then he climbs back onto the ice on all fours. Stands up. His eyes start to go back into his head so they're all eyewhites. But he keeps trying to tell me something.

The Cobray's quiet, so I ask dad what's wrong. What's he trying to tell me? Instead of talking, he's gargling. Dad's got a blood mustache now. 'Trans . . . fer . . . trans . . . fer . . . fun,' he tells me, falling slowly to his knees.

I follow him in my sight to see what he'll do. In my hands the Cobray is jumpy, going ratatat. If dad lived he'd be so embarrassed about me, I'd have to shoot him again. Mom doesn't care what people think of her or me, but dad has a reputation to uphold.

Dad is a good swimmer. He rolls over on his face and starts to do a crawl. He can do the crawl without moving a muscle. And I'm thinking, he's sending me a message that will really help me, transfer fun, but I don't know what it means. He just sinks and won't come up. I wait to see because I have so many questions but he stays down there. There's a thick, oily spot where he went down. Dad's an oil spill.

# CHAPTER TWENTY-ONE: CRISSIE

## Saturday: February 27, 1990: 2:20 p.m.

Driving the Cherokee is so different than driving the Tercel. I feel like I'm in a moving living room. It floats, you feel so protected, but like dad says, never forget you're running a dangerous machine weighing thousands of pounds. He's right, too. There was this boy I knew who got out of high school a couple of years before me and went into the navy, Jerry McAnn. And this one time on leave he got into a drag race with Warren Semanski at three in the morning down this hill outside Accordia that's a straight drop past the pizza place, and his car just took off. They said he was doing 130. Anyway, his car went out of control, and they said pieces of him were on the roof of the pizza place and other pieces were clear across the road. A car door was in a tree. Everybody used to joke about how they were still finding parts of Jerry McAnn, but I never laughed. Dad is right about stuff like that, protecting yourself.

I'm surprised how calm I am. I'm super calm, going about my business. If I have to drive all the way to Tuscarora to the police barracks I'll do it. I'll give them the address of the cottage and a complete description of Maurice and probably nothing will happen at all, he probably didn't shoot anybody really. He was just trying to show off. Psychiatrists are always saying people with schizophrenia are less likely to get violent than the average person, and I think it's true. Look at the stupid bar fights every Saturday night at the Accordia Inn. So if I just do the right things everything will turn out okay. Which I'm doing.

As I drive I keep an eye out for the sheriff or a trooper. Driving at forty-five it's easy to see everything, and I'm not doing more than that or I'll fishtail the Cherokee into a ditch or something. I pass Bare Bottoms, which used to be The Stick Willow Bar until these guys from Schenectady bought it and tried to start a topless club. They brought in strippers that they advertised were 'all the way from Utica'. That cracked me and my friends up. They even tried to run a ladies night where I guess you got to stick dollar bills into the leopard skin g-strings of some weight-lifting hunks. Maybe they were from Buffalo. People around here went crazy, the churches and everything, and one night the place burned down. Christian arson, mom said.

My socks are soggy; my toes are frozen.

To say the least, I resent having to drive around like this. I know after this thing is over, Maurice will do something else to drag me down. If I stay in town after I graduate, mom will be begging me to talk him out of his latest episode. My whole life will be spent watching mom get older and dad get madder and Maurice get crazier. I'll just be the good, sane sister who everybody thinks is so self-sacrificing. No thank you. It's not like I need any more reasons to get away for good, but this new thing with the gun, that's way too scary for me. (He wouldn't really shoot anybody, I'm sure now that I've calmed down. He was just trying to show off.) And when it's over, dad will find an excuse, and even mom, too. She'll say the shrink didn't keep an eye on Maurice's medication, as if there is no Maurice, or he has no will of his own.

Then I see the trooper's cruiser. Just sitting there in the Stick Willow Quikway parking lot. Carefully, like I'm moving in slow motion, I edge the Cherokee into the space next to the smokie. I have this sinking sensation that no matter what I do, I'll smash up the Cherokee and dad will give me this look that says, Yeah, it's inevitable, she's a fuck up, too.

The light in the Quikway is so bright it makes you blink. One girl, her hands in clear plastic gloves, is slicing ham. Hunched over, she has a back as flat and wide as a door.

A guy with a backwoods beard watches her make his sub. 'Slice me up some cheese with that. Lettuce, tomato, raw onion, Sandy.'

The trooper is leaning on his elbows at the counter, chatting up the other girl, who has a long nose. She reminds me of an anteater. He's buying a container of chocolate milk and no-brand cigarettes. You can see she's dropping her cookies cause a trooper is paying attention to her. For a second I get in line, like I'm dreaming. Like it's the polite thing to do. Then I catch myself.

'Excuse me sir, I've got sort of an emergency.' I talk like I'm underwater.

The trooper turns around, and he looks just like Donald Duck with a mustache. I mean it. I almost burst out laughing. He's the funniest looking guy I've ever seen with this little dead red mustache stuck to his face, and I realize he can't be more than twenty-five. He looks like a baby, too young and stupid to help anybody with anything.

We go over to the ice cream freezer for some privacy. Automatically, I check through the corner of my eye to see if they have any Cherry Garcia. They don't. I explain what's happening, but he doesn't seem to grasp it very well.

'You say he's armed, Miss?' He pulls on his wispy mustache as if he doesn't believe it's still there.

The phrase doesn't sound right. I mean, he is armed, but I don't think he's really dangerous. 'Did I? Yeah, he's got some kind of gun. He was shooting with it, but he wouldn't use it, I mean, to hurt anybody. I couldn't see it very well. It was squarish. Black. I'm no good about guns.'

Why do I think he won't hurt anybody? If he does anything to mom, I'll die. But I don't think he will. I get so nervous all of a sudden.

He pulls his notebook from his back pocket. 'Now tell me as best you can where this is located. I want to put it out on the radio.'

I start to tell him, but then I realize something. He may have a hard time finding the place without me, especially in the storm. I try to concentrate. 'You know where Baumgarten's is?'

'Building supply?'

'Yeah.'

'Well, you go back behind the store and there's this fork, and one of them is Willis Creek Road, on the right, but don't take that one . . . Take the other one . . . There's no sign, but that's the one . . .' I'm practically stuttering. I sound retarded.

'Yeah?'

Maybe I'm not thinking straight. 'You could get lost back there,' I say, trying hard to get him to understand. 'You might never find it.'

'I know the back roads pretty good, Miss. I'm from Merwinville.'

'He could go off and you'll be driving around in circles!' I don't know how loud I'm talking til I hear myself.

'Okay, Miss. Let's calm down. You can ride with me.'

The girl at the counter with the sharp nose looks mad, like I've stuck my tits in her boyfriend's face or something. Like I'd really want to steal Donald Duck from her, right?

The trooper tries to get me to give him directions again, but I can't, it's too confusing. It's funny how the camp can be so close to town and so isolated at the same time.

When we get into the cruiser Dick Dibbet, that's his name, turns on the flashing light on the roof and we start flying. 'Don't worry, we got studdeds on these cars,' he says, smiling like he's a genius who's solved all the world's problems. 'You say he wouldn't hurt nobody?'

'No, he started shooting, but it was probably just to scare my mom and dad.' My words sound like they're not mine, my voice I mean. It's like somebody else's voice on a telephone.

The body brush snapped and I felt so sorry I started picking him up and petting him, forgetting to put on a robe at first. I'm down there with him in a smelly pile of laundry trying to make him feel better after what he did to me. It made no sense, but that's the way it always is with him. Then I got an idea. I said, 'Let's bury it.'

'You won't tell?' The bridge of his glasses was cracked right in half and there was a big spreading bruise on his forehead. His right eye was starting to close. I knew I could get him to lie, but I wondered whether he'd hold a grudge. A long scratch from the splintered plastic ran down his cheek. Like a bad cat scratch. How could I do that? How could he forget?

'Say you got into a fight, okay?'

'Yeah, if you won't tell. You've got to promise never to tell.'

I promised and we took the pieces of the body brush down into the cellar, which is really half a crawl-space. The beams of the house are rough logs down there, and there's a big boulder mom says is holding the whole thing up. There are old *Medaglia D'Oro* cans and plastic seltzer bottles mom forgot to return all over the place. We used an old tin coffee can lid to dig.

'Hey, Cris, it's a funeral for a brush,' he said. I wanted to kill him, but it's so hard not to forgive him.

'Say you were in a fight. Otherwise, I'll tell.'

'How'd you know?' Dick Dibbet asks me.

'Huh?'

'How'd you know he won't hurt nobody?'

Suddenly, this awful pressure starts building up in my head. They could be dead, all of them. Maurice could have shot all of them. They could be lying on the floor of the camp house cottage, bleeding to death. I want to tell the trooper to call an ambulance, but all of a sudden I can't say a single word. I'm thinking fast, though, realizing that I can point which way to go, even if I can't say anything. It's the most bizzare thing. I have to point down my throat and shake my head, shrug my shoulders. The words are stuck down there, and they refuse to come out. But I don't cry.

'Tell me when we get near, I'll call for back-up. Shit! You're in shock little girl, you know what shock is?'

I can't stand the way he calls me little girl, but he must be right because I feel as if I'm in a cottony cocoon, and I can't say a single word. I want to tell him to drop me off before he gets there, but I can't get a word out of my throat. But I keep trying, it's like if I can clear my throat the words will come bursting out. I get to where I start to make grunting noises. It's so embarrassing. But by staying calm, I tell myself I'm making progress. Thinking positive is free. That's what dad always says. I'll get my voice back before we get there, and I'll tell Donald Duck to let me off in a safe place.

The trooper's calling everybody he can think of. The barracks. The sheriff's office. Ambulances. He sounds like he feels very important, and he keeps his Donald Duck face on like a mask. He has a handful of freckles on his cheeks. His ears are small sea shells. Too small for his head. I keep pointing.

'Now I want you to get out when we get nearby, far enough away, anyway,' he says. 'Keep you out of the line of any fire.'

Thank God, it's like he read my mind. I nod my head up and down like a fool.

But he worries me, too. He's getting so over-excited he could cause an incident when probably Maurice is already chilled out and dad has the gun and is talking to him in that low, murmuring way he uses when Maurice has done something wrong.

But when we get to the long drive above the cottage, I get so scared, I start making stop signals with my palms, and these grunting noises that aren't words. I jab my thumb towards the side of the road. Donald Duck nods and starts to slow down so I can get out. Then we see Ben's van bouncing up the road. That's a good sign, I guess. The whole mess is probably over, and Ben is driving home. Probably he's got Maurice and dad in the back with his stupid Sicilian donkey cart.

I nod and smile like everything's okay. God, I must look grotesque, but I keep smiling and pointing to myself to let him know things look okay.

The van swerves to a stop and scrapes our bumper, and I think I see Ben driving because I want to see Ben driving. But he isn't. The trooper leaps out of the cruiser with his gun poking in front of him. Then he has no head. Or part of a head. His body stands with part of a head longer than you might think. Why doesn't he fall? He falls.

And there is Maurice in a black hood with a black gun in

his hand, and he is going to kill me. I am alive for one more second. He must be definitely holding a grudge. How can a life be so short? I think of Harry and his stick legs in the rubber, knee-high farmer's boots. His white chest without a single hair. Logarithms. A designer blouse with fake pearl buttons I found at the label shop. A Pee Wee Herman tape I used to love when I was nine. Chicken with broccoli at the Great Wall in the Merwinville mall. French verbs. Soccer. Fuzzy slippers. Dusty, the horse. As these things flash through my mind I'm squeezing my eyes shut, waiting for the bullets to make the world end. Then I hear pounding on ice.

'Crissie, don't be upset,' Maurice says, taking my arm in such a gentle way you'd think he was saving me. 'I'm driving this bus.'

I do whatever he says I'm so thankful to be alive. When I squeeze in next to mom, she falls on me and grabs me, crying but trying to stop, practically choking me.

I wonder if I'll ever go to college. I wonder if I can rip the gun out of his hand. But I'm too afraid. As he drives, Maurice holds his awful gun in his left hand, aimed right at mom's head. Every time we hit a rut, the barrel jerks.

The van rumbles up the driveway and skids onto the back road. Every pathetic, broken-down house looks like heaven. I see the whole world in a new way. Precious, precious world.

Sitting between me and Maurice, mom is hyperventilating, but I see she's trying to get a hold of herself. It's like she's doing one of her yoga breathing exercises. She closes her eyes for a second, and I have the feeling that she's looking way deep inside herself. Dad always made fun of her California hippie stuff, but I'm glad she has something to hang on to. I have nothing. I can't even speak.

My words stick in my throat. They stick together down there like a blood clot. It's sort of funny. Without words, how can I save myself?

'You know, dad said living's a life sentence,' Maurice says, laughing at his own joke. 'That's why I want you to live forever mom. I'd never hurt you.' His voice is dripping with sarcasm. And I'm mute, I can't even beg for her life. 'Who's my father, huh?'

I don't know what he's talking about, but he's way out there, not even vaguely Maurice.

She opens her eyes and grips my knee, her fingernails digging in hard, telling me she loves me. Her loves pours into me through her fingernails. 'Nathan's your father, honey. Why don't you drop Crissie off. I'll stay with you til you feel better.'

'Tell me, mom. Maybe then you'll live forever.' Everything he says sounds sarcastic, but I try to think of something to say in the old way. *Moccorico. Riccomocco*. I have to stick my fingers down my throat and pull the sticky words out.

Whatever's in the back of the van rattles so loud I get a headache. Up ahead the white road vibrates.

'Nathan, honey. Nathan was always your father. He's a good man, your father. He cares a lot about you. Why don't you drop Crissie off in town? She needs some school supplies.'

'He fixed the barn for me, didn't he? They could have put it in a magazine. He told me that.'

I think she's succeeding in changing the subject. I hold my breath. My head is pounding so hard I'd scream if I could.

'Maybe we could stop at the Grand Union. I need some bandages.'

'I'm not stupid, mom. Don't play games with me. You know if there's one thing about me it's that I'm not stupid. In the sixth grade they said I had a 168 IQ, remember? Mrs Kiacheck?'

'I remember, honey.'

'I know quantum mechanics. A particle can be in ten dimensions at once. In ten different universes. This isn't even me maybe. This is my simulacrum from another universe. My father could be a particle from the Crab nebula.'

We're sailing right through the heart of Accordia, but there isn't a soul on the street, and we're going too fast for me to fling myself out the door. Valerie Van Dam's father was driving this house trailer down the hill from Stick Willow, and he lost his brakes, so he dove out to try to save his life, and he landed on his head and killed himself. I can't dive out. I could snap my spine and end up in a wheel chair. The town goes by in a blur, and we're out on the highway again.

I start praying even though I don't know how to pray. I pray the troopers will find us, I pray Maurice will let us go, I pray mom will talk him into giving up. I pray I'll see Harry. I pray I'll have the nerve to fight for my life. Balanced on the dashboard in his left hand, the gun holds steady now, pointing right at mom.

Outside of town Maurice swings off of Route Eight onto Stillbeck Road. Up ahead Gaiter's blue and yellow domed silo stands on a slight rise, visible for miles. I pray I'll have the courage to fight for my life. I pray and pray, wondering how to do it.

'Are you hungry, honey?' mom asks.

To my shock Maurice says, 'Yeah, mom. Maybe they've got something over at the Gaiters'.'

In the winter, the Gaiters' farm is empty. The Gaiters, who are from Manhattan, own it now, so it's not really a farm at all. Just a showplace for a few months when the weather's decent. These are people who never got cow shit on their boots. Dad says they can't tell a vulture from a crow.

When we get into the Gaiters' front yard, Maurice herds us out of the van and pushes us in front of him. Right over my shoulder he shoots the lock out of the front door. I think I'll go deaf. What can war sound like? I hold onto mom, we hold each other up as we stumble into the kitchen.

Maurice rifles the cabinets, coming up with a single box of crackers. He starts to rip the packaging with his teeth when I see myself lunge at him.

I move in slow motion, trying to knock him down, but I have no real plan.

It's a feeble attempt. All he does is crack me in the face with the gun and I crumple up, my mouth filling with warm blood. A streak of pain rings up and down my jaw, then Mom is on top of me, hugging me, pulling me up.

'Don't cry, it'll be fine,' she whispers in my ear. How can

I stop crying? I'm coughing up phlegm and crying at the same time. Can I speak again?

Clearing my throat, I start to cough up words that don't make sense.

'Maurice, now stop that. Don't hurt your sister,' she scolds, changing her tone completely. No more honey this and honey that. It's like she's baring her teeth all of a sudden.

He backs off, leaning against the sink. That's when he sees the first cop car pulling up. He starts pushing us to the back door when I notice one of my front teeth is loose. Exploring it with my tongue, I can feel it wobble. Shit. It'll cost mom a fortune to fix.

'I'll need a cap,' I croak.

# CHAPTER TWENTY-TWO: JULIA

## Thursday: August 10, 1987: 1:10 p.m.

In the cool, vaulted barn Moira sips out of the plastic cup, a beer mustache forming on her upper lip. The auctioneer rattles on in an incomprehensible patter, holding the bag of bull semen aloft, and, I suppose, singing its virtues. The farmers have their eyes glued to their tout sheets, judging the quality of the liquid seed before them. We've already seen the parade of heifers and calves – 'Dairy Fashions' they call it – Moira cooing especially at the young ones. I've always wondered if she liked animals more than people.

She showers affection on her horses and her dog. She can tell you in minute detail what sort of bacterial infection or stool disorder each of them has at any given moment. Of her feelings for Crissie and Maurice, I can never quite tell.

'How about the horse pull?'

'Good idea,' she says, laughing and wiping her mouth with the back of her sleeve.

A great pan of dust, the fairgrounds reflect the searing sunlight. High above the grandstand, a swollen, anthropomorphic cloud rises rapidly, as if it were made of helium.

The county fair fills me with nostalgia. I can still remember the first time I saw horses drag huge stones across a dusty ring, my father holding me up on his shoulders so I could get a better view. How old could I have been? Three, four? Sweet nostalgia, that gauzy distortion that contains within it a sweet poison.

We pass the sausage stand, the cotton candy stand, the hot dog stand, the mixture of frying meat and the sickly sweet tightening my stomach into a hard ball.

'I love the Clydesdales. This was such a good idea, Julia, thanks for calling.'

In her crisp peasant blouse, turquoise earrings and matching necklace, her lipstick painted with the hand of a professional artist, Moira looks years younger than she is. Her ebullience is a little shocking, considering Maurice's condition, but I'm not surprised. As usual, she doesn't see through to my real motives, some of which are far from altruistic.

I touch her elbow. She smiles back. 'I wouldn't go with anybody else.'

'Oh, how about some fried dough?'

'How can you eat that stuff?'

'Well, it's the closest thing to a *zeppole* I can find in this God-forsaken place.'

'I'll take a bite.'

'You're a stick, have a whole one!'

Finally, I relent, but I can barely get the sticky dough down. I wonder at her exuberance, especially after the way they found Maurice in Syracuse. About that she's been unusually close-mouthed. I know I'll get more out of her if she keeps drinking, so I buy another two cups with an eye to passing mine to her after she gulps the cheap swill down. Beer has always reminded me too strongly of bubbly urine.

The first pair of Clydesdales, chestnuts with rippling haunches, lug three stones the required distance. Apparently, we've shown up for the final round, the crowd of farmers in their K-mart jeans and cheap synthetic shirts, the downstaters in their muted country outfits by Land's End and Banana Republic. Moira, at home on either side of this divide, clutches her program and jumps up and down as each new team struggles to make the mark. A new stone is added and the pressure rises, three teams failing to reach the finish line.

Doffing their suspiciously expensive-looking cowboy hats – some of these horse pullers are really professional performers who travel from fair to fair – the winning team trots around the ring.

'How is he doing?' I ask as we wander towards the small barns featuring 4-H Club goats and calves.

Flush from the excitement of the horse pull, she says, 'Oh, fine. The doctors say he only needs to stay a few more weeks. They were more worried about him recovering from exposure than anything else.'

'But he got over that months ago,' I point out, injecting a sliver of reality.

In the stunning sunlight we wander past the kiddy rides.

I know she is dissembling, or even lying to herself, but I let it pass for now.

Standing in the wind tunnel of Rose Lane in his black-hooded Gortex jacket that made him look like a strange, austere monk, Nathan told me about the allegations, but he insisted they were absurd. The other man was just a derelict, and who knew how long he had been in that condition? But he also told me about the ripping denim, and I can't get that out of my mind.

'Ferris wheel?'

I go along with her suggestions, drinking in her energy, passing her my half-full cup without a word. By now nostalgia has given way to weary familiarity with the tacky attractions, the cackling sound system promising a sky jump and a demolition derby.

As we're about to board the Ferris wheel, she sees him. 'Vincent! Over here!'

At first, even as she is introducing me to the dark man almost feminine in his beauty, I think, it can't be *that* Vincent. What would he be doing here? Isn't he living in Manhattan? Wouldn't he avoid Moira's world at all costs?

With the practiced grace of a ladies' man, he kisses her lightly on the cheek. The shy boy at his side, nine or ten years old, looks awfully familiar, though I've never seen him before. 'This is my son, Lonnie. Lonnie, this is Moira and . . .'

A knowing, worn-away look makes Vincent terribly attractive, if you care for the type. Nathan is handsome without being so pretty, and less dissipated.

'Julia, oh I'm sorry I didn't introduce . . . So what are you doing up in the boonies?' Visibly blushing, Moira speaks with a breathy nervousness. Rarely have I seen her so flustered.

'Actually, I just bought a house on Redbone Road. I'm thinking of setting up a practice here.'

'Oh, that's wonderful,' Moira says as we edge towards our swinging seat.

Vincent and Lonnie get on before us. Over his shoulder Vincent says, 'Yeah, fighting for the guilty finally burned me out.'

After a few coughs, the old carney Ferris wheel lifts us skyward. Tossing my head back, I watch the clouds drift over us, trying to keep my excitement at bay.

'Oh God! Oh shit! Shit! Shit! I've got to get away from him, Julia. He's going to be living here, I'll see him everywhere. He'll shop in the Grand Union. He'll show up at the bank. How could I avoid him?'

'I can see why you always talk about him.' Easily, softly. No need to press.

'Doesn't he have the most beautiful eyes? Oh, if he came up here it means he's given up, he was so ambitious. I'll just have to ignore him.'

I almost laugh out loud at this. As far as I know, they've kept apart because they can't resist each other. But she hasn't seen him for years, or so she's told me.

'He knows you live up here?'

'Of course. He was stopping by til a year ago. Just a few times.'

The arrogance of beauty once again. Could there be any question of his motivation? She doesn't even entertain the possibility that he could have moved for another reason, even another woman.

'Well then.'

'Did you see his son?'

'Who's the mother?'

'Oh, some lawyer. A real bitch on wheels.' This is rather out of character for Moira, who loves to forgive everyone but Nathan. 'She's suing him for sole custody. I always thought that was so cruel, I mean unless there's abuse or something.'

Her vehemence makes me wonder. And how does she know they're divorcing? 'Who told you?'

'Oh, a mutual friend.' This is less than convincing, but she does seem genuinely shocked at Vincent's sudden appearance.

Running her fingers through her long, straight hair, she falls silent, brooding as the wheel descends for the last time. Just above the ground, she says, in a low, desperate voice, 'I've got to get away from him.'

Her arm hooked to mine, she waves half-heartedly to Vincent, who is waiting expectantly at the exit. Then she bolts, weaving in and out of the shambling crowd, dragging me past the cotton candy, the penny toss, the shooting gallery, the ring toss, the vertical gong. The mob, rushing excitedly to some fresh attraction, runs in a powerful wave against us.

A roar of engines practically deafens me. I can barely hear Moira shouting in my face. 'Demolition derby! Let's get out of here or I'll die!! Let's go!'

'Imbeciles. How about the reservoir?'

By the time we're backing out of the vast parking lot marked out in a back field, the derby cars are crashing, scraping, ripping into each other to the delighted roar of the fans.

A few miles out of town Moira turns off onto a road that changes from asphalt to gravel to a dirt track. I showed her this back road to the reservoir years ago, the road to the old creamery. Misch's Creamery. Behind it was the hall where they held dances in the summer, dances with local fiddlers and guitarists and singers. Standing on the shore, I imagine the general store, the barber shop, the churches, the mill, our house drowning beneath the glassy green water. Ducks float over my old roof.

'I'd like to dive down there in one of those diving bells. Or skin dive with an oxygen tank. The things I'd find.'

From her bag she pulls a small bottle of brandy and a pack of cigarettes. 'Like what?'

'Oh, I don't know. Moldy books. Old albums. Hats and shoes. I don't know.'

'At least you have somewhere to go back to, even if it's underwater. I'd never go back to the midwest. They put my father's liver in the Milwaukee Museum of Modern History. My mother, totally *non compos mentis*. You can't see her through the cloud of smoke. That woman smokes five packs a day, I swear. She talks about relatives I never heard of . . .'

As I take a sip from her bottle, Moira looks fixedly out at the water. 'Oh, I probably told you this a hundred times, when the nun with the underbite came to my house?'

'No.'

'This will give you the picture. You'll laugh, but it's true. In eighth grade a nun from St Barbara's showed up at my house, we were about to take this placement test for high school. The old lady was bowing and scraping all over the place, "Yes, Sister" this, and "Of course, Sister" that, and I was going crazy wondering what it was all about.'

'Uh-huh.' Moira goes back to the church the way I sink into Willistone.

'So they called me out from my room where I'd been listening to them anyway, and my mother, who's had a few in her teacup by now, puts on this phony, proper Irish lady voice of hers and said, "Moira, Sister wants to ask you a favor." I'd seen this nun before in the office and whenever I looked at her underbite I thought, that's why she became a nun. So the nun said, "Moira, there's a drawing part on the test tomorrow, and we don't want you to draw too well. It might hurt some of your classmates' chances. We want everybody to place well."'

'No, that's hard to believe.'

'I couldn't figure it out either. But my mother was bowing and scraping and swearing I'd listen, and I was thinking if I don't do what the nun says I may burn forever. I totally believed that. Really physically burn without falling apart. That way the pain keeps going on forever. Everything's on fire. Even your bones. The next day I got to the drawing problem, something very simple like a suburban street scene, a house with a yard. Maple trees. I saw just how to do it, where the shadows fell, the perspective, and I was sitting there, terrified. Burn in hell till the end of time or draw the picture just right.'

'You're making this up.' But her eyes look glazed, and her mouth hardens, and I accept every word.

'Primitive, right? It took me a long time. I started doing it badly, but I hated myself for even trying it. Anyway, I wasn't sure how to draw badly. Finally, this . . . this thing welled up in me, it just took me over and I was drawing and drawing and when I came out of it I had something I thought was absolutely beautiful. And I didn't care anymore.'

'About burning?'

'I was ready to fry,' she laughs. 'Vincent went to public schools, but it was all the same. Don't get above yourself. Who do you think you are.'

Now I understand. In some sense, this story is about her affair, not about the church at all. She smokes, furiously now, taking in deep lungfuls. We stare out at the glittering lake which obscures the things I truly love. I try to explain what happened, at the same time listening for the other story I've hidden even from myself.

'The Army Corps of Engineers would come in and nail an eviction notice on your door. The dam was coming and Washington didn't give a fig for your farm or your house or your business. They were doing it without an act of Congress, too. Some towns fought and won, but some didn't.'

I feel the undertow of watery streets and drowned gardens.

Under there, in classrooms filled to the brim, in the inundated bowling alley, in Victorian towers awash in fish and underwater foliage, I am myself truly. This dry, adult husk craves the moisture of the past.

But Moira isn't listening to anything but the sound of her own voice.

'You know that sequence in *Pennies From Heaven,* the one with Christopher Walken, where he dances on the bar and sings *Let's Misbehave*?'

As usual, she isn't really listening to me, and I feel like saying, 'I've touched every secret place on Nathan's body.' With me, for me, he gets an erection that is so hard he says it's painful. He likes me to suck his nipples, which I do though it's vaguely embarrassing, and dig my fingers into his small, tight behind while he's having one of his teeth-gritting, tormented orgasms. But of course, I don't tell. It's none of her business anyway.

I take a small sip of the brandy. On top of the beer I managed to swallow, I start getting slightly tipsy. 'You've shown me the tape three or four hundred times.'

She laughs deep in the back of her throat, a rich and moody laugh. 'Well, Vincent can be like that. Very dirty and a little mean. But he has this completely different side. High-minded really. I thought he'd become a judge and write great opinions about civil liberties. Or play a judge on TV, something. Ha. Things turn out smaller, don't they, smaller than you imagine. What did you think of the son?'

'Very attractive, like his father. Not as dark, though.'

An open expression on her face, she looks directly into my eyes. 'Doesn't he look like Maurice?'

And so he does. That's why he looked familiar. 'Somewhat. Not that close, though.' Evading, I lead her on.

'Well, Vincent could be Maurice's father. I started screwing him again a few months after I got married. In California. Isn't that disgusting?' The way she just spits this out takes me aback. Her hostility and self-loathing. A queer smile plays on her lips when she sees my reaction.

I do think it's disgusting, so I don't say a word. And it's not the sex, it's the level, the horror of the betrayal. The infidelity of the long-married is another thing entirely. Dignified in its own way.

'And the second we're alone, I'll start fucking him again. I don't care.' Immediately, she contradicts herself. 'I've got to get away from him, Julia. How can I if he starts living here?'

What a strange mixture of defiance, self-hatred and surrender.

'It's none of my business, Moira,' I whisper.

'Oh yes it is, you live to find these things out. It's your whole purpose in life,' she bursts out.

Stung, my spine arching, I throw my shoulders back. 'Definitely. I was hoping to get the carnal details as a matter of fact.'

'Well, he has a really thick one, not that long, and when he comes his eyes roll back into his head like he's having a fit.'

I turn to stone, stare straight ahead, but naturally I am glad to find out all about it. I know more than Nathan now, knowledge my sharpest weapon against his cool indifference. Nathan with his dark blade of a face and his clinical gaze. What do we talk about but Moira and Maurice?

Still, there are the random compliments.

You could have been a real historian, Julia. You've got a nice little ass, Julia. Nobody knows how funny you are, Julia. Moira could never read people the way you do, Julia. Moira always spit it out in a tissue. (Thank you for sharing that with me.) You're so much more rational than Moira. (I am the Flower Queen's antithesis.) Moira used more curry. Moira likes mindless situation comedies. Moira never gets constipated. (I was particularly pleased to hear that one.)

Mercurial, Moira puts her arms around my neck and kisses me on the cheek. 'Oh, Julia, I'm so sorry, I didn't mean that, please forget it. Please.'

Now I know I can get everything out of her. 'You never stopped seeing him, did you?'

She shrugs. 'Almost never. Except for the last few years. And for a while when he was married.'

'But then, too?'

She offers me another sip of brandy, and when I refuse, she takes another long swallow. Yet she seems as sober as I've ever seen her. 'Then too. So what? We'll all be fertilizer soon anyway. Yeah, when he was married. I used to go down to the city for the gift show or some of the conventions at Javits. I'd stay at the Howard Johnson just over the George Washington Bridge. It was convenient. He could zip up and back. Do you know what Nathan told me?'

I'm startled to hear Nathan's name, and in a brief moment of panic I think she is about to confront me. 'What?'

'Maurice had a shrimp fork with him. He took out that man's eyes with it.'

'What?' I have heard her every word. 'What man?'

'The derelict under the bridge. He was a street alkie. Imagine that? When they found Maurice in Syracuse he was living under the bridge . . . maybe with this man, we could never tell, or maybe the corpse of this man. During the day it got above freezing and the body . . . the man was wearing a jean jacket buttoned up to the neck, and after the body started getting rotten and blew up . . . inflated . . . the detective said to Nathan that when he found it he could hear the denim ripping. Wasn't that nice of Nathan to lay that on me?'

'The eyes, that sounds a bit far-fetched.'

'I know, but they found the man's eyes in Maurice's knapsack, in one of those small zipper compartments. Dried up, I suppose. Like winter grapes. He had a calculator in there. You know he loves numbers.'

At this my craving to know turns in on itself, nauseating me. This is the unspeakable act which Nathan has been hinting at for a long time. There is nothing to say or do but look at the still water and let the horror seep into my pores. How she can stand knowing her own child did something like this I cannot fathom. I'd never be able to stop thinking about it. I'd never be able to pick up a fork again.

A palpable sadness falls over us, and for a while I just hold her hand as she quietly weeps. I am grateful for her agony and even, in moments like this, sense it as my own.

My boys are so mundane, so effortlessly normal, my life so littered with small dissatisfactions, my rare spats with O'Bannon so petty, that I feel numb half the time. It is Maurice, Nathan and Moira I worry about, their anxieties and terrors reflected, however faintly, in my own mind.

Again she tilts the small bottle to her lips, then lights another cigarette. Shaky smoke rings drift from her lips. I always thought Maurice looked like Nathan, but now I see his pinched, haunted face in a new, burning light. Entirely unto itself.

'Oh, I'm sorry, Moira. I don't know what to say.' The small thrill of words that may even be true. The pleasures of self-analysis are beyond words.

'You know, when I started going back to Vincent in California I'd always forget my diaphragm. I mean, it seemed too calculating to take it along, as if I intended to do what I knew I shouldn't do. So I'd trick myself into thinking it wouldn't happen at all. Or if it happened, it would be so spontaneous that it would be impossible to stop it. It would be out of my hands. It wouldn't be my fault. Do you know what I mean?'

'There was a competition for spontaneity then, wasn't there?'

'A demolition derby is more like it.' Her voice takes on a hard-bitten quality. 'But I always remembered to get the jelly when Nathan came on to me. Like clockwork I'd remember to go to the john and stick that stupid piece of rubber up.'

Now I know almost everything. A dizzy excitement takes hold of me. I'm hot and giddy as her secrets go down inside of me. But I can't help pushing her further, as far as she'll go. 'Does Vincent know?'

'Oh, I think he knows, but he doesn't want to know. I never told him. It seemed like the right thing to do at the time. Keep it to myself. Anyway, it's different for men. They miss all the fun of having a baby's head rip their cunts apart. The babies are ours, not theirs.'

I am drunk now, too, starting to lose my restraint. 'Why did you keep it up all those years, I don't understand.'

'Fuck you, Julia. After you get everything, you want more. If I knew, I'd be a different person.'

Her outburst sears me, but I refuse to show the slightest vestige of anger. I won't let her intimidate me. 'It's just a mystery to me.'

With her boot heel, she grinds her cigarette into the stony shore. 'One time he called me from California and I was in bed with this guy, before Nathan and I were separated, in bed with this stranger who was all ribs, it was wretched, and he's lying next to me while Nathan's at the bank and the kids are at school, and I hear Vincent's voice on the phone from three thousand miles away, just his voice, and it was as if I went into a trance. I put on my clothes and drove to the airport and took one of those propeller planes out of Albany to Kennedy and then I flew all night and ended up in his bed in San Francisco. He had a flat on Portrero Hill then. There was this strange smell from some factory and the air smelled like chemicals and fish. It was as if I was completely deranged. It wasn't romantic. It was like a compulsion. I didn't want to do it. The whole time I was worried about the kids.'

'It hardly sounds like you.'

'That frightened me. Really scared the shit out of me. But most of the time it was more as if Vincent and I were married, and I was having a rocky affair with Nathan. I knew Vincent longer than anybody, he knows about my whole life. He's my family. We didn't even always have sex, but even then we were lovers. Because if we went to dinner it always felt like a date. Don't I sound like a woman's magazine? But I'd have to look good for him, I'd feel this nervous excitement with him. And I'd be so interested in his life, what his cases were. He had this pollution case in the South Bronx ten years ago. He did it *pro bono*, and I don't think it's settled yet. Don't you think Lonnie looked like Maurice?'

'Somewhat. A bit.'

'He looked like the sane version. I'm so afraid of him, Julia, he's still supposed to come over on weekends. How can I live with him anymore?'

How can I live without telling? How can I live if I do?

# CHAPTER TWENTY-THREE: MOIRA

## Saturday: February 27, 1990: 4:20 p.m.

'Don't worry, honey. Warner will fix it. He does nice work.'

'What if the whole thing falls out?' She fingers the front tooth. 'It's so loose.'

Maurice herds us into the barn. It's so odd. I am outside my body looking at my body as it puts one foot in front of another. The eyes in the head of this body search for the troopers, but they must still be out front in the yard. Locked shut, my jaw grinds my worn-away teeth. What was it the dentist said? 'Lotsa mileage on those molars, Mrs Coleman. Lotsa mileage.'

Why did I keep Nathan's name? I loved his pure black eyes and his chin. Oh, God, Nathan's chin is gone. On the pond, it's true, the shots, don't think. The California Nathan with his Jewish Afro, who I loved and didn't. Did for a time. Can't think about it. Crissie.

I wrap myself around poor Crissie, wishing I could lick all the blood from her bleeding mouth. She is crying, wiping blood with the back of her hand, and I feel so helpless. Don't.

Crissie. In a mantra I run through the names of wildflowers. Wood Lily. Pinesap. Calypso. Wild Columbine. Pink Lady's Slipper. Crested Dwarf Iris. Passion Flower. Painted Trillium. Dutchman's Breeches. I wrap myself around Crissie, and I wrap the sounds of wildflowers around myself.

In the distance sirens whoop and burp.

I wonder if I should shout for help, but I'm afraid to incite Maurice. No, not Maurice, the Shell. My mind outside my mind finds this helpful. If we die we will be killed by the Shell, not my son, not her brother.

I can't hate my own child the way I hate the Shell.

'Hurry!' The gun pokes me hard in my kidneys. The Shell speaks. 'Get inside!'

'Mom, mommy,' Crissie sobs. I stroke her head, pull her deeper inside my body.

We enter solid blackness. Could we run, dissolve in the dark? But suddenly the Shell switches the lights on. But peeking over my shoulder, I can't deny what I see. An ordinary boy, a shade pale, death twitching in his hand.

Foxglove. Spicebush. Spotted Wintergreen.

The barn is antiseptically clean, a pair of new western saddles hung over a railing. So new there is something obscene about them. The Gaiters board their four horses for eight months of the year in Swallow, outside of Tuscarora. How did they make all that money? Nathan once told me it had something to do with chemicals, but I can't remember which ones. I shouldn't think of Nathan. Erased Nathan who can't be erased. He is woven too tightly into every thought in my mind. Nathan wouldn't approve, Nathan would think, Nathan would explain, Nathan would protect, Nathan would cut down, Nathan would be hard to kill, Nathan would not die, would he? I shut it off. Go cold.

'Be quiet, mom!' Maurice hisses.

I don't even know I've been talking to myself. Frightening. Or has Maurice reached that stage? Remember what Dr Greenberg said: 'Demystify the illness. Think of it as diabetes or high blood pressure with certain predictable symptoms.'

Why is this impossible? Seething hatred of the Shell boils up in me.

'Get into the stall! Go ahead. Two moo cows in the stall!'

We follow his command, huddle, shivering against the beaten slats. Totally still, the barn is stone-cold. What would Nathan do in this situation? He would say, 'Let's look at the alternatives. What's the most productive strategy?' But even my mind outside my mind is paralyzed. All I can think of is rushing Maurice blindly, flinging myself on him, just ripping him apart so Crissie can escape. But would she? Responsible Crissie who went into a fury when her twelve year-old girlfriends giggled behind Maurice's back, who stroked his head and called him 'Moccorico'. That was it. Moccorico.

'We have to do something, mom,' she whispers. Even though she is shivering, a sheen of cold sweat on her forehead, she is gathering herself. With the back of her hand she smears blood, rubs it in, a runny crescent forming on her cheek. In the depths of my coat pocket I find an old tissue, reach out and pat the stain away. Almost. She breathes deeper and deeper, trying to gain control. We hold fast to each other, swathed in our sweaters, sweat-shirts and winter coats.

'We will, let's watch him first,' I say, flooded with irrational hope. 'Let's see what he does.'

'What're you saying? Be quiet!' he roars, stepping towards us. 'Stop staring!'

Certain predictable symptoms? But only Maurice believes the stars are the eyes of the universe and every one of them is trained on him.

'Nothing, honey, what do you want? Why don't you let Crissie go? I'll stay with you.' The wispy voice that comes out of me is the voice of another creature, but I'm amazed it comes out at all.

'Maybe. Maybe later.' Under the dim bulb, his black, silky hood pulled back, he looks cunning and far too sane. 'Who's my real father, mom? Huh? Who's the real one?'

Is there an answer to this question, one that won't set him off? 'Nathan raised you. Who would you like it to be?'

'My real father is Max Planck. He invented quantum mechanics. No, no, he's too old. Was Max Planck dead before I was born?'

'I don't know, honey.'

He starts marching up and back in front of the stall, getting more and more agitated. In his gesturing hand the gun points to the ground, straight ahead, fleetingly at us, up to the rafters. Barely attached to his hand, the dark weapon spins in the air.

Again the barrel sails in our direction and instinctively we curl up, press against each other.

The explosion of shots cuts through me, and I'm certain I've been riddled with bullets. But I don't feel a thing. Like a hen I scramble to sit on top of Crissie. We topple over in a heap. I peek. Maurice has shot holes in the roof.

Calmly, he reloads.

Crissie quakes next to me, gasping, weeping uncontrollably. I help her up, shake her shoulders. Terror has overcome her now, her whole frame trembling. Again, blood pours freely from the corner of her mouth. I shake and shake her, a raging intolerance welling up in me.

'Go cold! Go cold!' I slap her, long searing slaps across her cheek. Going cold, our only hope. I am at the bottom of myself.

Bleary-eyed she gazes at me, unable to understand.

'Go cold!' I slap her one more time, as hard as I can. 'Go cold!'

Nodding her head, she tries to suppress her sobs. Slowly they subside.

Pacing up and back, Maurice shouts, 'Who is he, mom? Who is he?'

'A lawyer, a nice man. You'd like him.' If he thinks his father is alive, maybe what he did to Nathan will change. It won't be so terrible. Or is this desperate logic? Racing thoughts.

'What're you talking about, mom?' Crissie disentangles herself from me.

'Shhhh, don't worry. Wipe your face. I'll say whatever he wants.'

'Well, let's call him up, he can join the party. Is there a phone around here?'

'We could go back to the house and make the call.' Standing again, my feet feel the flat earth. I breathe and breathe and breathe.

Suddenly, a harsh, amplified voice from nowhere barks at us: '. . . quietly with your hands up. You're completely surrounded, there is no way out. Surrender any firearms or weapons of any kind and come out peaceably. Surrender any firearms and come out peaceably.'

Brilliant light slashes through a crack between the barn doors. These squawking orders will set him off for sure. Every drop of air squeezes out of me. My heart beats like crazy. Hummingbird wings in my chest.

'If you have any hostages, release them now. Then surrender any firearms or weapons of any kind and come out peaceably.'

Forgetting us, Maurice races to the doors and peers out. Without thinking I grab Crissie's hand and rush to the back, the depths of the barn, hoping there is a way we can scuttle out. Instead, we plunge deeper into darkness. Madly I pat the walls to see if there is a side exit. A splinter pierces my finger, but I barely feel it. There must be a door. Desperate, I tap, grope, trace the rough boards with my palms. Nothing, nothing, nothing.

I am a cornered animal. I claw at the wall, rip it with my

fingernails. Magically, my fingers find a door frame. Groping, I discover the shape of the door knob in my hand. With every ounce of animal strength in me I grip it and turn, wrench it up and back, yank it towards me. Senselessly. Somehow it is jammed, jammed or locked or nailed shut, but in the blackness I can't see how. I fumble for a latch or bar, my eyes adjusting to the gloom, but all I feel is rough, splintery board under my fingers, against my palms.

Dizzy with fear, I realize we've made a fatal mistake. Our rush to escape will only anger him. He'll shoot us as soon as he sees us scuttling back to the light. But we must. Choking on fear, I crush Crissie's hand and drag her back out of the blackness. Underfoot, the barn floor is smooth as kitchen tiles. A downstate floor in a downstater barn. Crissie and I are one gasping animal, leaping in fear for the light.

As we approach the stall, Maurice gets off more gunfire, and we freeze in mid-flight. Fall. Birds shredded with shot. He's killed wild turkeys with Nathan's shot gun, why not us? I wait for the cold metal to penetrate my skull, I wait for pure emptiness, I die without dying.

He's still at the barn door. Crissie is still clutching my hand. Crouching, racing, we make it back to our haven, though I can't say why we've returned. It's so hard to think at all.

His face is the color of bleached flour. 'Come on, come on, I gotta show both of you to them. They don't believe me. Say I'm armed and dangerous. Tell them to stop watching me.'

Armed and dangerous, it doesn't begin to describe what he is, but he wants me to say it. He puts the barrel of the gun up against Crissie's temple and we walk, still attached, crab-like towards the slit of light.

Outside, blinded by floodlights, gasping, I get the words out.

Behind the brilliant light the voice speaks. 'Easy young fella. Who you got there, mom and sis?'

'Stay back! Where are you?' Maurice ducks his head, squints. Like us he can see nothing.

Then a man steps before the burning floodlights. Hatless, he is wearing civilian clothes, a leather jacket. For some reason this irritates me, as if without his broad-brimmed smokey's hat he will not convince Maurice he is real. In his hand is a cell phone, which he holds out like a peace offering.

He keeps walking, walking right up to us, and I am certain Maurice will shoot his eyes out.

'Here I am. I'm Officer Montgomery.' His cheeks are spattered with a rosy pattern of broken blood vessels. What's the name of that disease alcoholics get? Roseate something. Can't remember.

A strange sensation. The cold nose of the wretched gun pressing against the base of my neck.

'I want some walnuts and V-8. Can we get a pizza? No anchovies. I hate anchovies. Shelled walnuts.'

'Sure, whatever you want, Maurice. Why not let the ladies go, and we'll get you whatever you say.'

'What's his name, mom? What's his name?'

The gun barrel pushes deep into my rigid neck, and I notice I am crying. Just a few tears, though. I have nothing left. 'Who, honey? Who?'

'The man you were talking about. I want him to come down.'

'I don't know—'

His voice rises to the whine of a petulant teenager. 'You know, the lawyer! Who is it?'

'Vincent. Vincent Vitale. He may not be around, Maurice. He may be down in the city.' My first thought – ludicrous but true – I don't want Vincent to see me this way. All puffed up, my face must be the size of a watermelon. But to see Vincent one more time before . . . My knees cave in, but I grit my teeth, fight the swoon. I hang on to Crissie, who, feeling me go weak, stiffens, holding me up.

'Ma, mommy!'

'Call Vincent Vitale,' Maurice shouts, mispronouncing Vince's last name.

'Sure, we'll get him for you. Does he live around here?'

'I remember him. He was in my house. How about some Genny Pale Ale? A six-pack?'

'No, no, no booze. We've got to talk. Give me a minute, I'll order the food. Sure you don't want to let your sister go? That would help everybody. She'll be grateful to you, won't you, Cris? It'll make it better for you, too Maurice, better all around.'

Maurice ignores this quiet request as if he never heard it. 'Get me some shelled walnuts. Oh, and a deck of cards. Okay?'

Out of his back pocket Montgomery produces a second cell phone. 'How bout something to drink. Sodas?'

'Yeah, drinks. Mom likes Sprite, it doesn't have caffeine. Crissie, what do you want?'

'Dr Pepper?'

'You call us if you need anything else,' Montgomery says, edging closer, the phone in his outstretched hand. 'You're feeling bad, call us. Anything bothering you, call us. Anything at all. We want to help you. We've got a direct line. Just turn it on. Press the button. See?' He demonstrates. 'We're here to help you and get this thing to turn out right. Nobody gets hurt, okay? Unless you want to relax, come over to the house now. Nobody'll hurt you.'

Maurice just turns his back.

In the frigid barn I retie the knot of Crissie's hood. Somewhere along the way she's lost her ski gloves.

When the pizza shows up, it's actually hot. I'm astonished to discover that I have an appetite. Embarrassed, actually, especially after Crissie refuses to eat. 'C'mon, sweetie. Just one slice. We've got to keep up our strength.'

'I'll throw up, mom.' Her thick hair a curtain over half her face, she squats in the corner of the stall. 'How can you eat anything?'

I recoil at her disgust for me. It's deep, I know, but what am I supposed to do? Get so weak I faint?

'I don't know.' Chewing Avenoso's extra thick crust with intense pleasure, I wonder, How can I do it?

But the food gives me strength and strength ignites my hatred.

Maurice passes the time marching up and down the aisle, eating shelled walnuts, scattering handfuls, muttering to himself, checking on us every minute or so. Once or twice he starts to say something, then thinks better of it, turning on his heel and marching away again. Just when I'm catching my breath, suddenly, he bursts in, a look of mad excitement on his face.

'I've got an idea. Let's play cards.'

Cards are a good idea. Games keep him on an even keel. 'Good idea. What would you like to play?'

'Strip poker. Me and Crissie.'

'I'd rather die! I don't care!'

'No, you wouldn't. She'll play, Maurice, if you really want to. But it's freezing in here. And she's upset, isn't she? You don't want to play if she's upset, do you?'

But he appears not to hear me. His voice takes on that manic note I fear most. 'Deuces wild! You know what dad always says? Transfer fun! He has the right idea, we should listen to him more.'

What is he talking about? A chill runs through me. Waves of cold nausea. I try to beat back the thought, but it rises to the surface. If he doesn't know what he did to Nathan, he won't know what he's doing to us.

It's too grotesque, I can't allow it. Crissie will be sickened and humiliated beyond imagination. Then it occurs to me, disgusting as it is, that Maurice might get turned on in the course of the game, and I could get the upper hand, take the gun away from him, something. 'Maybe it's a good idea, Crissie. We'll have some fun.'

Catching my eye, Crissie seems to understand what I'm after. Visibly swallowing her disgust, she says, quietly, 'Yeah, okay. Maybe it'll be fun.'

A suspicious look crosses Maurice's face. Ingenious, he senses a trap in my cooperation. 'Naa, how about hearts? You remember how to play, Cris?'

Squatting just out of reach, he tears the cellophone off the package of cards. I try to calculate how far I can lunge, but I see myself falling far short of him, my body twitching in the gunfire. God, I don't want to die. My hatred of the Shell concentrates until I am nothing but a skinful of venom.

'Yeah, sure,' she says, barely above a whisper.

We play a few hands before he gets distracted again. Scooping up the cards he withdraws to the aisle, muttering and casting furtive glances at us. Everything slows down and lasts forever, every second. Despite herself, exhausted, Crissie starts to doze off, but I will never sleep again. I'm afraid I want to live too much.

I want to live, the craving is beyond imagination, but I want her to live more. I'll let him kill me to save her. The truth of this stuns me. I won't let her die before she lives, no matter what, I feel it in every fiber of my being, and the conviction makes me feel stronger. Maybe Nathan was wrong all along about me. Or I'm not what I thought I was.

Half the night Maurice marches up and down the aisle between the stalls. But he keeps returning and squatting near us, muttering in an angry whisper. I think he's running all of my crimes against him through his mind over and over, and every time he lifts the gun and scowls at me, a fresh wave of terror seizes me. But I'm so exhausted even fear has become a dull and distant feeling.

How Crissie sleeps I can't fathom. The cold is so penetrating, even in the stillness of the barn.

In this state Maurice can stay up half the night. If he would only sleep I could tear into him. A savage thing is growing in me, begging to escape. I'm so afraid and so filled with rage at the same time, I can barely contain myself. All I can do is think of my daughter. Every second.

At dawn the cell phone rings, Crissie jerking in my arms. Stunned, I realize I've finally fallen asleep too, at least for a few minutes.

'Coffee, momsie? They've got Egg McMuffins if you want. Cris, you want donuts?'

His voice is maddeningly perky, but the dark stubble on his emaciated face gives him a menacing look. 'Lookit this. Two space heaters! I asked for them!'

He drops the metal boxes at my feet and returns hauling a long extension cord with an adapter at the end of the wire. I plug both of them in and place them at our feet, but even waves of electric heat can't seem to penetrate the barn's solid cold.

Silent, sullen, even Crissie eats now. Unable to control myself, I devour my McMuffin in two bites and pour coffee down my gullet.

Only then do I hear Maurice dictating his will. He seems to believe that Vincent is on the other end of the line, but I don't. They must be tricking him. How would he know, anyway?

'It's warmer anyway,' Crissie says, holding her hands over the space heaters. A wan smile flutters on her lips.

Taking both of her hands I rub them, kiss them. 'We'll get out, I know it.'

'Sure we will, mom.'

I can't tell whether she's being slightly sarcastic or trying to comfort me. Either way she's getting her courage back.

'All toasty now?' Maurice says, his pistol in one hand, the cards in another. The perfect host.

'Sure. Great. Thanks a lot.' Surreptitiously, she squeezes my hand. Hope. I will myself to feel it. Perhaps, together, we can overcome him. I know I can risk it, I even want it. I see him shooting me over and over as Crissie goes through the barn doors, and seeing it I'm elevated, passing into an ethereal calm.

'A lot warmer, huh?'

'Definitely.'

'So how bout some strip poker?'

Crissie gets that sick look on her face again. 'Let's play hearts, that'll be more interesting.'

'Dad says transfer fun. Strip poker or nothing,' he says, his voice hardening. With his grubby, two day beard, he looks more and more like a terrorist. He is a Shell. A terrorist. Not Maurice.

'How about regular poker? You're good at that, honey. Remember how you used to beat the computer?'

'Butt out, mom. This is our game. We used to play, remember, Cris?'

'I was six then, Maurice. It's different now.' Her voice quivers, but she holds her own.

Ignoring her, he pulls his sweatshirt over his head. 'I'll start. Pick a card, any card.'

'You don't—'

But Crissie cuts me off. 'It's okay, mom. I mean, what's the difference?' She lifts the deck. 'Seven.'

'Lucky number, lucky number. And I get . . . four! My turn again! I'll give you my . . . rubber bootie . . .'

He loses again. 'How bout my socks? I'll put my feet in the electric fire.'

In an unspoken understanding now, we know what to do. We watch him intently, seeing if he gets tangled up or puts the gun down. But he sticks the weapon between his legs as he unties his duck boot, eyeing us all the while. Briefly, Crissie and I make eye contact. We're going to do something soon, something desperate. My blood pounds in my ears.

In the next round, Crissie loses. 'I'll give you my coat.'

'Do you still have that mole? Don't tell! Don't tell! Whoops, lost my belt.'

'Which mole, Moccorico?' I haven't heard her say it for

years, that strange childhood name, and I'm oddly embarrassed to hear it. Her voice drops low, seductive. I catch her eye and nod.

'The one your boyfriend licks. Likes, I mean. Don't tell, don't tell. I have a girlfriend, too. You don't know her, but she went to high school with me. We're getting married. Hey, pick a card, pick a card. You're not playing!'

'I'm playing.' She turns over a card. 'Look, I lost. What should I take off?'

'Uhhh, your boots. Put your feet near the heater.' He wiggles his own bare toes. 'It feels good.'

Maurice draws a deuce. 'My turn. I think I'll give up . . . my sweater. Remember when you used to lose a hand and take off a barrette? That wasn't fair. I always wanted to see your friend Laurie. What does she look like now?'

'She lives in Florida. I'm not sure.'

'She's very pretty, Maurice. I saw a picture of her,' I say softly, entering his childhood, too. But this is dangerous because I want to think of the Shell, not the Monkey Boy. The Monkey Boy makes me ache inside my bones.

When he has to take off a garment now, Maurice puts the gun on the floor behind him, still out of reach. He is mad, but far, far from stupid. I rise to a squatting position, bounce on my toes, the muscles in my thighs tightening.

'Who else do you think is pretty, Mocco? Any of my friends?' Crissie asks. Our eyes meet again and I nod.

But all of a sudden he gets flustered. 'Don't ask me about them! Play the game! Don't tell! Pick a card!' His brilliant black eyes focus directly on Crissie again. My stomach turns at what he may want.

Now Crissie starts losing one draw after another. Heavily layered, she sheds her white Irish wool cable-knit and then the black turtleneck underneath. Beneath that she's wearing her World Wildlife Fund t-shirt with the panda on it.

I grope for something to say, but I don't want to set him off.

Crissie draws a king to Maurice's Jack, and he's forced to pull off his black jeans. Stick-thin, his bony knees appear pointed. He clacks them together over and over, in brief flashes revealing his stained jockey shorts. I'm unnaturally calm and clinical. At first I'm not sure, but then I can see it clearly. The outlines of a teenager's skinny hard-on.

I slip towards him on my behind in tiny increments.

Her legs naked, Crissie shivers in her t-shirt, the panda rising and falling on her chest as she gasps for breath. Then she loses her t-shirt as well, exposing her black sports bra. She prefers these because they crush her breasts against her chest, helping to hide them. A rim of baby fat peeks over the waist-band of her black panties. No wonder she's been complaining about her weight. I never took her seriously.

I blink. The panties are mine. She's been in my bureau again.

Maurice draws a three of clubs and in a flash pulls his rugby shirt over his head. In that moment I edge closer still, but not in time to grab the weapon which he places, for a heart stopping second, behind him. His chest is a bird cage, his skin so white it glows blue. His legs jiggle, he bounces up and down on his ass. In his excitement his thin lips suck inward, disappearing.

As I slide closer, the circle of three contracts. I can almost touch him now. My calmness glows inside me. I'll do anything to keep her alive, I don't care.

Crissie draws a six of diamonds to his seven of hearts. She brushes her hair back, squares her shoulders, and stares right at me, as if Maurice weren't there. 'Do you want to see, Mocco?' she asks quietly.

Speechless, he nods.

With a shrug, she reaches behind herself and releases her heavy breasts. Maurice gasps. His fascinated eyes grow wide. I have enough time to see his fingers loosen on the pistol as her breasts fall.

'Tell mom what you did,' she spits suddenly.

'Don't tell, don't tell!' Cat-like, he pounces at her. An unnatural howl comes out of him, so piercing it hurts.

For a blind moment I am concentrated rage. In a fury I fall on him, blocking his leap, and tear the gun from his loose hand. I am growling, kicking, punching, driven by a powerful rush of adrenaline. But he is so angry and so strong he shoves me down, flattens me, my head banging against the stone floor. Breathless, I hear a dull ringing sound inside my skull and I black out for a second. Only the animal noise in my throat keeps me from passing out entirely, a growl I can't believe I'm making. I vibrate with a rage to stay alive.

Twisting under him, I cling to the pistol, but he grabs my shoulders and pounds me against the floor one more time. With my last ounce of strength I knock the gun and both our hands on the cold stone and bite his wrist as hard as I can. I'd bite right through an artery if I could.

'Yow! Mom, why'd you do that?' Leaping to his feet, he looks with disbelief at the wound.

The pistol slides a few feet out of his reach.

'Mocco! Mocco! Look! Kangaroo's pouch! Kangaroo's pouch!' Crissie shouts. Above us she spins around, stark naked, food for his starving eyes. She's hopping, kicking, dancing around. She's taken off everything, and in an instant I understand how sickening it is for her. Her eyes are glassy as she spins and spins, showing herself off.

Her beauty stuns him for the smallest fraction of a second, but in an instant, he leaps towards her, grabbing her neck. They roll across the stone floor, wrestling, flailing, but for a split second she gets the upper hand, mounting him and smashing him hard in the face. Tangled, they're like lovers tearing each other apart. The cat yowl pours out of him again, he pulls his arm way back and punches her as hard as he can, right in her eye. Clutching her face in both hands, she falls off of him, and before I can do anything he's on top now, both hands around her skull.

He pounds her head against the cement floor over and over. The sickening sound of bone cracking. This can't be happening, it is happening. One terrible cry and she goes silent, her body limp. Still, he keeps banging her battered skull against the cement floor. He'll keep pounding it forever if I don't stop him. I'm ready to die, yet so calm I can't believe it.

I scramble to my feet, and get a strong grip on the heavy automatic, feeling the tension of the trigger. It's more difficult to pull than I expected. I'll have to squeeze hard, but my hands are strong and I'm fully aware of what I'm doing. I'm not excited, I'm not afraid as I aim with unbelievable care right for the back of his head. But my right finger won't move. Now I put my left hand on the weapon, and my left finger on the trigger. But my hands won't listen to my mind.

The gun weighs so much it starts to droop, even as I jerk my arms to hold it up.

Maurice, the Shell, drags himself to his feet. Down to his jockey shorts he is so white he makes my eyes ache. I am the still point in the storm, aware of Crissie's lifeless body in a pile at my feet. She is dead now, and I want to shoot my son. Going cold, I know what I'm trying to do. I won't lie to myself at least.

The muscles in my arms ache; my hands aren't attached to them. If only I could make my fingers work. Then the gun explodes on its own, the recoil knocking me back, the bullet ripping harmlessly through the wall.

Maurice springs from Crissie's body and backs away, cowering. 'Don't shoot, mom! I didn't mean anything!'

She means nothing? How despicable. She means everything. Cold rage wipes out every thought, every feeling. Calculating cold rage.

He turns his back and races towards the crack of light between the barn doors. No thinking. After all this torture, just reactions. Rushing after him, I crouch and squeeze the trigger. With two hands it's easy now. Aiming low this time, I know what I'm doing. I'm killing my son. The Monkey Boy. I'm shooting him in the back. One, two, three shots. The Monkey Boy. He's defenseless. The Monkey Boy. A thousand bullets fly from the black gun and I fall back, stumbling over Crissie's body. It doesn't move. It. She. This is happening, it isn't happening. I'm so calm it's excruciating. A siren whoops but it's far away. My head is stuffed with cotton.

# CHAPTER TWENTY-FOUR: VINCE

## Sunday: February 28, 1990: 9:55 a.m.

'You stay put, Mr Vitale. We'll tell you when we need you.'

Maurice digs into the snow bank, his skinny ass in the air. If I blink he disappears, and all I can see are snow-covered fields. Blink again and his scrawny legs flail away. It takes a fucking century for the troopers to slog across the pasture in their heavy boots. Finally giving up, Maurice collapses in the snow, his head and shoulders reappear, and he raises a scrawny arm like he's protecting himself from bullets. Moving forward at a creeping pace, the troopers surround him. I think I hear him crying, but it could be anything. A screech on a two-way radio. A truck signaling it's backing up. A beeper going crazy.

Montgomery spins me around and aims me back at the house. Grateful, I follow his orders. I don't really want to see what's inside the barn. The kitchen is the safe place. There have been too many shots during the siege to entertain any hope. Anyway, I can imagine what's inside without having to see it with my own eyes.

Instead, I focus on Moira doing a twisty step at a Mongo Santa Maria concert at the Avenue D projects. Lower East Side July sunlight blasts down on her. She's so hot herself that the Spanish guys in strapped t-shirts have their mouths hanging open. In a Motel Six outside New Paltz she does Patti LaBelle, dancing and holding a pair of miniature soap cakes against her nipples. It's all a jumble. Moira drinking cheap Portuguese wine and laughing in my Berkeley kitchen while I cook some dog food I call a *paella,* Moira singing *A Foggy Day* in her croak-perfect Louie Armstrong imitation, Moira finding used condoms on top of a closet in our cheap Barcelona hotel and laughing and throwing the dried-up rubbers at my head.

I push open the door to her freezing upstate bedroom and she's standing on her bed, looking beautiful and beaten. Maybe it's that slightly flat nose of hers, or her puffy face, but she looks like she's gone more than a few rounds with a heavy hitter. Somehow, though, it just makes her more magnetic. In her cracked alto she sings again:

We come, we go
Just like ripples on a stream

There were shreds of chicken and black beans on the end of a fork. I could smell the bug spray in the *comida criollas* and the blinking fluorescent light was giving me a headache. I could have said, 'Don't say no. The license is running out. No hidden agendas.'

But why was I so sure she'd ruin me?

'I don't feel as if you mean it, I don't know why,' she said.

She was trying to save us by keeping us apart, and for a second I wanted to marry her more than anything. 'What can I say, what do you want me to say?'

'This . . .' She picked up a bottle of hot sauce and gestured towards the rows of formica tables. 'It'll never be this romantic, honey,' she laughed. 'Now I can't resent you for not taking care of the kids. I like not resenting you.'

I tried to frame an argument but gave up before the tinny words left my lips.

Instead I started talking about the beautiful Afghani girl who came to my office with two perfect black eyes. Her ex-boyfriend had climbed in her window in the middle of the night and raped her, as far as I could tell, but she was afraid to go to the police. I talked about the case as if my life depended on it.

Memories and rage mix inside me like a poisoned cocktail. I've got to get out. I pass through the kitchen into the living room, turn the doorknob and I am in the front yard where the police are bumping into each other like lost livestock. Why should I stay? Why should I have to witness a sickening scene I have no stomach for? Won't the permanent disappearance of Moira be enough? That faint presence dead people leave behind. My mother left a handful of fake pearls, pop beads and cheap watches. Joe the Barber's estate added up to a two-bit policy, Army discharge papers and a baptismal certificate. His surgical shoes still held the shape of his feet a year after he was dead. Why should I have to witness Moira's fucked-up parka, her winter wools, and her last ski socks? Slipping and sliding in the muddy slush, I make my way to Mackey's patrol car and sink into the beat-up front seat.

At the same time I'm in the North Beach Café when she took a match to our first marriage license. The day, a decade later, when the second license expired, both of us too cool to even mention it. Instead, we went out to see *Dog Day Afternoon* at the Carnegie, the revival house around the corner from the recital hall. Afterwards, we ate Indian food on East Sixth Street, lamb sag and lamb kurma. The food was dirt in my mouth.

We both knew the date, but we never mentioned it. We took a cab to Puffy's in Tribeca where Paul, the smooth, silver-haired bartender served us vodka martinis with a twist. On stools at the counter we set up our drinks and stared out at the street where a very thin, very drunk man pissed against a loft building. In the window I watched a reflection of Moira's broad, perfectly expressionless face. At midnight the license died, but we were too cool to say a word about its demise.

I had just settled a pair of whiplash cases and was getting a nice reputation for the spinal cord in lawyers' joints up and down Montague Street. Hot little paralegals in platform shoes played simple games in the backs of cabs, in Ocean Avenue walk-ups and East Flatbush basement apartments. I woke up one morning surrounded by a cat clock, a cat lamp, a cat cup, and a harem of live cats on the bed, having no idea where I was. I couldn't remember the name of the woman smoking Kools next to me.

Marriage seemed like the right thing to do, but it was far away. For Moira's coolness on the subject I was secretly grateful. Then the question faded again. All long before the Martini case, long before Janet and Lonnie and Maurice made a wicked triangle in my life. Paralyzed in the patrol car I watch our other possible lives unfold. If I had married her, if I had left the firm, if there were no Redbone Road, no schiz with a cheap semi.

This is happening, I tell myself, but it doesn't do any good. I can't get myself to believe it.

Thinking back all those years, I look as flat as a cartoon character to myself. What the fuck was I thinking, what the fuck was I doing?

Two ambulances rush past me, chugging around the house and heading for the barn, and before I can stop myself I'm sloshing through the mud, racing right behind them, vaguely aware of the icy muck leaking into my sneakers. An ambulance chaser in clown pants. By the time I plow my way around the house, two red-coated volunteers are lifting someone onto a board and fitting a collar around her neck. Bad news. Without thinking I know that it's Moira. Her red-brown hair hangs straight as string over the sides of the litter, the familiar shape of her body rolls past me. I remind myself not to hope. Hope is my enemy.

When I reach her I'm stunned. Half the woman's face is Moira's, half a bashed-in, dark bruise. Makes me think of the last eggplant in the bin. One eye is closed and swollen, the other stuck shut. Her right arm hangs loosely over the side of the backboard. Subdural hematoma? I've seen a dozen at Bellevue. I had one case, a brick fell off a building on Great Jones Street and hit this poor sonofabitch in the head, and Bellevue stuck him in a hall and forgot about him for twelve hours. He got lucky and died, otherwise he would have been a total vegetable.

Hazy, I look, force myself to gaze at the smashed-in face again and Moira fades away. This can't be Moira, this woman is years younger, I must be losing it. Sonofabitch, the kid. She could be paralyzed. Beaten simple. They've got to stop the swelling. Keep the pressure down. I hope these bozos know what they're doing. At least they have the sense to collar her.

A stretcher on wheels stands empty at the doors of the barn. Volunteers, detectives, smokies mill around. Suddenly, I realize Moira's body is inside, she's been dead for hours, a whole day. Every burst of fire, every random shot we heard, every round that Montgomery swore was pissing in the wind ripped through her head, her face, and her heart. The boy killed her over and over. No fucking doubt. They'll ask me to identify her, and I'll do my duty without looking at her. Oh, crap, looking at her corpse I couldn't stand.

A siren begins to wail. Shouts, roaring motors, clashing noises. I race towards the barn, my knees dissolve, but I shove on. Pushing my way through the knot of cops, I plunge towards the sliding barn door. No one lays a hand on me. Noises separate into voices, voices into words. Some sort of argument is going on. A volunteer has his hand on the sleeve of a tall woman who's shaking her head.

I try to plod around them when I hear my name.

'Vincent, maybe you can talk some sense to these men. I'm not getting in an ambulance. It's absolutely unnecessary.' The old intransigence is unmistakable, her calm, matter-of-fact tone completely jarring. She speaks in a peculiar, slow cadence, but no doubt it's Moira herself.

Her feet planted in a swamp of ice and mud, she refuses to move an inch. I almost say, Marry me now, right here, it will make up for everything, but the words die before they come out. Her face is a white prune. She looks a hundred years old. I know who I am and sainthood would fit me like a cheap suit.

'I murdered him, Vincent. Everyone's dead.'

Then I see it. She's in walking, talking shock. 'No, he's alive, Moira, everybody's alive.' My words gurgle out of me. Maybe I'm as wacked out as she is.

'Oh, no, no they're not. The lake, oh well . . . But it's nice of you to say so. I'm the only one alive. Why should I get into an ambulance?'

Quietly, I take her arm. The three volunteers in their red coats are all smoking and looking down at their shoes. 'How about you let her sit up front, boys? The lady's been through hell.'

No one has thought of this simple solution. A volunteer with a beard down to his chest and a manic, biker voice says, 'Hey, good idea. Sit up front with me, lady.'

I take her elbow and half lift her into the cab. Squaring her shoulders she shoots me a defiant look through the window, a look that says, I can stand anything, even this. The worst delusion of all.

'No visitors, Vince,' Connie says from behind the plastic panel.

Last year I got the county to drop a second DWI against her husband, Frank, so you'd figure I'd have some leverage. 'C'mon, Connie. She walked out of there.'

She shakes her head firmly. 'She's sedated.'

There isn't a single patient in the waiting room, typical of Sam Booth Memorial, Accordia's bankrupt hospital. The bank owns the paper but can't figure out what to do with it. Mackey looms behind me, shuffling, hacking away with his smoker's cough.

'Who's up there with her?' The air stinks of Lysol and formaldehyde. Knee-weakening hunger hits me. When was the last time I ate?

'Larry.'

'A Physician's Assistant?' Upstate medicine. I can't fucking believe it. 'You don't have a CT scan, do you? Where's Murphy?'

'It's Sunday, Vince,' Mackey puts in, laying a hand on my arm. I brush him off.

'Just for a minute?'

'You're not kin, you know that.' Connie smiles slightly, and I realize I haven't even said who I want to see.

The elevator doors clank open and Larry Nivens steps out,

a wild look on his freckled, innocent face. Too innocent. He doesn't know shit. 'Hey, Larry, what's up? Is Crissie . . .'

He frowns and doesn't meet my eyes. 'We're moving her to Tuscarora, I was just on the phone with Wallowick. We don't have the facilities to handle this.'

'Handle what? Is there bleeding? A lot of swelling?' I'm preparing for the worst now.

'Hey, Vince, let the man do his job. We ought to get out of here,' Mackey says.

'She's reacting to stimuli,' Larry says, guarded.

'Is she fixed and dilated? C'mon, I had cases. I had to study this shit myself.'

'Uh, no, not really,' he answers, so unsure of himself I figure he didn't check her pupils.

'Maybe you should look again. Where's Maurice? He here?'

'No, they sent him straight to Tuscarora. He was shot up, I heard.'

'They take the shooter to the good hospital, and they leave the vics behind?' Now Mackey is pissed off, too. 'That girl could end up brain dead if you don't watch it.'

Suddenly, Larry blows up, his white bread face flushing. 'I'm watching it, damn it! Why don't you jerks let me do my job!'

All this time I haven't noticed Julia, who has gotten off the elevator with Larry. She's wearing a big fur hat. Her head swims in it. 'Julia, did you see them?'

She nods slowly. 'In there. We can talk.'

First, I get into Larry's face one more time. 'You better get them to Tuscarora, bud, or I'll have your fucking license, understand?'

Mackey gives me a good hard shove, knocking me back on my heels. 'That's enough, Vince, he's gonna move 'em as soon as he can.'

'We're just waiting for an ALSP to ride onboard,' Larry explains.

'Now get out of here before I do something I don't wanna do.' Mackey sticks a stubby finger in my chest. I brush it away.

Blindly, I follow Julia. Off the emergency room there's an immaculate nursery. A red plastic slide. Two playpens. A Sesame Street Ernie puppet sits on a shelf. One eyebrow is torn off. We sit on low children's seats and clasp our hands.

Through a small, square window in the door I can see a fragment of the hall. Two volunteers in their red coats amble past.

'Crissie is still unconscious. Larry can't tell a thing except that she's breathing and her blood pressure's not bad.' She speaks in a flat, controlled voice. Dry, curled-up finger paintings hang on the wall behind her head. 'Enid told me this morning, Enid told me . . . Maurice . . . Nathan's dead.'

She rocks, a visible shudder running through her slender body. It's hard to explain, but when she puts her face in her hands, even when she's losing it totally, she does it with undeniable class. I reach out and touch her shoulder. What a tiny, sharp-boned shoulder.

'How would she know? Maybe it's just a rumor.'

For a while she cries softly, taking shallow gasps of air. 'Harlan saw it. He was back there . . . in his stupid snowmobile. It was really rather thoughtful of her.' Her laugh is short and bitter. 'She wanted me to know before somebody less well-intentioned told me. She wasn't sure, but some stupid fool volunteer told her. But I knew something was strange this morning.'

In my numb condition, I don't quite understand what she's getting at. I keep an eye on the blank hallway. I listen for the sound of vehicles starting up. When're they going to move them?

'You don't understand, do you?' Now she lifts her head and looks straight at me in a raw, defiant way. Not Julia at all. 'I thought Nathan and I had been so clever and careful. I forgot where I was living.'

My back aches from sitting on the miniature chair. Scrawny Julia wrapping her legs around Nathan. It seems impossible. 'Oh.' That's all that comes out of my mouth.

'I went to get O'Bannon his blueberry muffins this morning at the café, and I heard Maureen say, "He wasn't very-well liked anyway." And I had no idea what she was talking about. She had this supercilious smile on her face . . .' She starts crying again, this time full-force, but I can't break the barrier between us. Some other woman I would touch or hold in my arms, but not Julia, she would resent it, I'm sure.

Wet with snow melt, the fur hat bobs up and down.

Recovering again, she blows her nose with a tissue. 'She won't see you. I just talked to her.'

'Connie let you up?'

Standing, she smoothes her long, wool skirt. 'Maurice is your son.' There is something almost triumphant in her tone.

'What?' Outrage. As if I've never heard this before. 'On what basis?'

'Because Moira told me. A long time ago. I thought now, with Nathan . . . I don't think I'm going to get over it.' She breathes very, very deeply, reaching for her last shred of control. 'There's an empty place next to me . . .' Her arm waves stiffly.

'I'm sorry for your loss.' As soon as the words slip from my mouth, I realize I've recited the standard cop lingo.

My eyes fall on Julia's tattered, gnawed cuticles. A sharp jolt of fear hits me in the gut. It could be true, even if a lunatic and a woman crazy with grief say so. My son. Sharp hunger pangs make me feel faint. 'So you're telling me about Maurice so I can do what?'

'Do whatever you'd like. Personally, I think we all ought to look at ourselves in the mirror.'

This is bullshit. She means I ought to look at myself in the mirror. For what? For fathering this murdering lunatic? For running away from him? I'm still sitting in the kid-sized chair, looking up at her, and all of a sudden she looks very self-possessed.

But I'm not giving in to her assault. She could be making the whole thing up. She could be certifiable for all I know.

'I'm going to need a lot more than your word before I believe it. Being Maurice's father . . .' My paternity could be a fact, but no, the chances are negligible. No, not negligible. Maurice was born in New York. How many months after Moira left Berkeley? Who knows after all these years? 'It's absolutely without foundation. Moira was on the pill or something.'

Nothing like lawyer talk to make me feel secure. Then I start kicking myself. Why even admit to the relationship? I notice that I'm more shaken up than I thought.

She smiles with bitter satisfaction. 'You're an expert on birth control, too? I'm sorry, but it's the truth. Actually, Moira asked me to tell you. She couldn't do it herself.'

'That's not what you said a minute ago. A minute ago you said she told you way back when.'

'You're not really going to insist it didn't occur to you.'

'Absolutely. The timing was all wrong.' Sure, in the distant past the thought had crossed my mind, but I just assumed Moira would have come clean with me. And then I forgot all about it. California wasn't connected to me anymore. Some other guy who looked like me had lived there. The destruction this could leave behind . . . What it would do to Lonnie . . . It's out of the question. Even if it's true, which I definitely doubt, I'd never admit it now. Why should I?

The hunger pangs won't let up, I haven't eaten much, and I'm woozy as hell. There's a lawyer I know, Marvin Something or Other, who's a genius at this paternity shit.

'She thought you'd have a right to know.'

'Well, that's thoughtful. Why didn't she wait another twenty years? Why would she do this to me? Do you realize how awful . . .'

Now I swing in the other direction, certain that little fuck Maurice is mine. Why else have I tried so hard not to consider it? What is it Marvin does? There were always rumors.

As far as I can tell, they're all sitting on their asses out there. It's time to take things into my own hands, otherwise these bozos'll kill that poor girl while they're having an extra discount cigarette.

'She doesn't want you to do anything. She just wants you to know. She's not going to tell anybody, if that's what you're worrying about.'

When I stand up, my head is spinning. I'm so hungry I could eat a horse. 'I am worried about it. And anybody who even makes the vaguest reference . . . who even whispers this will have a slander suit on their hands fast. Do you understand? And while I'm at it, why didn't you tell Nathan if you were so sure?'

'I said we all had to look in the mirror. I was afraid he wouldn't believe me, or he'd get rid of me for telling him . . . I don't know . . . Maybe I'm a coward like you. He raised your son. Why should he be blamed for this? Have you ever thought of that?'

Trying to stay upright, I find my hand on a spongy bulletin board. 'I never blamed anybody. Anyway, Nathan can't be hurt now.' If I can get a hold of Larry, I'll rattle the shit out of him.

Julia's aristocratic routine suddenly disappears, and in an angry whisper she says, 'He most certainly can. He's been dead less than a day, and it's all over town that he did something to that boy, or it was his rotten genes, something. When all he did was kill himself for years to save your son. Then there's the business at the bank, which they were always talking about but nobody has ever proven. They'll turn him into some sort of fiend. People love doing that. I've lost as much as anyone,' she adds, her face white as chalk.

I fight off a rush of dizziness, but I'm hungry, in pain, lightheaded all at once. Maurice's strangled voice fills my head. Does the medication do that? It doesn't seem right that some hot poke twenty years ago should add up to this. But even if it's true, I didn't raise him. Marvin Something or Other, he has friends who do these tests, he can get urine and blood samples for a price. No, no, you get caught doing that shit, it's big time. Disbarment at least. My brain feels like it's being squeezed in a vise.

'This is bad for all of us, Julia.' I'd like to rip her head off, but better to get rid of her.

If Larry's still dicking around, I'll get on the damn phone myself. I've seen the neuro wards at Bellevue. Mouths frozen wide open.

'Pardon me. How terrible for you.'

'Don't get nasty with me, lady. Enough of this crap.'

When I get to the door, the room suddenly contracts, expands, the lights go off and on, off and on, I fight it, grit my teeth, thinking oh no, not this shit again, not this after all these years. Staggering, I grab onto a low desk, but my body snaps like a whip and now I'm on my knees. The floor's hard, scratched-up linoleum, but there's nothing sharp down there. With every ounce of will I have I'm fighting the thing, shoving it back down, but it keeps boiling up, making my legs and arms and my whole body jerk faster and faster.

I try to remember whether I've taken my dilantin, and yeah, I'm pretty sure I did, so I get up again, the second or third time, and sonofabitch if I'm not walking right towards Connie's desk, wondering if there's a candy machine. Bam! I'm on all fours again, but I've shrugged the blackouts off a hundred times. Connie's gone, so I keep going like a fucking locomotive. I bounce off a wall. Who cares? You can't stop me.

Outside the parking lot's a skating rink. I'm going on tiptoes. Where are the ambulances? What'd I do with my car? Gusts of wind drive the snow into my eyes. Probably a good idea. I'll wake up. Opening my mouth wide, I swallow some. I'm doing better except for the hunger, the swelling hunger that feels like it's filling every cavity in my body. A jolt from a Snickers sometimes does the trick.

# CHAPTER TWENTY-FIVE: MOIRA

## Monday: October 18, 1990: 4:30 p.m.

I shut up the house and started driving. Stick Willow. Merwinville. Verona and Wittsboro. The crumbling towns blow away behind me like dry leaves. Tuscarora. Linden. Chesterfield. Main streets with strings of dead stores in wormy frame buildings. Abandoned churches. Churches turned into insurance agencies or artists' studios or places with high ceilings for Chamber of Commerce events.

At first I don't know I'm going to visit my animals. Driving calms me, and without thinking I follow roads I already know to the creatures I've shaped into life. I want to see whether my creations are surviving the hard winters, or whether they've been killed by ice. Many of them are owned by friends whose concerned faces barely register. They want to know how I'm feeling, as if I could even describe it, as if it mattered at all.

*I sense he is following me, but I know he'll never catch up.*

The Three Wolves' tails are far too full, but I clip and clip until they point straight back in the wind. The clipping is a medieval fugue in my head. I use my own shears, the

Felcos with the spongy handles, my hands in goat-skin gloves I've used for years. The Molinaris, Giselle and Jack, offer to let me stay longer, but I need the soothing road.

It's hard to tell The Giraffe from a camel when I get to Sandra's place, but I show her again how to exaggerate essential features, and to use the clippers in a decisive but delicate way. Wander, ponder and prune. Use thinning strokes. Jerry Zelakowski is too busy blowing glass and playing golf to take care of the Giant Turtle – he used electric shears and it's full of brown patches now.

Clipping boxwood wipes every thought from my mind.

*I know Vincent is following me, but I dart in unpredictable directions.*

In between stints at old friends' houses, I stay at motels. I love everything about motels, the little cakes of soap, the commercial landscapes in cheap frames, the bulbous lamps. I've always been taken by the slight shabbiness of these places, even the upscale types with their five-by-five conference areas and their blond, pressed wood desks. You're so alone in a motel, no one tries to help you. I can't think of any greater freedom.

When I go to see Maurice, I stay at the Seven Dwarfs Inn. It's actually called that, and the path to the office is lined with cute lawn dwarfs. Inside, for some strange reason, a sink is bolted to my bedroom wall.

I turn on the shower and Nathan's voice pours out. Under the weak spray I scrub my skin till it's raw, listening, arguing, thinking, trying not to remember. Nathan says, 'Emotions are cheap, only action counts.' The pictures come before I can stop them, the pictures, the wind and the snap of a red pine crowned with ice.

*I never imagine that Vincent will find me here, but when I hear his voice on the motel phone my skin breaks out in bumps. Still, I feel more than well. It's time to see him.*

I make sure my shower cap is on tight. When Vincent comes, I want him to notice the new auburn hair I just got out of the Revlon bottle. I wash my breasts and stomach, I wash between my legs, I wash my thighs. Grief has given me beautiful thighs. I couldn't swallow a thing for months. I don't want to feel what I feel. Instead of feeling I become Dinah Washington's voice.

Blue gardenia
Now I'm alone with you

I'm singing so loud I don't hear the knocking. Vincent's voice barely penetrates the door. I can't allow him to see me like this, absolutely not. I have to fix my face. I have to organize my thoughts. Go over all the boundaries. Oh, God, let this be quick and clean.

'Go away! You're never early! Go out to the pool!' The tables around the empty pool are shouldered by Sneezy, Grumpy and Sleepy.

I hate having to get ready fast. I snap open the Clinique eyeliner case and spit on the water color brush, my tripe-0 sable hair from the art supply store, but I'm rushing, the eyeliner smears and I have to start all over again. I stipple the bottom line in with dots, and then rub on some light ivory foundation under my eyes, over the bridge of my nose and under the arc of my eyebrows. Then I get into my freshly washed gardening pants with the kneepads to show I don't care how I look.

Now I have to sit on the end of the bed and concentrate. The spread is Mondrian-goes-Walmart. My palm skims its slick, synthetic surface. I remind myself that Vincent is a lawyer, not just my ex-lover. I almost say ex-husband, but he is both and neither. How would you describe what we were?

I look out the sliding window to see him leaning on his car, gazing out at the wooded hills. Bands of intense orange maples ripple through the forest. The red maples vibrate. How would you describe what we were?

I open the door, blood rushing to my face. He stands there, a familiar smile playing in the corner of his mouth. He stands there in his worn rust-colored suede jacket, in his Italian knit polo shirt, in the small powerful body I know so well – yes, he stands inside his own body – and his physical presence is completely unreal. The force I fear most streams through me.

He smells like cigarettes and scotch. 'You're smoking again?'

'Yeah, well, a walk on the wild side.' He shrugs with that self-deprecating gesture that is nothing of the sort. But his voice is tight. With a shock I realize he's as nervous as I am. In his hands he lifts two Diet Pepsis.

I look around to turn the TV off, but the screen is blank. 'So, you're all right? I heard you had a blackout.'

'Mind if I have one?' He puts down the sodas and pulls

a packet of Marlboros from his shirt pocket. 'Yeah, well, I'm fine. They just upped my dilantin. Eidetic seizure disorder they call it. That's a fancy way of saying they don't know what's wrong with me. In other words, I'm like everybody else.'

'Well, that's a relief. Oh, sure. Go ahead.' I take one too and wait for him to pull out his silver lighter. 'Sit.'

'You must be out in the sun all the time,' he says, appraising me from under his heavy eyelids. 'How're you feeling?'

That ridiculous, numbing question. 'Oh, Vincent, not you of all people.'

'Yeah, sorry.'

Flustered, I let the words come out in a rush. 'I gave birth to him. Look at what he is . . . Nathan's gone. It's impossible. Poor Ben. I think people ask me as a form of entertainment. If I say I'm in mourning, they'll check to see if it's deep enough. If I say I'm surviving, they'll say I'm a cold bitch. There aren't any words for this.'

Now I've embarrassed him, but so what? 'Hey, hey, I understand. Sorry. How's Crissie? I heard she's doing okay.'

Why not tell the truth for once? It won't kill him. 'Well, actually she wasn't very good for a long time. The head injuries weren't too bad. All she had was a bad concussion. Ha. Listen to me. All she had . . . But she was getting what the veterans have?'

'Post-traumatic?'

I have nothing of the sort. But I see pictures of the frozen pond, I hear the wind. City people don't know that the wind can howl as if it's in a movie. 'Something like that. But it went away after a couple of months. I never thought she'd be able to go to school on time, but I suppose she wanted to get away from me so much she managed. She's even forgiving me a little, I think. I visited her in Geneseo. Dorm rooms are like cubbyholes.'

'Forgiving you for what? You saved her life, for crissakes.'

'Well, she doesn't see it that way. She's very angry at me, Vincent. But we're talking. She's alive, she's herself. You can't comprehend, nobody can. I can't and it's happening to me.'

'Angry about what?'

'Oh, everything, for shooting Maurice, for giving birth to him. Everything I can't change. Every night she'd tell me how I'd neglected her and every night she couldn't sleep alone. It doesn't matter how much I apologize. She says it's too late, and I suppose she's right. She accuses me of being too hard to rebel against.'

'I'm a walking, talking apology myself.'

A few more inhales and I'm loopy. 'She'd come into my bed and kick me when she was sleeping. Or maybe she was awake.'

'She's supposed to kick you. She's what now, eighteen? It's in her job description.'

'Let's not be clever, Vincent. That she's just alive is so incredible . . . that she can put herself together when I don't have a single answer for her . . . What can I say? I admire her.'

Reaching across the rickety conference table, he touches my hand, but sympathy is the last thing I want. What were we? He withdraws, but with his subtle, practiced grace. 'Come outside,' I say, 'I want to show you something.'

The hatch of my Civic is laced with rust. Half-peeled, the bumper sticker that says PRACTICE RANDOM KINDNESS AND SENSELESS ACTS OF BEAUTY makes me wonder who I used to be. All of my tools are in an old canvas satchel. Rummaging around, I find the clippers. When I turn, Vincent looks completely out of place against the brilliant hills. His darkness belongs in a narrow street, at a café table in the shadows. Nature can be so extreme, so unnatural.

I hold the shears up, the metal blades giving off a dull shine. 'This is what I do. I make things with them. And I go to see Maurice, too. It's almost impossible, but I face him, and I never could before. Isn't that strange? And I'm paying for Crissie and helping her out when she'll let me. I sold the horses, I'm selling the house.' My hands are clipping in the middle of the air. 'How do I feel? It's the wrong question. I can only do what I have to do, certain things for my family. That's it.'

He looks away. 'I could see him, too. Anything you need from me. Help with the HMO, I'll run those sons of bitches ragged. I'll make them pay.' It wouldn't hurt to have Vincent on my side, but I can't tell how much of this is acting. 'Hey, I left my bag inside . . .'

'It's quite cut and dried. She's alive. She'll be fine. I have my work.'

'You're going to keep driving around like this forever?'

I have no answer to this. I haven't thought about it.

The room feels so small now. I stub out my cigarette in the glass ashtray. People even smoke in the non-smoking rooms in motels like this. Smoke comes out of the pillows when you rest your head.

Sitting on the edge of an orange swivel chair, he opens his briefcase without looking at me. 'I'll look into the coverage. I know a guy. Meanwhile, I've got to know what's what. Was Julia telling me the truth about the paternity issue?'

'Is that how you think of it?'

'Sorry, yeah, what a way to put it, huh? But this has serious ramifications. When I go out with Lonnie I'm monitoring every move he makes . . . he's doing great but he's way too touchy. Brittle, like a piece of glass.'

'Like Maurice?'

'Well, I've got a right to be concerned.'

Quick and clean. Wasn't that the way I wanted it? 'It's possible. It was all so long ago . . . But that's entirely my business.'

'Probable?' This is all he really cares about. It's written all over him. But I can stand this because everything is so simple now. Crissie. Maurice. The animals. I'll drive forever.

'Possibly probable, how's that? I wasn't exactly the book-keeper type back then. Anyway, after all these years it has nothing to do with you.'

'Yeah, well. So you don't know for sure.' He rummages around in his briefcase for a moment. Under his olive complexion, he blushes. When he coughs into his fist, I know something's coming. But what does it really matter? I have everything I need.

'I've got a document here. To tell you the truth, I'm

embarrassed as shit to do this, but . . . It says I'm not his father, and I'm not responsible. Since you're telling me you don't care and you're not totally sure.'

I'm angry, I think, but this is what I want, too. 'Legal papers? What a surprise!' I grab a magic marker out of my bag and scrawl my name across the bottom of the papers. 'There! I declare you innocent of any and all congress with the witch.'

'Thanks, I really appreciate this. I mean, it's what you want, right?'

'You already said that. A lawyer till the end? I hear Nathan's voice, but I see you. I feel you.'

He looks away, unprepared for my words, unprepared as I am. But I can say anything because I feel so much better. I've never been so crystal clear. I can stand anything.

He looks at me, then at his shoes. 'I don't know . . .'

I smell the chemical stink of a burning filter. His Marlboro is finished. 'Oh, Vincent, who were we? What were we? Did we make this happen?'

'Of course not. You didn't make him sick. He was born that way.'

I think of Nathan's lovely Berkeley punch, but I can't come out with it. Not now anyway. 'So nothing I ever did or didn't do meant anything at all? Is that what you're saying?'

'No, not exactly.'

I never wanted to see him again, but now he is inches from me. 'We let a marriage license expire and never even talked about it afterwards. Don't you think that's strange? Don't you ever think about that? What were we doing all these years? I said I was willing to do it, I said I'd marry you, and then it all just . . .'

'Hey, it's funny, but I could say the same thing.' Vincent gets up, circling me in the tight enclosure. 'I wonder if we should even talk like this. Actually, it scares the shit out of me.'

'Why not? It's all we, it's all anybody has left, isn't it?'

'No. That's not it. We've got to deal with the situation.'

'Then tell me what we were. It's all a bunch . . . of disconnected memories to me . . . a beautiful slide show or something . . .'

'We were lovers.'

'Oh, that's so easy. Way too easy, Vincent. We were lovers for so many years. We lived with each other without living with each other. We were married without being married. Why?'

'We're too much alike.'

I get up, unable to stand still. 'Too easy. We've said that a hundred times.'

He follows in my steps. 'We were afraid . . . if we got too close . . .'

'So we had a twenty year one-night stand?'

'No, no, that's not true. I always wanted to see you, I always thought about you, no matter who I was with.'

'I don't want to think about who you were with, thank you.'

'Likewise. After a point, what could we do? We had the kids. Suppose we had run away and left everybody else behind?

We would've destroyed everybody else. If we were such fucking monsters, why didn't we do that?'

'You're just trying to put a good face on it.'

'No, just realistic. Or do you think Nathan was always right?'

'Yes, yes I do,' I say, sinking back to the swivel chair. 'Yes, no, I'm not sure. What an idea,' I laugh, but it really is a shock in a way, Nathan being wrong. I fought with him and fought with him and never believed a word I said.

'Think about it. We'll talk,' he says, picking up his briefcase and heading for the door. I don't say a thing. I can let him go. But he stops in his tracks and looks over his shoulder.

Turning, he shows me his worn, charming, good-looking face. How could I berate him, this face says. This sincere, subtle, beautiful, intelligent face. 'Yeah, I knew. I didn't think about it so long I forgot, but I sensed it. I know now and you're trying to let me off the hook again. At least I can admit it to you.'

'Do you think that's all you have to do? A little admission? I'd like to I don't know what . . .' The rest of the words don't come out. I see Crissie whirling stark naked around Maurice, I see his skeletal back, so scrawny, so white, so defenseless. I shoot him again. I can't stop weeping, face down on that cheap, synthetic Walmart spread.

The bed sags. He touches me tentatively on the shoulder, but I brush his hand away, unable to bear the sensation. 'Stop! I'll be fine . . .'

But he doesn't go away. Instead, he sits on the edge of the mattress, a silent presence. Embarrassed, I get up and start for the bathroom. 'Sorry. This isn't the way I am now.'

His back to me, he says, 'I didn't even know it, but I knew it.'

Startled, I stop in my tracks. 'Then say it. Just say it, damn it!'

'Like you said . . . he's probably . . . he is mine, right?'

The pictures come all night, but I just surrender to them. I dare them to come. My heart stops, but I do not die. Even in loss our bodies, Vincent's and mine, fit together.

In the morning, unshaven, Vincent has the lined, grizzled face of a Roman soldier.

'Listen, do me a favor. Give me my briefcase.'

'You're going to work now?' Dazed, I hand him the satchel.

Carefully, he draws a folder out and thumbs through it with deep concentration. Finally, he pulls a single sheet out, gropes in the pocket of the pants he's cast over a chair, and pulls out his cigarette lighter. 'Fuck this,' he says, putting a corner of the document to the flame. 'Who's going to know?'

I take the burning paper from his hand and rush to the motel sink bolted to the wall. In a few moments, the paper becomes ash.

# CHAPTER TWENTY-SIX: MAURICE

## Sunday: March 21, 1993: 1:30 p.m.

I'm getting older, better and wiser. My beard is so thick I have to shave every day. I'm over six feet now, I grew an inch and a half when I was nineteen, and I weigh about 175 pounds at least. People like me do grow up, even if we're out of sight. We haven't died. We're just in warehouses all over the country, maybe in your neighborhood, stacks of us one on top of the other. The Center for Disease Control says it's an epidemic.

I think about things hard now, without any interruptions from wires in my head or Black Thinking. The latest meds are like sound-proofing for the brain. If another patient sends me a sizzler, it sounds as if it's coming from the edge of the universe. The meds make my wetworks go deaf.

For instance, I was thinking about how mom wouldn't go on TV. I found that out from Crissie, who started visiting me a year ago. She was telling me mom told the Channel Five reporters to go take a flying fuck, and some French TV people, too. We both laughed like in the old days when we were small and dancing to Blondie. Mom liked Blondie but dad hated them.

He said Debbie Harry was a dumpy non-en-tit-ty. That made us laugh. We thought he was saying she had no tits. Anyway, I was thinking about what Crissie said and how predictable it was that mom wouldn't talk to the TV people. She'd think it was gross, and I can understand that. People like mom look down on people who talk about their problems on TV because it's not dignified. She's probably right, too.

But there's another side to it. I was watching the other day when the parents of this carpenter with the harelip who shot all those kids in the school yard in Bogaloosa came right on the *Today* show. First I was thinking like mom. This is disgusting. The victims aren't even in the ground yet, and here are the murderer's parents trying to get attention or sympathy for themselves. But Katie Couric was so nice to them, and they seemed so sincere, and the father was a coach, and he was crying in a very quiet way that you wouldn't expect for a coach, and I realized something. People going on TV like that, it's good for them and the rest of us. It's like an American funeral on the *Today* show. With millions of people attending. They're the biggest funerals in history. They make us think about the terrible things we don't want to face. I was sitting there and crying, too.

As I get better I understand what I did. It may surprise you to know that I do understand how horrible it was, and when I think about it I twist in bed and grind my teeth until I get a headache even the stuff they make for migraines can't cure. In fact, when I think about how terrible what I did was, I grind my teeth purposely, to punish myself, knowing that it will be impossible to punish myself enough. At least I'll end up with nubs for teeth.

But they let me live, so I have to go on day after day. The therapy is good here, and with the new meds I can keep the Black Thinking at a distance when it starts. I can say, 'Oh, that's the old Black Thinking, it's not reality.' I even have a girlfriend, and I'm not talking about Kiki or some fantasy fly girl. Her name is Marlene, and she did something she never talks about. She's getting better, too.

There are places we can go to be alone. A whole wing of the hospital was closed down years ago. But it's easy to get in there, the orderlies do it all the time to drink wine and smoke pot. Once in a blue moon I sneak in with Rashid, he's some kind of nurse, and fire up, but it's only to prove I don't need anything anymore. Rashid and Larry go into that sealed-off section with patients and do the nasty on dusty mattresses in beds that crank up the side. The locks have been broken a hundred times. One room is full of pigeons. Woooossh. Woooossshhh. Don't open that door.

Marlene and I go into that wing, but we bring clean sheets in a gym bag, and pillow cases. We go all the way down a long hall that's almost closed off by a pile of metal furniture and tables on wheels.

I like to think about the beginning of time, when the world was almost infinitely small and infinitely dense, and the end, too, when energy will just leak away. When I think about these things I forget where I am, and the day-to-day annoyances of being locked up fade away. With my new perfectly quiet mind

I could be like that prisoner on Alcatraz with the birds, if they gave me birds. Who cares then if breakfast tastes like wallpaper paste or lunch is a single slice of baloney on white bread?

On visiting day mom comes with the lawyer now and sometimes with Crissie. They've been telling me the lawyer is my step-father, but I know it's just to make me feel better. So I'll think I have a father again, but that doesn't seem like good therapy to me. He's very nervous when he's near me, but the lawyer is trying to help me. Or that's what he says. But Crissie used to say dad was full of promises, but never trust him. I think the lawyer is like that, I don't think he means what he says. Crissie says mom thinks the lawyer looks like Al Pacino, that's why she married him, but to me he looks like that old baseball announcer dad used to laugh about. Phil Rizzuto.

I guess mom and the lawyer have their own room down at the end of their own long hall.

We go out on the grass that's really more like a sandy infield than a lawn, and mom brings fried chicken and fresh French bread and pickles and salads. She brings me brown mustard that they don't have in the hospital. She touches my face and says she loves me. She doesn't cry or anything when she says this. At first when she came to visit she couldn't even talk to me, and I started wondering if she was going to get the room next door. (Joke.) But now she looks me straight in the eye. I can't look back.

## If you enjoyed this book here is a selection of other bestselling titles from Headline

| | | | |
|---|---|---|---|
| FEAR NOTHING | Dean Koontz | £5.99 | ☐ |
| SCARLET | Jane Brindle | £5.99 | ☐ |
| CHANGELING | Frances Gordon | £5.99 | ☐ |
| PASIPHAE | William Smethurst | £5.99 | ☐ |
| AFTER MIDNIGHT | Richard Laymon | £5.99 | ☐ |
| NO HEAVEN, NO HELL | Jane Brindle | £5.99 | ☐ |
| BLACK RIVER | Melanie Tem | £5.99 | ☐ |
| THE RISE OF ENDYMION | Dan Simmons | £5.99 | ☐ |
| CADDORAN | Roger Taylor | £5.99 | ☐ |
| A DRY SPELL | Susie Moloney | £5.99 | ☐ |
| SACRAMENT OF NIGHT | Louise Cooper | £5.99 | ☐ |
| THE SILVER SCREAM | Ed Gorman | £5.99 | ☐ |

Headline books are available at your local bookshop or newsagent. Alternatively, books can be ordered direct from the publisher. Just tick the titles you want and fill in the form below. Prices and availability subject to change without notice.

Buy four books from the selection above and get free postage and packaging and delivery within 48 hours. Just send a cheque or postal order made payable to Bookpoint Ltd to the value of the total cover price of the four books. Alternatively, if you wish to buy fewer than four books the following postage and packaging applies:

UK and BFPO £4.30 for one book; £6.30 for two books; £8.30 for three books.

Overseas and Eire: £4.80 for one book; £7.10 for 2 or 3 books (surface mail).

Please enclose a cheque or postal order made payable to *Bookpoint Limited*, and send to: Headline Publishing Ltd, 39 Milton Park, Abingdon, OXON OX14 4TD, UK.
Email Address: orders@bookpoint.co.uk

If you would prefer to pay by credit card, our call team would be delighted to take your order by telephone. Our direct line is 01235 400 414 (lines open 9.00 am–6.00 pm Monday to Saturday 24 hour message answering service). Alternatively you can send a fax on 01235 400 454.

Name ......................................................................................

Address ..................................................................................

..............................................................................................

..............................................................................................

If you would prefer to pay by credit card, please complete:
Please debit my Visa/Access/Diner's Card/American Express (delete as applicable) card number:

| | | | | | | | | | | | | | | | | | | |
|---|---|---|---|---|---|---|---|---|---|---|---|---|---|---|---|---|---|---|

Signature ...................................................... Expiry Date ..............